STEP INTO A PERFECTLY PROPER WORLD . . . OF DARK SUSPICION, SCANDALOUS SECRETS . . . AND MURDEROUS REVENGE

White collar crime takes on a whole new hue . . . when a scheming accountant discovers the secrets of success.

Curious neighbors take matters into their own hands . . . when buried treasure leads the way to fatal suspicion.

A picture is worth a thousand words . . . and a movie reveals the secrets of a fifty-year-old murder.

Little girls with long memories learn that revenge is not a spectator sport . . .

Thirteen of today's most skillful mystery writers spin tales most clever of murder most cunning.

Other Books in the
MALICE DOMESTIC *Series*
from Avon Twilight

SHARYN MCCRUMB PRESENTS
MALICE DOMESTIC 7

Margaret Maron

PRESENTS

MALICE DOMESTIC 8

Contents

CONTENTS

Introduction:
Down These Clean Streets . . .
—A Look at Domestic Malice

Margaret Maron

It was ten years ago, at the very first Malice Domestic Convention. Carolyn Hart, Susan Dunlap and I had stepped into the elevator together, each of us wearing our Malice Domestic name tags.

The hotel was also hosting a large gathering of trial lawyers that weekend, and the elevators were full of attorneys in sober business suits and ties. One of them looked at our name tags, instantly deduced that we were probably social workers or mid-echelon civil servants and said, "Malice Domestic, hmm-mm? Is your conference about violence in the home?"

"You could say so," Susan replied with a perfectly straight face.

Indeed.

For ten years, Malice Domestic has celebrated the traditional mystery, i.e., crime with a distinctly domestic face: no Mafia shootouts, no evil masterminds pulling strings for world domination, no sewer rats crawling up from urban cesspools. Violence here is seldom by random chance. Should a drive-by shooting actually occur, we soon learn which of the victim's nearest and dearest has access to a black sedan. If someone keels over in the chocolate mousse, the poison usually comes from Grandmother's enameled pillbox. The knife is seldom a switchblade. It's more likely to be an antique Persian dagger that hung over the sideboard and was used to slice the cheddar before turning up in hubby's chest.

In short, victim and perpetrator know each other. If they are not related by blood or marriage, then they work together, are lovers (or ex-lovers), are rivals for the same desirable plum, are privy to the other's darkest secrets.

Think Christie instead of Cain, Sayers rather than Spillane.

In the last ten years, Malice Domestic (the convention) has honored some of the best modern practitioners of this side of the genre: Elizabeth Peters, Patricia Moyes, Charlotte MacLeod, Aaron Elkins, Anne Perry, Dorothy Salisbury Davis, Ellis Peters, Peter Lovesey, Carolyn Hart and Robert Barnard.

For the last eight years, Malice Domestic (the annual anthology) has presented stories by these authors plus dozens more who write wittily and perceptively of personal relationships gone awry.

This year's collection continues the tradition.

Enjoy!

In 1992, Margaret Maron swept all the mystery awards—Agatha, Anthony, Edgar, Macavity—for Bootlegger's Daughter, *her first novel featuring Southern judge Deborah Knott. Since then, Maron has continued to garner critical acclaim for her Knott books and those featuring self-possessed New York police lieutenant Sigrid Harald. Maron lives on her family farm in North Carolina.*

Venus Rising

Nevada Barr

It was July. He'd been watching April since February. The play of months amused, then confused, then frightened him. The emotions coming so hard, each upon the heels of the other, hurt his brain. Squealing, he squeezed his temples between the palms of his hands to squish out the disorder.

February was brown, a time his world began to grow heavy. July was yellow, glaring and clear. He could think in July. April was a girl. Not a girl; a woman. Old enough to be his mother. But not a mother. April was perfect. She would never be a mother with all the blood and slime that entailed. He'd seen his cat be a mother once. He loved the kittens, kept all seven, but he was glad when his brother got her fixed so she'd never have to do it again. April, he was sure, had either been fixed or wasn't ever broken in the first place.

Now a cloud had come over his personal sun, over April. That man had come into her life.

In the hall outside his room he could hear his brother Rob talking with the nurse. "Nurse." She called herself that. Rob played along. But she was evil. Her breasts were too big and her eyes too far apart. When she laughed, they rolled around, rattling into opposite corners of the room like pool balls smacked all different directions. They weren't even exactly the same color. One was blue and the other kind of greenish. Rob said her name was Dolores, and she had "Dolores" written on a little plastic pin she wore over one giant boob. Jeremy didn't believe it. A Dolores would have gentle brown eyes and wouldn't hurt him.

"He's been having nightmares," Rob was saying. "I think he's having trouble telling the difference between the dreams and reality. It's scaring both of us."

Jeremy wished he wouldn't tell her that stuff, wouldn't tell her anything. She used it to get inside your head and mess with you.

"Has he been watching the news? I know it's giving me nightmares," Not-Dolores said and laughed. Jeremy pictured her eyeballs rolling down the hall, bouncing down the stairs into the living room.

"TV's about all he's got. That and his computer. Jeremy's a genius with computers."

"That's as may be." Not-Dolores's mouth would be crimping down, making snake-lips. "But you've got to remember he has the emotional development of a ten-year-old child."

"I'll watch him," Rob said.

They didn't know anything. Rob snuck out at night. Had a weakness for the ladies was how he'd said it once. But while he was out, Jeremy was watching, and it wasn't TV.

Jeremy turned to the computer console on his desk. "Are you sleeping?" he asked. "Time to wake up."

*   *   *

"Computer nerd" was a term April disliked. "Computer guru" was the title she favored at present. Electronics had achieved its much-deserved glamor. Paint, ink, charcoal were as obsolete as the stylus and wax tablet. Even pixels were passé. Art was a matter of light and color, of signal without substance; hard copy a mere formality required by the uninitiated. Her works soared through cyberspace, viewed in Finland and Newark, New Zealand and Fresno within a heartbeat.

Repositioning herself so the sun wouldn't strike the monitor on her Micron Millenia Pro2 Plus state-of-the-art system, she clicked on Netscape. Six thousand and change. Worth every penny: memory for days and color as true as a Polaroid ad. April began to download a piece she'd recently added to the gallery on her web page. In the past she'd scoffed at artists who referred to their work as their babies, but this one was dangerously close to triggering the maternal instinct. This picture spoke to her. *Venus on the Half Shell* with a futuristic slant, a woman seated at the edge of a clamshell of a spaceship in an alien Eden, her helmet under her suited arm. Well, not a helmet, precisely. April hadn't the software yet to create that image. She'd settled for a globe, green and glowing with a sense of inner peace, a light as personal as it was soothing. In place of a spacesuit—also not available on clip-art—she'd opted for a red sheath dress. With contrast, light and shadow, the reflection of the salmon-colored blossoms, April had created an aura of sublime innocence. Not the new innocence of the ignorant but the reborn awe of the jaded brought again to their God. Creatures, both animate and inanimate, exuded the ambience of that old World War II song, "Someone to Watch Over Me." Never too impressed with subtlety, April had put in a literal someone to watch. Half hidden in fronds of sunlit green in the foregrounds was the silhouette of a panther. Not a pouncing, biting, bone-crushing predator but the childhood fantasy of tens of millions of little girls raised on Snow White: an animal that would nestle in one's skirts, lie down as a pillow when the ground was hard.

Tentatively, she'd entitled the work *Venus Rising*.

Following a complex set of commands that never failed to strike awe of man-made magic in April's heart, the picture would take a minute to download. She passed the time by playing with Wanda's tail. Instinctively attracted to the altar of the moment, Wanda, a Russian Blue with a coat any starlet would lust after, curled in a neat circle in an emptied drawer at April's elbow.

Feeling childish, but enjoying the sensation, April wouldn't let herself look at *Venus Rising* till it was complete. Wanda had grown tired of adulation and begun returning friendly nips for strokes by the time the picture had finished downloading. April turned her chair and looked at the monitor. The familiar sense of joy in her own creativity, that delicious, wicked smugness an artist knows when the work is right, wasn't forthcoming.

Disease.

That was the word April was looking for. The picture looked diseased. And it caused disease in her, discomfort. "Damn," she whispered.

It happened; art revisited becomes garbage. "Damn." She stared awhile before she saw it. The picture had changed. Little things: light, once soft, had become harsher; clouds had darkened, become foreboding.

Something was wrong with the computer's color mechanisms. In all her years as a graphic artist, April hadn't run across this particular virus. Hadn't even heard of it. A minute more, and she knew it wasn't merely malfunction. The kindly panther spirit was smaller, slipping away into the undergrowth. The green globe, a shimmering metaphor for self-acceptance, had floated from the woman's hands, appeared to be drifting away over the water.

Powerful as her computer was—and deeply as she believed in the wonders of technology—April knew machinery hadn't spawned the changes. Disease crept into her soul, trickling like poison.

Somebody was messing with her.

"Shake it off," she said aloud and tried to think of who knew her password, who had the skill to manipulate her work. Nobody. She lived alone. The password existed only in her head. Why would a hacker trouble himself to fiddle with a picture that was free for the taking?

The doorbell rang. April flinched. Wanda hissed and ran under the desk. "You'll have to get used to him," April said to the nose protruding suspiciously from between metal table legs. "This one might be a keeper." Switching to a screen saver of Mars, April banished the defiled *Venus*.

Steve had brought flowers. Not grabbed up from the neighbor's yard as a last-minute stab at cheap romance but a store-bought bouquet that spoke of planning and thought. April didn't care a whole lot for flowers, but she was impressed by the gesture. There'd been too many grabbers and stabbers over the years, guys who came late, canceled dates, had live-in girlfriends or otherwise slimed through relationships. At one time it had angered her. A year or two of bitterness followed that. Now she simply had no time or patience for it. In her ballpark it took less than three strikes to be called Out. So far Steve Davis was hitting home runs.

"Hey," April said, accepting the flowers and the kiss. He followed her in, and she abandoned the baseball metaphors, having exhausted her sports knowledge with the two allusions.

Steve Davis wasn't much taller than she, five foot eight at the most, and he was a few years older. Thirty-seven, he'd said, but she guessed closer to forty. His body was good. That mattered to April, who was decidedly carnal. Wide shoulders and well-muscled legs contrasted sharply with the balding head and bifocals. A short brown beard shot with gray lent him the amiable look of a small-town druggist or an accountant. Love was not yet a word she chose to bandy about, but April was rather taken with his humble ways and his wit, sharp but never cutting. Also, she admitted to herself as she put the somewhat stiff floral arrangement in an empty mayonnaise jar, with her, flattery would get you everywhere.

Steve had picked her up at the video store. Overwhelmed by her "idiosyncratic beauty," captivated by her "obvious intelligence." Not realizing she did so, April snorted at her own vulnerability and was surprised to hear Steve's laughter. He even found her snorting delightful. A man in a million.

"It's him," Jeremy said. He was at the window again with the field glasses Rob had given him. "It's him," he yelled. If Rob heard, he didn't answer. Maybe he was downstairs with the not-really-Dolores creature. Maybe they were having sex. Jeremy laughed at the image: Rob and Robo-eyes on the kitchen table like in that movie with Kevin Costner. Except Rob was better looking than Kevin Costner and Not-Dolores never looked as good as that lady actor in her wildest dreams.

April, her short red hair all shiny like cat's fur and her little summer dress sort of slip-sliding off her shoulders, was leaving with him. "Chrome dome," Jeremy tried aloud. He'd heard that somewhere before. For this guy he needed something new, something special. The actor lady, the one on the kitchen table, had been in a movie. *Dead Man Walking*, that was it. "Death Man." Jeremy thought about that as Steve and April walked out side by side. Taking Rob's camera from where he'd left it in waiting on the desk, Jeremy focused the zoom till he could see whiskers and ear hair. He clicked the shutter. Rob would take it to 1-Hour Photo for him. Rob thought it was a harmless hobby.

"Nope," Jeremy said.

"Death Man" was too classy for a short bald guy. He watched as the man opened the door of his Jeep. It was brand new with fat, special-order tires and a shiny roll bar. Rob said men had to buy stuff like that when they had a penis the size of pin. "Bug Dick." Jeremy had heard that before too, but it made him laugh. And it made Chrome Dome less scary. "Bug Dick," Jeremy said to test it out. "Bug Dick" it would be.

"Don't do it, April, don't do it," he whispered as she climbed into the Jeep, her little dress flying up over tanned thighs. "You'll be sorry."

She did it.

Jeremy sighed and put down the glasses as the Jeep pulled away. The computer monitor beckoned, toasters flying through star-filled space. "Boldly go where no man has gone," he said and logged on.

Wind-blown, sun-kissed—all those lovely things women's glossy magazines tout—April and Steve got back to her house around four in the afternoon. Riding in an open Jeep had left her flushed and tousled. April abandoned Steve in the living room and slunk away to "freshen up." She'd actually said the words, like a debutante in a fifties movie. Staring at her reflection in the mirror, she admitted she looked pretty doggone fresh in an outdoorsy, California kind of way.

They'd driven south toward San Francisco, lunched in Benicia at a sidewalk cafe. There'd been flirting and compliments. The sun on the water, the sky devoid of the proverbial cloud, the ointment free of flies. Yet April had been unable to shake a sense of dread. It was *Venus Rising*, the darkness coming. The image soaked into her brain, touched everything she saw like a leprous King Midas. The ships in the Benicia ship graveyard, usually quaint and historical, loomed gray and scabby. Lunch in the cafe, charming and beautifully served, inspired her to look for hairs in her salmon salad, roaches skittering behind the cappuccino machine.

Disease.

"I'm coming down with a computer virus," she told her reflection and ran some water into the sink to keep her credit good with her date, should he be so crude as to be listening.

Even Steve, always cheerful, emotions sunny and easy to read, had caught it. On the drive back he'd teetered near sullen, reacting, she supposed, to her coldness and distraction. She'd not wanted him to come in, but there'd been no polite way to get rid of him. So she'd mumbled her excuse and scooted off to the sanctity of the bathroom. All she wanted was to be alone, to download *Venus* again, see if she'd gone mad or the changes were actually there.

Time was running out. Any longer in the john, and he'd probably dial 911. April turned off the water.

Jeremy couldn't sleep. He didn't have to pretend anymore. Rob had gone out; he'd heard the door shut between the house and the garage. Sleep had ceased to be his friend some time ago. Horrible things woke him up, pictures so real he wasn't entirely sure they hadn't happened. One night he dreamed one of the kittens had been beheaded in his brother's bathroom. The next morning he refused to get out of bed till Rob brought all seven of them upstairs and turned them loose in his room. He'd hugged and kissed and counted them over and over, but still he'd never summoned the courage to use Rob's bathroom again.

Other things weren't nightmares, they were real, but nobody believed him. Sometimes he didn't believe himself, but mostly he did. He'd learned not to tell anybody, especially the "nurse." She'd use it as an excuse to keep him locked up longer. Rob paid her to do it; she probably didn't want to lose the money. If he got well, she'd be out of a job and have to go roll her eyes down somebody else's brother.

His computer was having its own dreams, rendering images for cyberminds. The toasters were gone; he'd replaced that screen saver with another: April's face. She put her picture on her web site. She shouldn't do that. You never knew who was watching.

Pushing up the window, Jeremy slid his legs over the sill then felt the scratchy solidity of the roof under his feet. There was a moon over April's house. A hunter's moon? He'd heard that phrase on the evening news. The newscaster said that was when the killings happened. Light to kill by. Light showed up all the little animals, and they couldn't hide from the hunter.

A headache woke April just after five in the morning. Her night had been filled with furtive bumps and skritching sounds usually reported around Girl Scout campfires and attributed to a homicidal maniac with a hook for a hand. Steadfastly, she'd blamed all itinerant noises on Wanda, but she'd still had a lousy night.

Morning was looking little better. Rest being a fruitless pursuit, she padded downstairs to the computer. Last night, after she'd finally shot the door on an increasingly weird Steve, she'd downloaded *Venus*, but there'd been no more changes. For an instant she'd hoped the changes had been a fluke, a bad joke. Nothing had happened to blast that hope; it just faded under the pervasive evil that emanated from the despoiled Eden. Finally, she'd switched off the computer and gone to bed.

This morning Wanda was ignored. She resented that as keenly as she did adoration and sat beside the computer on the printer, batting at April's hands as she fingered the keys. The web site opened. Portfolio. April clicked on that, scanned down the list of her works and stopped at *Venus Rising*. Anxiety, nauseatingly close to fear, poured through her veins like ice water. For a moment it crossed her mind to erase it without looking, purge it from her hard drive. Bury it with a stake in its heart at a crossroads at midnight.

"It's only a picture, for Christ's sake," she said. "Right, Wanda?" Catlike, Wanda knew better than to commit herself. April clicked on the picture's icon and watched the screen slowly fill with color from the top down.

It had changed again.

The panther was gone. The globe had floated out of reach of the woman's hands. The sky was the red, not of sunset, but of coming fire. Water reflected the fire on an oily surface. Green was gone from the mountains, leaving black toothy relics. The ice water in April's bloodstream began to freeze solid. Tiny hairs on the back of her neck stirred, prickling outside her mind as fear prickled within.

"Stop it!" she whispered to herself and blanked the screen. She could not blank her mind. Crawling itched at her skin and her brain. No longer able to sit, she walked from the study into the living room. No solace there, she moved into the kitchen, wandering aimlessly through the familiar sanctity of her home. The counter by the sink was covered with broken glass. Sharp and glittering, shards cut across the Formica and spilled onto the floor. The flowers Steve had brought lay wilted in the ruin. In her haste she had forgotten to put water in the jar, and they'd probably died even before the wreck of the makeshift vase.

Wanda?

April bent down and plucked up one of the dying blooms, a peach-colored zinnia. The petals had been pulled off as if by a violent hand, the stem broken. The base of the mayonnaise jar was lying intact at the bottom of the metal sink. Wanda, wicked as she might hope to be, couldn't have destroyed the jar except by knocking it to the floor. This had been smashed on the edge of the sink. Something stronger and angrier than a cat's tooth had severed the heads of the flowers. Trickling fear turned to flood, and April ran through the house checking the doors and windows. The sliding glass doors onto the patio were unlocked. Surely she'd locked them before she'd gone out the day before. Maybe not. The routine was so automatic, she couldn't remember.

Had someone come in during the night? Destroyed Steve's flowers, broken the jar?

The news. A serial killer. The hunter's moon.

"Jesus," April muttered. Racing as if hordes of axe-wielding maniacs were charging her stronghold, April ran from window to window, door to door, checking and rechecking the locks. So much was glass. A brick, a stone, and she was exposed. Snatching up the phone, she poked numbers, then banged the receiver down. What would she tell the police? Someone was coloring in her pictures funny on the Internet? A jar was broken, a door left unlatched? With the news they must get hundreds of calls a day from hysterical women who fancied they saw shadows lurking in the bougainvillea.

"Get a grip," April told herself sternly. Without knowing why, she returned to the study, to the picture. Clicking on the monitor, she stared into the black and red hell that had once housed her secret self. Down in the right-hand corner, unnoticed in the terror that had gripped her on first seeing the changes, was the figure of a man, naked or nearly so—his back was to her—holding what could have been a staff. Beside him was her panther. The image eased her, though she couldn't have said why. The staff could easily have been a spear, a weapon, but his presence and that of the panther gave her hope.

"Hope for what?" she asked the computer. "Irrational hope," she told the cat.

Feeling a fool, she called Steve's pager number. In less than a minute he phoned back. He didn't mock her or pretend her fears were unfounded. The picture on the computer bothered him and she felt validated. When she told him of the changes, he grew as close to angry as she'd ever heard him. Anger was reassuring. She wished she'd reacted with anger and not with sniveling and running about from window to window like a demented Wee Willie Winky. Best of all, he promised he'd come over after work. This might be the night she'd invite him to stay. Fear was as good an aphrodisiac as any.

April fought anxiety the way she fought every violent emotion in her life: she worked. Under her intense gaze an alien world of depth and complexity was built on her computer screen. Layer by layer, piece by piece, she moved mountains and oceans, built and destroyed cities, caused moons to fall from their orbits and ships to trap themselves in the eternal amber of a distant world's ether. Once during the day she'd been interrupted by an E-mail message. Steve saying he would be there at ten on the dot, to keep a candle in the window for him. He'd signed off with the message "love."

Rob hadn't come back from work. Not-Dolores made Jeremy supper: chicken and instant mashed potatoes. It was good, but he pretended he didn't like it so she wouldn't get the idea she was going to stay around in the capacity of cook once he was well. From downstairs he could hear the TV. With that and free access to the beer Rob always kept in the refrigerator, she wouldn't bother him no matter how late his brother stayed out. Jeremy was relieved. She had to be gotten rid of, and if he did anything drastic toward that end, Rob would be mad at him.

Jeremy had tapped into April's E-mail. It wasn't hard if you knew the password, and through binoculars he'd watched her enter it so many times he couldn't count. Jeremy'd never tried it, but he figured he could even make calls from her phone if he wanted to. Bug Dick had ended his message with "love." Bug Dick was going to come to April's tonight. Probably they'd have sex.

Not-Dolores had closed his window as if the soft night air was poison. Jeremy shoved it up again and sat on the sill, his feet on the asphalt shingles. Raising the glasses Rob had given him, he looked first at the hunter's moon, then at April's window. He'd been at the computer all day. It was uploaded now; she would see it. He knew she'd check her web site after supper. She always did. Tonight her blinds were closed for the first time. She was learning. Too late now.

"You better be looking, April," he said.

Nine-thirty. Hating herself for her cowardice, April had pulled all the blinds before dusk and checked the locks a dozen times. In half an hour Steve would come. Till he did, she would suffer from the preternatural hearing that had plagued her since sundown. Creaks became footsteps upstairs, the squeal of distant tires the sound of a door opening just out of sight. Television couldn't hold her attention, and the words of her book blurred before unfocused eyes. She found herself once again in the study in front of her computer. She had to look. All day she'd stayed away from the web site. Why wiggle the tooth if it hurt? Whoever was changing the picture could only frighten her if she complied. If she didn't look, it wasn't there.

But it was.

Condemning herself as hopeless, she logged on and called up her web site. The mouse summoned *Venus Rising* and she watched the colors scroll down the screen. The globe had burst. Smaller globes the color of fire rained down on an oily sea. A blackened crag erupted in dark vapor settling in a radioactive dust, blighting the plants. The woman was standing, her arms thrown up as if she reached to pull back the light or to close the hatch of the ship before the fallout reached her. The native man was there, as was the panther. They looked not at the woman but past her, as if they, too, were helpless, their eyes on the sinuous swirls of smoke or dust coming from the mountain.

Bile rose in April's throat and her hands trembled on the keys. The hell was so personal it could have been snatched from the bleakest corners of her id. All the things she feared had come to pass in this Eden she'd made for herself. Coiling purple haze shimmering on the screen hypnotized her, and much as she wanted to, she could not look away. Something in the lines turning in on themselves, forming and reforming beneath a molten sky, tried to force its way through her paralyzed mind.

The doorbell chimed, and she twitched as if she'd been poked with a cattle prod. Heart pounding, she leapt to her feet, Wanda running for cover beneath the computer desk. Nine-forty-five. Too early for Steve.

He was punctual to the minute. April looked back at the screen. Smoke swirled in its frozen pattern, talking to her, but in a language she could not understand. The doorbell rang again. There was no peephole. Running upstairs, April jerked apart the blinds and looked down at the porch. A little roof over the front steps hid the identity of the caller, but a man's legs showed from the knees down. Unable to decide whether to be still and hope he would go away or to run back down to the study for the phone, April stayed where she was. Slowly the feet turned. Trousers black, shoes lightweight running shoes. He stepped out and looked up directly into April's eyes.

"Steve!" April cried. Relief in the form of laughter swept her down the stairs and across the front room. Chain unhooked, bolt turned back, she pulled open the door and looked into his dear and familiar face. Steve smiled and the smoke cleared, the dust settled.

The swirling lines from the mountain: they'd formed a face, she'd just been too blind to see it. Steve's face, leering down from a blood-clotted sky.

Laughter choked into a strangled scream, April slammed the heavy door. A meaty forearm stopped it before it latched and pushed her back. Suddenly the wood gave, she fell forward, her knees banging painfully on the tile. Scrabbling, she clawed up the oak toward the chain and the bolt. Her fingers closed around the chain as the door exploded inward, smashing her elbow, slamming her back into the living room. Steve had kicked it. Formless in dark clothes, he burst in with the shattering wood. April stayed on her back on the carpet. Down, she could kick with all the considerable force of thighs and butt. If she tried to right herself, to crawl away, he'd be upon her. He shoved the door closed, shutting out the world, any help that might come. In his left hand, black with leather, he carried a short, sharp knife, the kind used to gut fish.

"You let the flowers die." His voice was quiet, normal, but his face had the stiff look of a man who's suffered a stroke. "It's always something."

April didn't have time to wonder what failings the other women had, the ones he'd punished. He stepped into the room and she kicked out. He was too far away. Energy wasted. "Don't, April," he said. "It has to end the same. Don't be ugly."

Helplessness tried to rise within April. All the movies and books that featured impotent heroines flailing harmless and tiny fists tried to take her courage, open her arms to the knife.

"Ugly," April hissed and gave herself strength. "Filthy, damn ugly." Harsh words bolstered her. She bent her knee, ready to kick again if he closed the distance between them. With frightening dexterity born of practice, he tossed the knife from hand to hand, careful to keep away from her feet as he looked for an opening. Without warning, he threw himself on her. Full body weight down the length of hers, the force of his fall crushing the breath from her lungs. One kick landed somewhere on his leg, and she heard him grunt, but he wasn't slowed. Screaming, April scratched for his hands, grabbing his sleeves, trying to find the knife and keep it from her. Breath, hot and sweet, puffed in her face, drips of spittle falling on her cheek. His chin was close to hers. Rearing her head up, she sank her teeth into the fleshy pad beneath his lower lip. Biting was a meager weapon, but pinned beneath him, it was all she had. Ugly. She would make this as ugly as she could.

Grabbing her hair, he banged her head against the floor, but she didn't let go. Blood—his—poured into her mouth and nose, choking her, but she didn't let go.

Crashing filled her ears and the sound of wood splintering and shouting. At first she thought it was her skull cracking and her lungs screaming, but suddenly the weight was lifted from her and a man in blue was saying—rather ridiculously she thought—"Unbite, lady. Unbite."

Steve was hauled away by two large and to April's eyes beautiful policemen. The sergeant stayed behind to ask her questions, check her security and let her blood pressure return to normal. April made the policewoman a cup of coffee, the kind in bags like tea. The sergeant sat at the dining table with a clipboard, her hat on the checkered cloth at her elbow, letting April wait on her, seeming to know that would be more comforting than forcing her to sit still and be a guest in her own home. April told her all she knew of Steve and was embarrassed at how little she'd really found out about his life in the four weeks they'd been seeing each other. She told the officer of the pictures on the computer, how they had warned her. The officer doubted if Steve had sent them. His m.o. was low tech. None of the other victims had been computer users.

As the policewoman was leaving, the obvious question came to April. "Were you following him?" The sergeant looked confused. "Why did you come?"

"You dialed 911. The address comes up automatically even if you don't speak."

"Thanks," April said distractedly.

"Are you going to be okay?"

"Sure," April returned. "I've got a guardian angel."

The sergeant didn't bat an eye. Twelve years on the force, she had probably heard it all.

"Well, call us if you need to," she said, smiled and was gone.

* * *

Jeremy stayed in the window, watching, till the patrol cars all pulled away. His call on April's line had worked. "All right! Bug Dick goes down," he crowed. Tonight he would put her picture back the way it was. Except for the muscular guy with the spear. He'd leave him. Somebody had to watch out for her.

Rob came in close to midnight and sat on the edge of his bed. Jeremy considered playing asleep, but he wasn't really mad at his brother. Since Erin had left him, he'd been pretty lonely.

"Hiya buddy," Rob said and ruffled Jeremy's hair. Jeremy pretended not to like it, like he always did. "How ya feeling? Headaches bother you today?"

"Good. I feel good. I can go back to school anytime."

"We'll see. Hepatitis is nothing to mess with. I talked to your teacher today. She said if you can make up the work, you won't have to repeat fifth grade."

"No big deal." Not for the guy who brought down Bug Dick.

Rob sat in silence for a minute. Trying to think of something to say. Jeremy knew the signs. "I'm sorry I leave you alone sometimes," Rob managed after a while. "I get . . . You know."

"Yeah." Rob, his only family, was twenty-five years older than Jeremy and had taken care of him since he was three and their folks died in a boating accident.

Rob looked around the room as if he'd never seen it before. His eyes settled on the computer monitor. "New screen saver? That some actress or something?"

Jeremy had left April's picture up. "You know, it'd be easier having a little brother if you married somebody. I could use a sister-in-law," Jeremy said slyly as they watched April's face fade in and out against a background of leaves.

Somebody had to look after her.

A resident of Mississippi, Nevada Barr draws on her background in the National Park Service for her series featuring ranger Anna Pigeon. The first book in the series, Track of the Cat, *won the Agatha and Anthony awards for Best First Novel in 1992. The most recent title is* Blind Descent, *and the next Anna Pigeon novel will take place on Ellis Island.*

My Dinner
with Aunt Kate

Amanda Cross

My name is Leighton Fansler, and I am niece to Kate
Fansler. I have for a long time aspired to be her Watson,
but she cannot be said to have encouraged me in this
endeavor, despite the few stories she has managed to tell
me. Recently, realizing how long a time it was since she
had treated me to an elegant dinner, I called and begged
to be given food different from my usual fare. My usual
fare is rather boring because of scant finances and a desire to remain thin, a desire I am quite prepared to recognize as totally indefensible. Aunt Kate, whose
slimness, like her income, is inherited, is rather intoler-
ant of my dieting, though all it consists of really is eating
Japanese and Vietnamese food in particular and vegetables in general. Aunt Kate, who finds Far Eastern food
or vegetables as a main course unendurable is, however,
sympathetic about my finances. My father, one of Kate's
brothers, is certainly rich, and so shall I be, one day;

23

meanwhile, I earn a pittance and receive from my father an allowance that he thinks is generous because it would have been so considered when he was a lad. Kate, therefore, agreed to take me to one of those restaurants where you make a reservation weeks ahead and consider yourself honored that they remember it. I know Kate hates this sort of place, but she is willing to indulge me from time to time, and even she admits that the food is good.

I was, of course, in pursuit of more than a savory meal, grateful though I was for that. I wanted to wrest another story from her. But "wrest" is the wrong word; one does not wrest stories from Aunt Kate; one entices them, and then only if she is in a narrative mood. I was pleased to see that she seemed unusually mellow as the waiter took our drink orders. Kate ordered a martini, which I hadn't seen her drink in a long time; lately, it had been single-malt scotch and nothing else. I raised an interrogative eyebrow.

"It's actually a long time since I've been here," Kate said, looking around the fancy restaurant. "I connect the place with martinis, so why not?"

I ordered one too, saying I wanted to join with her in celebrating the long ago and far away. When we were sipping them from tall, iced, inverted glass pyramids, I began to introduce the subject of her amateur but hardly anonymous endeavors as a detective.

"Have you ever noticed," I asked, "how many cases you've been requested to solve where some person has disappeared or decided to take on a new persona or impersonate someone else? I always thought you were a specialist in academic and literary puzzles, but you do seem to have attracted types who are a little unstable in the matter of their identity."

"Is that so?" Kate murmured, signaling for another round of martinis, while over her countenance there crept that odd, intrigued look, transitory but fervent, which indicates that something, not always obvious to the onlooker, has caught her attention. "I never thought of that, at least not exactly in that way." A reflective look came into her eyes; I held my breath.

"I never told anyone about the strangest of all those identity puzzles; really bizarre, that was, and it fooled and mocked me to the end and, I regret to say, beyond the end."

I finished off the end of my first martini, handed the glass to the waiter, and touched my fingers to the stem of the second martini while gazing with passionate interest into Aunt Kate's eyes.

"You needn't put on one of your girlish looks of fascinated attention," Aunt Kate said. "And do stop calling me Aunt Kate; I've asked you several times."

"I know you have." I lowered my eyes. "But just plain Kate doesn't seem very respectful."

"Leighton," Kate said, glaring at me. "Spare me the hogwash. I'll tell you the story, but not because you're looking at me like a lovesick cow. I feel like telling you the story, now that you've reminded me of it. After all, who else would listen? We aging detectives have to seize what opportunities for reminiscences present themselves."

"Oh, come off it, Kate," I said, reverting to my usual expression. "Let's hear it."

"We must order first," Kate said. Which goes to show you how sincere I really was about wanting to hear the story. Because perusing the menu, making hard choices about what to order, is one of my absolutely favorite undertakings. I picked up the huge menu and disappeared behind it, lost in agonizing decisions. Kate, of course, merely glanced at it and had made up her mind. She asked for the wine list. I flipped a mental coin to decide between my two favorite offerings and then, as is my wont, resolved on the other. I always had the same appetizer: oysters, a dozen of them. Once the oysters were finished, I would lap up all the cocktail sauce after adding more horseradish. Kate was wonderfully tolerant of this habit, which is what makes her the absolutely perfect model of aunthood.

Kate, who was spreading pâté on toast fingers, watched me start on the oysters and then spoke.

"This was years ago, you have to understand, in a different era. Let me see, well, I don't know how long ago, but it was one of my first cases, as you call them, and I damn near muffed it. It was just about at that time that computers were coming into general use for commercial records; most people didn't have personal computers yet, but clever business managers installed these mainframe computers, I think that's what they were called. I remember that they took up a whole room and that firms kept all the company records on them. It was a situation ripe for deception, since the folks who ran the computers then were the only people who really understood them, and of course, a good deal of fiddling went on."

"Don't tell me you understood computers back then!" I gasped.

"Of course not, you idiot. I don't even understand them now, I only write on them and use E-mail. Anyway, at that time, most of the fiddlers were caught sooner or later, or mostly sooner, because they were rather stupid about what to do with the money after they had embezzled it; they knew computers but weren't very canny in the ways of the big wide world—except for one computer thief."

Kate paused to allow me to give my attention to the remains of the cocktail sauce. Once the waiter, smiling tolerantly, had removed my empty oyster platter, proferred the wine, poured it, and set down our main courses, she continued.

"In fact," she mused, with the odd scrunched-up look people get when they are racking their brain to pluck forth a memory, "it may have been your father who put me in touch with the people who had been robbed. Anyway, it was one of my brothers, and clearly he, whichever one he was, had offered me as a last, if dim, hope. I can imagine it: 'My sister likes to play detective from time to time, in a purely amateur way; she doesn't get paid. I doubt she can help you, but as a last resort, you might want to give her a call.' That sort of thing. Anyway, I went around and was given the sad story.

"Their chief computernik, a woman—which was still a little unusual in those days—had managed to transfer nearly a million dollars into her own pocket. No, don't ask me how; I didn't understand it then, and I don't understand it now. The problem they presented me with was: what had become of her? She had vanished from the face of the earth, the way you say people tend to do in the puzzles I'm faced with."

"Hadn't they gone to the police?"

"Of course they had, and the FBI also."

"How did the FBI figure in it?"

"There was the assumption that she had probably crossed state lines. Anyway, when business calls, the FBI listens. They talked to everyone she knew or had ever known. She'd been with the firm a good while. She stole money a little bit at a time, parking it in some account before transferring it bit by bit to her own pocket, something like that. The only point I clearly grasped was that she'd taken her time about it and had managed to hide her transactions from the auditors. The fact that she'd been with the firm a matter of years made it likely that she would have left a trail of some sort behind her when she departed, a far richer woman, but the fact is she didn't.''

"She hadn't lived with anyone?"

"She had, as a matter of fact; she had apparently lived in connubial bliss with a plumber, who had a nice apartment and a nice income, pleasantly supplemented by her salary."

"They were married?"

"No; you can live in connubial bliss without being legally married; at least you can in my stories. Do stop interrupting."

"Sorry; but if I really don't understand one or other of the basic facts, mayn't I inquire?"

"Oh, Leighton, eat your dinner and stop simpering. Where was I?"

"I don't know where you were; the thief was living in connubial bliss."

"And fingerprintless bliss, which was the most amazing fact. The plumber claimed that she often wore gloves at home—saving her manicure or the smooth skin on her hands, some such reason—which certainly suggested premeditation of flight."

"She wore gloves in bed and in the shower?"

"Leighton!"

"Sorry."

"Of course she didn't wear gloves all the time. On the day of her flight, after the plumber had left for work, she wiped everything in the place carefully—very carefully. There wasn't a print to be found. And I learned that if you use something like Lemon Pledge, some ordinary furniture polish, it doesn't remove fingerprints beyond the capacity of a forensic laboratory to recover them. This woman knew what she was doing."

"She was a hardened and experienced criminal."

Kate, who had stopped for a bite, decided not to groan at this remark. "It certainly suggested that she knew about fingerprints and what was necessary, so to speak, to avoid their being lifted. Anyway, the point the investigators had reached so far was that she had successfully disappeared, vanished, dissolved, leaving behind only the loss of a million dollars.''

"Didn't they think she might have gone to work in another computer room for another firm?''

"Of course they did; the police may not be the cleverest or most honest people in the world, but they're not morons. That was everyone's first idea after they found the apartment she shared with the plumber offered no clues. Neither, incidentally, did the plumber. He couldn't understand it, but seemed inclined to shrug off her departure, which needless to say aroused suspicions. But she never got in touch with him, and a complete search of his life, friends, jobs, provided no clues whatever.''

"Trumpets sound: Kate Fansler enters.''

"Hardly. I could barely get the police to give me the time of day. But with enough pressure from the big business types I was finally shown the whole file of the police investigation—not yet on a computer, by the way. I had to read through endless reports written in some language that resembled English only accidentally and only occasionally.''

"But you didn't complain or come on as an English professor?''

"Certainly not. I complimented them on their thoroughness and oozed gratitude for their generosity. We ended up, some of us, rather chummy, as a matter of fact, but that didn't matter then. I was, however, able to ask an occasional favor from them in later years, and they asked me how to get their kids into college, but that's neither here nor there. Where was I?''

"Just beginning, I think, having read the police files.''

"I'm glad you're paying attention. I quickly reached two conclusions: one, she was obviously too smart to leave a trail by working at computers or anything related thereto; second, if she was as clever as I thought she was, she wasn't going to live on her ill-gotten gains and blow the lot. She would want to find some arrangement which supported her and left the income from her theft for luxuries like elegant shoes and a convertible—that sort of thing.

"I decided she was still in the United States; she was unlikely to risk using a fake passport or a real one with her picture. I know that sounds a little weak, but if she wasn't in the U.S., I certainly couldn't find her, so I decided she was here. Anyway, I acted on that assumption. But "here" is a very large place. I had somehow to narrow it down. The most obvious thing for her to do was to marry, to tie up with someone rich, preferably without too many relatives."

"You're saying it's always easier for a woman to marry money than to make it."

"Let us remember, dear Leighton, that the women's movement was barely under way. It was well into the seventies that conditions for women, legally speaking, began to change."

"*Roe v. Wade* was 1973."

"If you keep interrupting and correcting me, I shan't say another word. In fact, I think I won't in any case. I'm ignoring this excellent and expensive dinner while you sit there guzzling away."

"Aunt Kate, Kate, please don't be angry. Who taught me to be a feminist? Who said that the trouble with the young today was that they didn't know any history and thought they'd always had the rights they now enjoy? I was merely showing you how seriously I took these admonitions."

Kate had the grace to smile. Anyway, she liked barking at me; it assured her that she wasn't getting sentimental or over-affectionate, attitudes to be avoided at all costs.

"Even if my conclusions were both sexist and obvious, they were all I had. And don't think for a minute that they were particularly helpful. The number of rich men looking for wives or mistresses is limited but still large enough to be uncountable. I did establish, from the plumber and members of the firm, that she was good-looking—graceful and on the whole agreeable as well as pretty.

"Don't say it. Of course she would no longer look remotely the same; she would have changed the color of her hair and her use of makeup. I doubt she would have gone in for anything surgical, since that leaves a trail, and not leaving a trail was what she was especially good at."

"Dentists."

"We couldn't find any. And even though the police used a sketch artist, it wasn't all that clear in the details. With her hair cut short, her face scrubbed—she wore a great deal of makeup, apparently—with spectacles added, she would have been practically unidentifiable."

"But still pretty enough to attract a rich man."

"That was my hope. I then thought of a folk saying or old-fashioned truth I used to hear a lot. If you're having trouble finding a man, go away and become the new girl in town. I decided—after all, what could I lose?—that this is what she would do: find a relatively small town, one that contained some rich men, and go there. So all I had to do was find some small towns with rich men."

"How did you define small?"

"Good question. I decided to start with towns of five thousand or less, where a new girl in town would be noticeable. I was only able to find figures for towns with populations of between twenty-five hundred and five thousand. There were twenty-six hundred of these in the U.S. Of course, not all of them had rich families. An urban economist friend of mine played with a few numbers giving income, correlated them with the number of towns, and came up with about eight hundred. I telegraphed (we still had telegraphs then) the newspapers in all of these towns and asked if they had had any marriages within the last months between an out-of-town woman and a well-to-do man. I offered to pay for the information, which sped the answers along nicely. There were twelve such cases. So I started off on a trip around the country. Reed came with me. We weren't married then, but he had leave coming, so we spent the summer toddling around to small towns.''

''And you found her.''

''No, we didn't. The whole process was rather drawn out. Once I had made the acquaintance of the newly-weds—sometimes we had to await the return from their honeymoon—I had to decide if the woman in question was the object of my search.''

''How on earth did you establish that?''

''I'm glad you asked. I did it by the patented Kate Fansler method: intuition. Well, not exactly intuition, more instinct really. Most of the women could no more have managed the workings of a mainframe computer than they could have discovered the planet Pluto. I didn't expect my woman to admit to a knowledge of computers, nor did I dismiss the assumption that she might be acting dumb to mislead me. But I will say that one thing my life as a professor has taught me is to recognize a mind used to the contemplation of complex ideas. You can't imitate it and you can't hide it. I counted on that.''

''Kate,'' I asked, deciding to satisfy my curiosity and throw caution to the winds, ''do you mean that you and Reed took off on this expedition with no greater hope of success than a mad idea about newlyweds in small towns?"

"Well, not exactly," Kate said, chuckling at the question, which fortunately she seemed to have found amusing rather than pert. "Reed and I wanted to go off somewhere, spend some leisurely time together, we both liked driving, and we thought we ought to see the United States, or at least that part of it that summoned us in connection with this endeavor. This search seemed as good a travel plan as any, so we adopted it as an excuse."

"Why did you need an excuse to drive around the U.S.?"

"Because neither of us wanted to just take off together—too big a commitment, too serious altogether. But when I mentioned this case to Reed, and as we talked about it, the idea of the journey seemed to amuse us both without any obligation upon either one of us to stay with the plan to the end. I could continue alone, either of us could decide to peel off, no pledge of any sort either way. As it turned out, we had a fine time."

"And you discovered, despite your decision never to marry, that Reed might just do."

"That's putting it a little emphatically. We didn't marry for quite a while afterward. But you are right: it was on that trip that I determined he was a good traveling companion in every possible way."

"Meaning as a lover, I suppose?" I like to act cool with Kate.

"Of course, but a lot else besides. He was never boring, he wasn't impassioned about sightseeing, and he was ready to consult road maps, which I have never been able to decipher, without acting as though he was about to take up cartography as a vocation. Above all, we laughed a lot. It is my belief that if you don't laugh when you're traveling with someone, you might as well go unaccompanied or not at all.''

"Imagine that! I'm glad I inquired.'' I'm always intrigued by Kate's and Reed's relationship. "What happened next?''

"The same as had been happening before. I couldn't locate a single woman who would have been able to run a chicken farm efficiently, let alone a computer program for a large company. No, I'm not putting women down, that just happened to be the way it turned out. But remember, we're still in the seventies.''

"So the story fooled you to the end. Don't tell me that's all there is to it. That's the story, then? That's it?''

"Not quite. It was just about this time in our travels that I had an inspiration. It struck me one night when we thought we'd take a walk. We usually stayed in motels, but we were spending this night in a country inn, charming, and as tends to be the case with charming country inns, a bit too gussied up with chintz and fluff, but at least one could leave the place and take a walk that didn't lead, after ten steps, onto a highway.

We set off, and the night turned out to be a bit chilly. I said I'd better go back for a jacket. Reed said, "Why bother?—you can wear mine,'' and he put it on me. We're both tall and thin, though he's a bit taller, and the sleeves of his jacket were long on me, but not uncomfortably so. I was wearing pants and English walking shoes—I particularly remember that detail for some reason—and it occurred to me that someone seeing us together with me in his jacket might think I was a man. Heaven knows why I thought that, but I never examine a sudden revelation as to cause.''

"So you suddenly thought that the computer thief was disguised as a man.'' Of course, I had seen this coming. We had both, by now, finished our main course and were being encouraged to have dessert by the waiter. I ordered a lavish piece of pastry, and Kate had coffee and a sambucca. "So," I ventured, trying to keep any sense of the anticlimactic out of my voice, "having had that bright idea, you went forth and found the woman."

"Yes, we did. Not that that was a lot easier. We'd been to several towns already, but now we had more exact questions to ask, and our inquiries to newspapers and other requests for information in the towns we hadn't yet visited were a little less general. We felt reasonably certain that the towns we had seen contained no such couple as we now envisioned. Reed and I talked about it, and we decided that what she/he would have to do would be marry a rich woman and one who might not, for some reason, have been likely to marry. Probably someone young, rich, and ill, who hadn't expected to marry."

"What on earth made you arrive at that conclusion?"

"It took a while, but we decided that she/he would need to marry fast and therefore would need to propose to someone considered more or less out of the marriage game. Illness or excessive homeliness or even being disabled seemed good guesses. I know, don't argue with me, Leighton, we were not being very enlightened; in fact, we were being damned sexist, but you asked for the story and that's how it went."

"And I'll remember it was in the early seventies."

"Good girl. We did succeed in finding just such a marriage with half the effort or maybe less than half the effort we had had to expend in our former pursuit, and we set off. We stayed in a bed-and-breakfast. I had nice gossips with the local ladies, and Reed played golf—which he played very well, though he's long since given it up—with the men, and before many days were past, we had all the details and an invitation to meet the newlyweds. The girl was crippled with polio, which she'd contracted in Mexico, having foolishly gone there uninoculated, but a highly intelligent, lovely person. She was in a wheelchair.''

''And her ''husband''?

''He was delightful; attentive to his wife, but not ridiculously so. They shared a number of interests, clearly, and were planning trips and projects. He/she was a handsome fellow.''

''And how, may I ask, did you suppose that he had won her over with no suspicion that he was after her money?''

''Watching them, and talking to her alone for some time, I decided it was not hard to decipher. She/he was, after all, a woman herself and knew how to please a woman, I mean really please a real woman, not just treat her the way popular magazines and movies suggested she wanted to be treated.''

''And sex between them wasn't really a problem since it didn't happen.''

''Intercourse probably didn't happen, but I'm sure there was sex between them; that's one of the things he/she understood so well, as I figured it out. And at the same time, she knew how to give her husband enough rope for him not to feel tied down. I couldn't help noticing how she/he stayed with her when she invited him, urged him, to run off by himself.''

''But instead of letting them live happily ever after, you pulled the plug, identified him to the FBI and the police and the big business folks, and tore apart their idyll.''

''Well, what would you have had me do, Leighton? The woman had stolen a million dollars; surely that had to be returned to its rightful owners.''

''Why? They weren't smart enough to know she was

stealing it until she took off. And what's a million dollars to a business like that? They'd write it off as a bad debt and charge the customers more. Really, Kate, I think you might at least have spied on them from time to time, the newly married couple I mean, and if their happiness flourished, leave them the hell alone."

"The truth is," Kate said, fishing out one of the coffee beans from her sambucca and chewing it thoughtfully, "we did just that. Reed and I talked it over. We both kept in touch with people we had met in that town; we kept inquiring about the couple, we probed. And as far as we could determine, which was pretty far, they went on enjoying marital bliss as much as most so-called happy couples do and more than most."

"And that's the end of the story, Auntie, and in fact they are happy to this day?"

"Not quite, not as a couple. She/he was killed when a tree fell on him; he died instantly."

"A tree fell on him? Come on, Kate. Are you making this whole thing up?"

"Not a word of it. Trees do fall on people, you know, particularly in storms. There's a famous scientist who was killed that way, though I can't at the moment remember his name. In California. A storm came up. I've forgotten the details, except that it was very sad. And so was this. This death was regrettable indeed."

I thought about the story for a while. I contemplated having a second dessert but nobly decided against so immature a move. We sat for a while in silence until I thought of something.

"But Kate," I said, remembering, "you told me when you began this tale that it fooled and mocked you to the end and beyond the end. What was that supposed to mean?"

"Well, it fooled me to the time when it occurred to

us that the woman might be masquerading as a man and mocked us for not having thought of that sooner.''

"And beyond the end?"

Kate looked at me a while, and an expression came over her face that I can only describe as sheepish, a most unKatelike expression. She waved at the waiter, asked for another cup of coffee and the bill, and started rummaging around in her purse for a credit card.

"Kate," I said with some emphasis. "Tell. Was it that you thought the young woman had found happiness only to have it lost to her through a freakish accident?"

"Not exactly; no. You see, we had figured out that the reason his "wife" had to be ill or disabled was to avoid their having intercourse, since that might have been difficult to bring off. I've learned since, of course, how many people do bring off this sort of thing, but at that time I was a lot less informed on such subjects."

"Plays like *Yentl* and *M Butterfly* hadn't come along."

"No, nor books like Diana Middlebrook's biography of Billy Tipton, who married about five times as a man and was a woman the whole time—both a husband and a famous member of a jazz band."

"You're saying she/he could have faked it, and so you figured the whole thing out on a basis that wasn't necessary, is that it?"

"Yes, that's it."

"O.K. So what happened beyond the ending?"

"Well." Kate didn't seem to know how to word this, whatever it was. "After she/he died, they discovered that she had been a he all along."

"What on earth do you mean?"

"I mean, Leighton," Kate said firmly, having made a determined effort to shed her embarrassed demeanor, "the woman who had stolen the money in the first place wasn't a woman. She was a man."

"A man pretending to be a woman."

"Exactly."

I thought about this for a moment or two. "But what about the plumber? Didn't he think she, or he, was a woman?"

"He did. But as the Chinese man/woman character says in *M Butterfly*, men find in women what they expect to find. You may remember the character has to strip nude to convince the audience, if not the judge in the play, that he is indeed a man who has been a kept woman for decades."

We started to get up from the table. "But Kate," I said, when we were out in the street, "you believed that the reason she or he was such a good husband was because she knew how to please a woman."

"I admitted all that, Leighton," Kate growled, heading off a rapid pace for her walk home and waving to me as she departed.

"Wait a minute," I called, catching her up. "In fact, you were wrong about everything in that case; you just wanted to traipse around the country dallying with Reed. You didn't really solve it at all."

"Nonsense," Kate said. "He may have been a man, but he had lived as a woman, so he knew what women wanted."

"Or what they were supposed to want." I couldn't resist saying that.

"The fact is, Leighton, I'm sorry I told you the story, I really am."

And she strode off, leaving me, who lived in the opposite direction, to smile to myself. Oh, well, I thought, she found the person, whatever the sex, and that person gave a woman happiness. Not a bad story after all.

But I wasn't sure it was really suited to me in my Watson mode. Oh, well, it was a sumptuous dinner.

It's an open secret that mystery writer Amanda Cross is feminist scholar Carolyn G. Heilbrun, author of several nonfiction works, including a biography of Gloria Steinem. In her Cross persona, Heilbrun has created forthright English professor Kate Fansler, star of Death in a Tenured Position *and numerous other novels, including the recent* The Puzzled Heart.

Just So Much Garbage

Mary Daheim

Serena Grover Jones, known as Renie to family and friends, crouched on the living room floor, dug in with her fingernails, and ripped the brown wrapping paper off what looked like a suit box.

"I've been expecting this outfit to be delivered for the last three weeks," she said to her cousin, Judith Flynn, who was sitting nearby on a big leather footstool. "Nordquist had to back-order it. I can't wait to wear it for my big presentation at the garbage dump."

"Knowing what you probably paid for it," Judith remarked dryly, "you'll need to start collecting garbage on your own, not just sell the city on your graphic design presentation."

"Yeah, yeah, yeah," Renie muttered, raising the lid of the box and removing the top layers of tissue paper. "Yikes!" she cried, recoiling. "This isn't what I ordered! It's a cocktail dress. Two, in fact—there's a green one under the blue. Ugh. I hate peplums." Renie stood up amid a fluttering of tissue paper. "I'm calling Nordquist right now. Where the heck's my garbage suit?"

As her cousin stomped off to the dinette to retrieve her cordless phone, Judith idly picked up the brown wrapping paper. "Hey, coz," she called, "this isn't addressed to you. It's to a Mrs. Alvin Masterson, down the street."

Halfway through Nordquist's number, Renie hung up. "What? Masterson?" She returned to the living room. "The deliveryman must have made a mistake. Damn. Now I'll have to rewrap this and take it down to the Mastersons." Her voice held a note of trepidation.

"Cheer up," urged Judith, assuming that Renie was worried about getting her outfit on time. "When's the presentation?"

Renie was distracted. "Huh? Oh, a week from today, next Tuesday." She got back down on the floor and began smoothing the discarded tissue paper. "You know, this is weird. I've been meaning to mention it for a long time, but I always got sidetracked. There's something downright spooky about that Masterson setup."

Judith's ears pricked up. While Hillside Manor, her bed-and-breakfast establishment on the other side of Heraldsgate Hill, kept her busy, Judith had a knack for unraveling mysteries that even her husband, Joe, a veteran homicide detective, grudgingly admired.

"Spooky?" Judith echoed. "You mean, as in mysterious or scary?"

"Both," Renie said, settling into her husband Bill's favorite chair by the window. "The Mastersons have lived in this neighborhood almost as long as we have, but nobody's ever gotten to know them." Renie leaned forward, pointing at the window. "See that Roman brick house across the intersection and two doors down? That's their place."

Judith had gotten up from the footstool to have a look. "The house looks all closed up."

"It always does," Renie said as Judith returned to the footstool. "An alley goes through the block, and the Mastersons usually go in and out that way. But once in a while—and bear in mind I'm talking about over a period of twenty-odd years—they park out front, and I see them go in that way. He's a tall, skinny guy and she's a big, big woman. Close to three hundred pounds, I'd guess. I think her first name is Marla. We've gotten their mail a few times over the years. They never have company. I don't think they have kids, at least I've never seen any. Then last week I saw a strange woman go up the front steps. I thought she must be selling something, but she went inside. I waited a few minutes, but then I had to get back to work down in the den. I never saw her come out. I realized that in the last year or so, she was about the third woman I'd seen go into the house. The first one was a big blonde with a chest out to here." Renie gestured with her hands. "Then there was a redhead, all swivel hips and high heels. The last one was brunette. Actually, she was nice-looking. I guess that's why I thought she was in sales, maybe real estate."

Judith didn't comment right away. "When was the last time you saw Mr. and Mrs. M.?" she asked after a thoughtful pause.

Renie grimaced. "I don't remember when I last saw them as a couple. A year or more, maybe. But I saw him three, four months ago, around Halloween. Once in a while I cut through the alley to come from the bottom of the hill. Mr. Masterson was working in the backyard."

"But no Mrs. Masterson?" Judith asked.

Renie shook her head. As usual when she was at home, the chestnut curls were uncombed, and the bedraggled black pants and rumpled sweatshirt were a far cry from the designer number she'd been expecting from Nordquist.

"Hey!" Renie said, jumping out of the chair. "Let me have another look at those cocktail dresses. Why would Mrs. Masterson order them when they never go anywhere?"

Renie reopened the box while Judith leaned over her cousin's shoulder. "Size ten," Renie said in awe, pointing to the label on the blue dress. "They're both tens. From what I've seen of Mrs. Masterson, she'd have to sew them together to cover just her butt."

Judith gazed wistfully at the tags on the dresses. "Size ten," she sighed. "I haven't been a size ten since I was ten. And even then, I was a twelve."

Renie repackaged the dresses. "Coz, you aren't really overweight. You're just—statuesque. And tall. I am neither of those things, since I verge on dumpy."

"Dumpies don't wear size ten. You do." Judith tried to visualize Renie's figure. It was in there somewhere under the ugly, baggy outfit. She nudged Renie. "Shall we deliver those little numbers?"

"Now?" Renie considered. "Why not? I've got the presentation more or less in hand. That's one of the reasons I have my graphic design business at home. I can keep my own hours."

The cousins walked down the steep hill in the bright February sunshine. It had rained the day before; it would probably rain the day after. But for now, the Pacific Northwest weather was kind. The daffodils were budding, and the forsythia was in its full golden glory.

"Who lives on either side of the Mastersons?" Judith asked as they crossed the intersection.

"The Chow-Fullers—that's a hyphenation—live in this corner house," Renie replied, indicating the two-story remodel with its floor-to-ceiling picture windows. "They have a couple of little girls, very cute. Mrs. Lyzincski lives on the other side in that light-green bungalow. She's quite elderly and has been widowed for a long time. Her son, Archie, looks in on her at least a couple of times a week.''

Judith had slowed her step, studying the Roman brick facade with the heavy drapes covering the big front window. ''It's well kept,'' she remarked, ''even if it has that deserted look. Who mows the grass?''

''Angel Rubirosa, the same one who does ours,'' Renie answered as they approached the ten curving steps that led to the front walk. The small rockery flanking the steps had been planted with heather, pot o' gold, various forms of sedum, and other low-maintenance flora. ''I've asked Angel about the Mastersons,'' Renie said, ''but he never sees them. He comes every two weeks, submits a bill, and gets paid by check. Of course, Angel hasn't been around since October. He'll start mowing again in late March.''

Renie led the way up the concrete steps and pressed the buzzer. The porch was small and unadorned. The cousins waited. Renie poked the buzzer a second time.

''Who is it?'' The voice that belonged to whoever was peering through the peephole was husky and abrupt.

''Your neighbor, Mrs. Jones,'' Renie called. ''I have a parcel that belongs to you.''

''Leave it,'' the husky voice replied.

''I opened it by mistake,'' Renie said. ''I'd like to apologize.''

''You already did. Good-bye.''

Renie and Judith exchanged glances. ''Rats,'' Renie muttered. ''Let's go.''

''Where?'' Judith asked in a whisper.

Renie shoved Judith in the direction of the walk. ''Hit it, move, let's boppin'—''

''I'm going,'' Judith replied a bit crossly. ''You sound like Bill.''

"I often do," Renie said as they went down the concrete steps. "It's what comes of having been married for over thirty years. You'll see."

Widowed by her first husband, Judith had been married to Joe, the great love of her life, for six years. She couldn't help but smile. "I'm enjoying the wait."

Renie, however, was moving uphill at a trot. "Come on. We can cross the street and watch the Mastersons' front porch from behind the Dierdorfs' rhododendrons."

The cousins reached the shrubbery just as the screen door to the Masterson house swung open. An arm clad in light blue reached to secure the package. The screen door swung shut.

"That was a dud," Renie griped. "Was it a man or a woman?"

Judith shook her head. "I couldn't tell, not even from the voice."

Renie returned to the sidewalk, with Judith right behind her. "Let's try the alley just for the heck of it. I haven't been down that way for a while."

Checking her watch, Judith saw that it was almost noon. "I should get home to fix Mother's lunch. You know how crabby she gets if I'm late with her meals."

"Aunt Gertrude's crabby when you're *not* late," Renie replied, heading along the cross street. "My mother merely plays martyr and guilt-trips me into submission."

"It works either way," Judith sighed, but dutifully accompanied Renie to the paved alley. "This morning my mother accused me of sucking out the cream centers of her Granny Goodness Easter eggs. I didn't even know she had any Easter eggs yet. Lent just started."

"My mother told me not to buy her any Easter candy this year," said Renie. "She doesn't expect to live that long."

"She will." Judith sounded resigned.

As they walked past the remodeled house on the corner, two small girls of Asian-American ancestry peeked out around the open gate to the Chow-Fuller backyard.

"Hi," Renie said, summoning up a smile. "Which one of you should be in school?"

"Me!" piped the taller of the two, raising a hand. "I'm Madison, and I'm almost seven. I've got sniffles." Madison glanced at her small sister. "This is Seneca. She's only four. She has to stay home to keep our mother company."

Judith started to speak to the children, but before the words could come out, a shaggy white puppy darted through the open gate.

"Rags!" Madison cried as Seneca pursued the dog on her short, plump legs. "Come back here! Seneca, don't go there. Mr. Bastardson will shoot you."

Renie and Judith stared at Madison. "What did you call the man next door?" Renie asked.

Madison was watching Seneca, who had retrieved the puppy. "Mr. Bastardson. That's his name. That's what my daddy calls him." The little girl turned innocent dark eyes up to Renie.

Judith had bent down, hands on knees. "Is that because Mr. Bastardson's not a very nice man, Madison?"

Seneca, who appeared to have a stranglehold on the puppy, jumped up and down. The dog managed to escape and began sniffing the cousins' shoes. "He's mean!" Seneca squealed. "He yells at us! He threw a rock at Rags!"

"Why was that?" Judith asked, scratching Rags behind the ears.

Madison assumed a very grown-up air. "Rags dug under Mr. Bastardson's fence and got in the yard. Rags likes to dig. Mr. Bastardson caught him and started throwing rocks. We heard Rags bark, so we ran down the alley and helped Rags get out under the fence. Mr.

Bastardson said if he ever caught Rags digging in his yard, he'd shoot him.'' Madison's eyes glistened with tears.

"Interesting," Judith remarked under her breath. "Is Mrs. Masterson—Mrs. Bastardson—as mean as he is?"

Both little girls looked bewildered. "You mean the big fat lady?" asked Madison. "I'm not sure. I haven't seen her since I was little."

Judith put a hand on Madison's head. "How little?" she asked with an encouraging smile.

"Umm . . ." Madison hesitated. "When I was five?"

Judith gave the dog another scratch, then guided him around the gate with the Chow-Fuller girls. Renie was already a few yards down the alley, cautiously approaching the Masterson property.

"A six-foot-high wooden fence," Renie noted. "There's the detached garage." She pointed off to her left. The doors of the wooden structure were padlocked. Renie gave the gate, which matched the fence, a shove. "It's locked, too. Can you see over the fence? I'm too short."

Judith looked around for something to stand on. A rock had been wedged under the fence, perhaps where Rags had dug his way in. Judith tugged and yanked until the rock came free. Then she stood on tiptoe, balanced precariously on the rock. "Mostly shrubs, low maintenance, like the front yard. An old apple tree—you can see the top half from where you're standing. It's kind of dreary, but . . ." Judith stopped, leaning against the fence. "That's odd. There's a big patch of grass that looks new, smack in the middle of the lawn."

Renie frowned up at Judith. "How big?"

Judith stepped off the rock. "Six feet by five? You don't have septic tanks on this side of the hill, do you?"

"Of course not." Renie seemed insulted. "We're as civilized as you snobs on the south slope."

Judith started to pick up the rock to replace it, but Renie stopped her. "I've got a better idea," she said, looking mischievous. She picked up the rock and dumped it in the garbage can across the alley.

Judith started to remonstrate, then thought better of it. "Where are the Mastersons' garbage and recycling bins?"

"Maybe on the other side of the garage. They don't have to be out in the alley except on pickup days," Renie explained. "Coz, what about that new grass? If you aren't much of a gardener, why worry about a bad patch?"

Judith grimaced. "Are you thinking what I'm thinking?"

Renie gave a faint shake of her head. "I don't want to, but . . ." She made a helpless gesture with one hand. "Is it even remotely possible?"

"Anything's possible, as we well know," Judith said in a grim voice. "If Mr. Masterson is still around, and nobody's seen his wife for months, how great are the odds that she's making mulch on the other side of that fence?"

"Ugh." Renie had turned a trifle pale. "Are you going to tell Joe?"

"No," Judith answered. "You know how he hates it when I speculate about things. Come on, let's go back to your place and talk this over."

Sitting in the Jones dinette, drinking coffee, the cousins reviewed what little they knew about the Mastersons. "That's the problem," Renie sighed. "We don't know much of anything. Twenty, twenty-five years in that house, and I've seen them maybe two dozen times. I haven't seen Mrs. Masterson for at least a year, maybe two. But that's really not unusual." Renie paused, rubbing her chin. "What is unusual, now that I think about it, is that I often saw them together in January. I remember, because I'd have the post-holiday blahs, and I'd catch myself staring down the street, thinking how bleak everything looked after all the decorations were down.''

''But not this past January or last year?'' Judith asked.

Renie shook her head. ''We had all that snow a year ago January. Nobody on this hill got out much. And this year, definitely not. Of course, I spend so much time in the basement den, working. They could come and go a thousand times, and I wouldn't know it.''

Judith was silent for a moment. Then her black eyes lit up. ''When do they pick up your recycling?''

''The fourth Thursday of every month,'' Renie answered, then jumped up. ''Day after tomorrow. I always put the bin out the day before. We all do around here, because they come so early.''

''Garbage?'' Judith asked.

Renie lowered her coffee mug. ''Every Monday, same as yours.''

Judith had gotten to her feet. ''I'll meet you at six A.M. Thursday in the alley behind the Mastersons.''

''What?'' Renie was aghast. ''You know I never get up before nine-thirty.''

''Try it once,'' Judith said with a sly grin. ''You may like it.''

''I won't,'' said Renie. ''But I will. Try it, that is. Once.''

Wednesday afternoon, Renie decided to talk to the Mastersons' neighbors. She called on Mrs. Lyzincski first, bearing a plate of fresh-baked snickerdoodles.

''I see you so seldom,'' Renie said in her most amiable voice, ''now that you can't get to Mass every Sunday. How is your arthritis?''

''Terrible,'' the old lady replied, sinking further into the mohair sofa. ''Aches all the time. How's your dear mother? I haven't seen her in ages.''

"She's fine," Renie answered. "You must call her. Mom loves to talk on the phone." Indeed, the picture that sprang to Renie's mind was of her mother with the phone practically screwed into her left ear. "I was wondering . . . how are the Mastersons? I haven't seen them all winter."

"Oh!" Mrs. Lyzincski held up her small, gnarled hands. She was a tiny woman, with beautiful white hair and keen blue eyes. "Keep themselves to themselves, don't they? Except for the music, of course. I wish they'd keep that to themselves."

"Music?" Renie echoed. "What kind of music?"

"Oh, I couldn't say. It's just *loud* music." Mrs. Lyzincski sniffed with disdain.

"How long has that been going on?" Renie asked.

"Oh, let me think—a few months. Maybe a year." The old lady smiled sadly. "It's hard to keep track of time when you spend so much of it alone."

Renie heard a sound from the rear of the house. She looked inquiringly at her hostess. But Mrs. Lyzincski didn't turn a hair. Deaf, Renie thought, and stood up. "Shall I take these into the kitchen?" she asked, pointing to the cookie plate.

"How nice," said Mrs. Lyzincski. "Thank you, dear."

Renie gave a start when she saw a balding man about her own age taking off his jacket and cap. "Archie?" she said in an anxious voice.

Archie Lyzincski grinned at her, revealing a gap between his front teeth. "That's right. You're the neighbor from up the street, right? Mrs . . ."

"Jones," Renie offered. "I brought your mother some cookies."

"How kind of you," said Archie, and grabbed one of the snickerdoodles. "My favorite."

"I was just leaving," Renie said. "Your mother and

I were talking about the Mastersons. Has she ever complained to you about the Mastersons' loud music?''

Archie chewed thoughtfully. ''Yes, she has. The volume must have been turned up high. Mama's a bit deaf.'' Archie uttered a little laugh. ''I'd never have guessed it until lately, but the Mastersons must be party people. Mama had a spell a couple of weeks ago, and I had to come over here about two in the morning. I've misplaced my front door key, so I had to use the one for the back. I came through the alley, and Mr. Masterson was closing the garage. He was all duded up, like he'd been out on the town. I missed seeing her. She must have gone on ahead of him to hit the lights. They went on just before I pulled into Mama's garage.''

In a thoughtful mood, Renie left the Lyzincski house. The cocktail dresses certainly backed up Archie's belief that the Mastersons were a pair of party animals. But nothing else fit, especially not the size tens. Renie glanced up at the Masterson place on her way to the Chow-Fullers. It looked the same as before—unwelcoming and shut off from the world.

Jackie Chow-Fuller was a pretty, vivacious woman in her early forties. She greeted Renie warmly and insisted on making a fresh pot of coffee.

''My girls are in the family room, watching TV,'' she explained. ''Maybe we'll have some peace and quiet.''

Renie told Jackie about meeting Madison and Seneca in the alley the previous day. ''I was appalled,'' Renie said, hoping she didn't sound like a phony, ''when they told me Mr. Masterson had threatened to shoot Rags.''

Jackie laughed. ''I'm sure he was teasing. Oh, a couple of years ago, I wouldn't have said that. Mr. Bastardson—'' She stopped and put a hand over her mouth. ''Sorry. That slipped out. My husband and I have to be more careful around the children. But that's what we used to call Mr. Masterson before he mended his ways.''

"He did?" Renie was surprised.

Jackie nodded. "We've lived here for over ten years. Up until a year or so ago—except for the incident with Rags, and frankly, that puppy is a terror when it comes to digging—neither of the Mastersons even spoke to us. But lately, he's become much more friendly. He even apologized for yelling at the girls."

Renie was nonplussed. "What about Mrs. Masterson? Has she warmed up, too?"

Jackie was pouring the freshly brewed coffee into a pair of Moonbeam mugs. "You know, that's the strange part. I haven't seen her for ages. I always felt sorry for her. He was so grumpy, and I know he must have given her a hard time."

Renie made a face. "I hate to ask a dumb question, but did you ever hear loud music over there?"

"Sometimes," Jackie replied. "But it's always in the morning, so I try not to let it bug me. It's not rock or anything like that, but there is a lot of shouting."

"By the Mastersons?" Renie asked.

Jackie shrugged. "Could be. I honestly can't tell."

By the time Renie headed back up the hill, she was more confused than ever. "How," she demanded of Judith on the phone ten minutes later, "could Mr. Masterson do such a turnabout and suddenly become nice?"

"It definitely sounds odd," Judith agreed. "Maybe he retired recently. By the way, what did you say he did for a living?"

Renie tried to think, to remember. "I don't know," she finally admitted. "I don't think I ever knew. But he could have taken early retirement. I'd guess the Mastersons to be in their fifties, about our age."

"This just keeps getting stranger and stranger," Judith said. "I've got to fix the appetizers for my guests. See you at six A.M."

Renie groaned.

* * *

It was still dark the following morning when the cousins entered the alley. "Bill thinks I'm crazy," Renie muttered, huddled in her black parka. "Doesn't Joe wonder where you are?"

"He thinks I had to run up to Falstaff's Market to get some missing ingredients for the guests' breakfast," Judith answered.

The alley was now lined with large, heavy plastic bins, reserved for paper and aluminum. Hooked onto the front of each bin was a separate container just for glass.

"I'll dumpster-dive," said Judith. "You check the glass stuff."

"That's easy," Renie said, clicking on a small flashlight. "There's not much in here. A half-dozen fancy juice bottles. A mustard jar. A lightbulb. Some broken glass that looks like it might have come out of a picture frame. That's it."

In the bin, Judith was finding newspapers, magazines, catalogues, and the usual junk mail. But as she strained to reach bottom, she felt something stiffer than newsprint or an advertising circular.

"Look at this," she said, holding up an eight-by-ten photograph that was badly creased, perhaps in an attempt at destruction.

Renie shone the flashlight on the photo. It was of a gray-haired, heavyset woman, who looked as if she was mad at the world. Or at least at the photographer who had taken the picture.

"I never saw Mrs. Masterson up close," Renie said softly, "but I'm sure that must be her. I'll bet the picture got thrown out with the frame and the broken glass I just found. Whoever did it must have been angry."

"Or vindictive," Judith murmured. "This is getting ugly, coz."

"Save that," Renie ordered. "Much as I hate to say it, it could be evidence."

Judith made one last dive, disturbing some of the newspapers clutched in her fist. Thin pieces of paper fluttered to the bottom. "Look at these," she said to Renie, gathering up the small, flimsy sheets. "They're off W-2 forms, those things you get in late January to file with your income tax."

There were three in all, listing not the Mastersons, but other names. "Evelyn Barrett," Renie read in the flashlight's wavering beam. "Jeanne Sorenson. Diana Marchant. What the heck . . . ?"

Judith's expression was grim. "You saw three different women go into the Masterson house? I wonder if any of them ever came out. Alive. And that includes Marla Masterson."

Feeling shaken, the cousins walked back to Renie's house, where Judith had parked her car. A faint line of pale gold was showing above the mountains to the east.

"So," Renie said, as cars began to trickle down the hill to join the morning commute, "Alvin Masterson killed his wife." The thought was too appalling; Renie couldn't go on.

Judith nodded solemnly. "Then buried her in the backyard, and—"

"Lured some other poor women to the house, where he murdered them for their money," Renie put in with a gloomy expression. "If the third one is still alive, we have to warn her. Maybe you should tell Joe."

They had reached Judith's Subaru. "I'm still leery of telling him," Judith said. "I wonder if we should come back tonight with a shovel."

Renie looked horrified. "You mean—dig up their backyard? How do we get in? The fencing goes all the way around to the front, so you can't get through."

"A ladder," Judith suggested. "You and Bill have

several, including the step kind for stuff around the house.''

Renie grimaced. ''Dare we? The Chow-Fuller kids said he had a gun.''

''Didn't Jackie Chow-Fuller tell you he was teasing?'' Judith retorted. ''It may not be true.''

''And if it is?'' Renie wiggled her eyebrows, never having acquired the knack of raising just one.

Judith locked glances with Renie. ''You got us into this mess. Your call, coz.''

Renie sighed. ''Okay, but on one condition. The Mastersons have to be gone tonight or whenever we execute this extremely stupid, dangerous, self-destructive caper.''

Judith clapped Renie on the shoulder. ''Now you're talking. And if we find a body, we call Joe ASAP.''

Renie neither looked nor felt comforted.

To Renie's chagrin, the Masterson garage was empty when they came down the alley around midnight. ''I'll hold the stepladder,'' Judith volunteered. ''You go first, and I'll pass the shovels to you over the fence.''

Renie balked. ''*You* go first. I'll drop the shovels and run back home.''

In the end, it was Renie who clambered up the steel stepladder and clumsily lowered herself to the ground. Judith delivered the shovels, wooden handles first. Then she, too, flopped into the Masterson backyard.

''Oof!'' she exclaimed, remembering to keep her voice down. ''I'm not as young as I used to be.''

''But maybe as old as you're going to get,'' Renie said with a wary glance at the darkened house. ''I still think we're insane.''

Judith, however, wasn't deterred as she shone the pocket flashlight around the grass. ''It's too late to turn back. Ah! That looks like a patch of newer grass.'' She paused, gritting her teeth. "Wow. It certainly is about the size of a body."

"Must we?" Renie said in a feeble voice. "I'm squeamish. I'm cold. I hear my mother calling me."

"Of course you do," Judith agreed, making the first pass with her shovel. "Your mother is always calling you. The phone will still be ringing when you get home in an hour or so."

Renie's face set. "Why did I ever mention this to you? I must have been nuts." But she, too, began to dig.

The cousins hadn't dug much deeper than a couple of inches before they hit something hard. The winter rains had made the ground so soft that it didn't take long to uncover what looked like a large leather chest. Judith and Renie stared at each other.

"Dare we?" Judith whispered, reaching for the metal clasp.

Renie shook her head. "We don't. It's going to be horrible and it's going to smell bad and I'm going to be sick all over the place. We call Joe. Now, from our house." To prove her determination, she whirled around and started for the fence.

Renie didn't get far. She tripped over her shovel, which caught on Judith's and clattered onto the top of the chest.

"Oops!" Renie staggered, her big brown eyes fixed on Judith's startled face. "Damn!" she breathed.

The lights went on in the Masterson house. Judith and Renie froze. The back door was flung open, and the figure of a woman stood outlined on the threshold.

"Who's there?" The husky voice carried menace.

It had never occurred to the cousins to plan an escape route from the backyard. But as one, they raced to the gate. The catch was complicated, impossible for anyone unfamiliar with its mechanism. Judith and Renie sensed the woman marching towards them.

"Hold it!" she ordered in that deep, almost masculine voice. "Who are you?"

Renie turned. "I can explain—" She stopped and stared. It was the woman she had seen go into the Masterson house the previous week. "Who are *you*?" Renie demanded, curiosity overcoming fear.

The woman, who was somewhat above average height, with a slender figure and smartly coiffed brown hair, bridled at the query. "Don't try to throw me. Who do you think I am? I'm Marla Masterson. And why are you trying to steal my old clothes?"

Judith had been known to fib in a good cause. But even she couldn't come up with a story to explain away the nefarious doings in the Masterson backyard. Thus, the cousins were forced to tell the truth, a stumbling, rambling, and most embarrassing narration. They had almost reached the conclusion when Alvin Masterson pulled into the garage.

"Hey, Marla honey!" he cried, rushing through the gate. "What the hell is going on here? There's a stepladder out on the other side of the—" He saw the cousins and stopped.

Marla, looking beleaguered, threw up her hands. "Now that you're home, darling, I'm going to let these two wackos come into the house. If you believe their story, I won't call the cops."

Inside the Masterson living room, with its neat if somewhat old-fashioned furnishings, Judith and Renie went over their explanation at a much slower pace. Alvin and Marla listened in silence, though they both frequently shook their heads and exchanged quizzical looks. When at last the cousins had finished, Marla tapped her fingernails on a cherrywood end table.

"After so many years," she sighed, "The misery of all the weight, then all that dieting and exercise and cosmetic surgery! And now this fiasco! Maybe I should have stayed fat.''

Her husband wagged a finger at her. "Don't say that, Marla honey. Have you forgotten all those years when you were so hard to live with because the fad diets failed time and time again? Every January, when you went in for your annual checkup, you'd come home and cry for a week. You beat yourself up because you could never keep the weight off, and then you'd take it out on me. We were miserable. Now everything's changed. Aren't you as excited as I am about going to visit the kids and their families?''

Marla's handsome features softened. "Of course I am. I was ashamed to let them see me all these years because I was so huge. That was wrong of me. Neither Carrie nor Don cared how I looked. I was still their mom.''

Alvin turned to the cousins. "My poor sweetie burned all the pictures of her when she was overweight. I tried to save the portrait she'd had taken a few years ago, but she ripped that up, too, and smashed the glass.'' He chuckled softly. "A lot of memories down the drain, I'm afraid.''

"Mostly bad ones,'' Marla put in. "That's why we buried the clothes instead of burning them or giving them away. It was symbolic, like the death of the past. Those clothes were just so much garbage left over from years of unhappiness.''

Renie found the courage to ask a question. "What about the other women I saw go in here? A blonde and a redhead.''

The Mastersons exchanged puzzled looks. Then Marla laughed, a rich, throaty sound. "That was me. While I was losing weight, I experimented with my hair, my makeup, all those things. I had a different look about every six months. But this is the one I like.'' She patted her sleek brunette coiffure.

"I like it, too," Alvin smiled. "And I'm darned glad that Marla can lay off some of those more strenuous exercises. The music from those videos drove me crazy. Ever since I gave up my office downtown, when they wanted to raze the building for a new high-rise, I've been working at home. Those tapes with the instructor shouting all the time kept distracting me."

Judith raised a tentative hand. "Don't tell me—let me guess. You're a tax accountant."

Alvin was mildly surprised. "How did you know?"

"Oh . . . just an intuition." On the sly, she nudged Renie, who sat next to her on the muted plaid sofa.

Alvin was nodding. "Late February, a busy time of year. I've been making house calls, which is where I was tonight. Some of my clients are elderly and can't get out much."

Renie was getting up. "I can't tell you how stupid we feel," she said. "Our imaginations carried us away. We'll go out the back way and collect our shovels."

The Mastersons walked the cousins to the rear door. "I'm sorry I was abrupt yesterday when you brought that parcel," Marla said. "I was on long distance, talking to our son, Don, in Houston. I'm taking the dresses with me when we visit him and his family and then our daughter, Carrie, and her gang in Indianapolis."

"No problem," Renie said. "Have a wonderful trip."

Alvin showed the cousins how to open the gate to the alley. When he had gone back into the house, Judith and Renie looked at each other.

"We're idiots, coz," said Renie.

"Better to be safe than sorry," Judith noted.

"We weren't safe," Renie responded. "But we're sure sorry."

"No, we're not," Judith said, folding up the stepladder.

Renie didn't comment. She had reached into her parka

and was pulling out the mutilated photo of Marla Masterson. Then she raised the lid of the green receptacle.

"Garbage," she said, and threw the picture into the bin.

Mary Daheim draws on her knowledge of her Seattle hometown to write two mystery series, one featuring bed-and-breakfast owner Judith McMonigle Flynn and the other newspaper publisher Emma Lord. Her most recent novels are Legs Benedict *and* Alpine Kindred.

Jack and Jill, R.I.P.

Jonathan Gash

The hottest day of the year might not sound much for East Anglia, but I found it hellish. Standing in the Woolwich Building Society queue without shade made it doubly so.

"This is simply murder," a smallish lady remarked.

"No," I replied. "Kill somebody, you're paroled after ten years."

She smiled. "Not in Victorian times."

As the queue shuffled in, we continued talking. This is unusual—strangers speaking without formal introduction, for heaven's sake?—but she made a chance observation about Culver Street and the town's Old Library. I said I remembered it, so many changes now.

"I know you!" she suddenly exclaimed. "You gave a talk there!"

These sorts of encounters embarrass me. I wished the queue would go faster, but the teller girls are always slow on Saturdays. I prayed they wouldn't up and off to coffee just as my turn came. Truth to tell, I don't suppose I was very gracious, until she remarked that she once lived in Arlesford Manor. This made me look at her. I felt a definite desire for further acquaintance.

The upshot was that I made sure I held the street door for her as we left. We spent an interesting half-hour over coffee in Purdey's cosy lounge.

She seemed a merry soul, admitting to having a couple of decades on me. We played the usual middle-aged game: I recall Head Street before Mr. Wesley's old chapel went, surely you're too young to have seen the Jubilee procession, all that. By the time we parted, I'd gleaned enough to find her again without stalking her. I was relieved. Stalking is always so time-consuming and troublesome.

The library's Local Studies section provided me with the Register of Electors back to heaven knows when, old phone books, rate records, quite sufficient to identify some lady who'd grown up in Arlesford Manor. A mere nine cross-references later, and I had her. Mrs. Jill Leanderton, now of Goldhanger Road.

That evening I posted her one of my novels, inscribed *To the Lady of Arlesford Manor*. Signed on the title page, in today's pompous fashion, but people who buy the books seem to like it, so who am I? I had the wit to include a short note, what a pleasure to encounter you and so forth, with my address. She wrote politely three days later, and we were off.

For once I kept control, did things right—in short, I'd not bungled the "relationship" (such a hateful word). It felt full of brilliant promise. Reason? She alone knew something really rather special about where someone was buried. That secret ought rightfully to have been mine, not hers. I deserved that information. She, frankly, didn't.

*   *   *

The next fortnight was depressing. We met for lunch once, had dinner at the George, our best hostelry. Not that she was a poor conversationalist. She was quite outgoing but unhappily was given to those extraordinary reminiscences so beloved of country folk. I simply wasn't on her wavelength. Different origins, you see.

She hunted. She shot. She rode to unspeakable hounds. She even fished, for God's sake. She held strong views on the training of golden retrievers. She discussed the obligations reed cutters had to waterways. Can you believe, she knew a great deal about artesian wells? She had a few witty anecdotes, saving me from total boredom. Frankly, I'm a townie and believe you can't have civilization without pavements. So I sat opposite, watching her attractive mouth move and wondering how long it would be before I got what I wanted. I became increasingly desperate.

At our third meeting—supper in the Donkey and Buskin tavern—she at last began to reveal some personal history. Twice divorced, she still saw her second husband, "so useful with my accounts." Jill was disarmingly frank about her sisters-in-law, speaking of them with that tranquil hatred only women can affect. Her daughter lived locally. Jill was currently engaged in disputing the right of an angling club to construct a ramp beside a lake leased from her estate. Her dearly loved father had left everything to her. "Serves my sister right, the cow," she said with what I can only call satisfaction.

When I dropped her off at her door that same evening, she shyly invited me to lunch the following Tuesday. At her place! I accepted, though it called for urgent changes to my calendar. For the first time I felt optimistic. Meanwhile, I read everything I could lay hands on about Jack the Ripper.

* * *

Someone told me there were over six hundred volumes devoted to Saucy Jack, as Jack the Ripper called himself in one of his taunting notes. History has accused virtually everyone in Victorian London of being the perpetrator, from members of the Queen Empress's own family to police, from insane American vagrants to Members of Parliament and quasi-mystical Masonic plotters. It's quite an industry. I dug out an old newspaper article. It set me thinking. Under the headline I GUARD JACK THE RIPPER! was a photo of a smiling lady, Arlesford Manor in the background. My memory was right. It was Mrs. Leanderton. She claimed, said the article, to own feudal rights to the site where Jack the Ripper lay. Roguishly, she had declined to tell the reporter precisely where.

Within a month the story seemed to have atrophied. Crime enthusiasts—they're always pests—developed earnest theories, then moved on. Local people whispered that Mrs. Leanderton had gone rather dotty, from inevitable ancient family troubles. I was particularly glad when that Suffolk bobby, now famed, recently developed the idea of the Ripper as America's first serial killer, because its crude plausibility distracted attention from the lady of Arlesford's newspaper claim.

If Jill were willing to share her secret knowledge with me, I would be on a winner. We crime writers live constantly between hope and helplessness. I became quite saucy myself, confident that pretty soon I would be the only crime writer who really *knew*. In a word, I'd make a killing. (Only metaphorical and literary senses, please, and I mean that most sincerely.) Unfortunately she made no disclosures when we dined at her house. I waited hopefully.

Time passed. Weeks turned into a season. Six months became nine. I grew testy and developed tactics, one of which was to persuade Jill to show me round her old haunts. She was thrilled to oblige. We visited the creek at Arlesford, the seashore where she used to gather samphire to fry for supper, where Daddy trained his bloody dogs for the East Anglian Show. Bored sick, I stared at the fence where she'd fallen on some damned nag. I acted impressed, but her numbing county-set lore beggared belief. My dislike of countryside swiftly became hate. Not a single word about Jack the Ripper's resting place, and I was too canny to mention it. Last thing I wanted was to scare her off.

Many times Jill would say mischievously, "Why on earth do you bother with me?" It became her playful catchphrase. My reply was always something like, "Can't I simply like you, for heaven's sake?" In fact I was really quite fond of her by now, though beginning to glower at myself in mirrors over wasted time. A year further on, I'd read everything about Saucy Jack. I had a few notions of my own about Jack's identity, but Jill *knew*.

We became lovers one wet Thursday after I'd collected her from choir practice. She sang alto, always the shakiest section of any mixed choir, at the Charter Hall. I'd intended taking her for supper—probably for yet more mud-and-mulch memories—but instead drove her home when she said she was tired. She insisted I stay for a drink, and one thing led to another. Making love that first time, I was astonished at her verve. She insisted on our bathing together afterwards. I stayed the night and awoke about four the next morning to find her propped up on an elbow regarding me with rapture. It was moonlight. I was pleased the way things had gone. Jill was thrilled.

Some days later—us regular lovebirds—she relented and at last began to tell me about Dr. Gull. This highly esteemed Victorian doctor was not at all difficult to look up. The facts are public. He lived as a lad in Landmere, a stone's throw away down these low estuaries. Born in 1816 in St. Leonard's parish, Colchester, trained at Guy's Hospital, London, he got the Gold Medal for his M.D. He rose to become the grand Sir William Withey Gull, Queen's Honorary Physician no less. His cottage at Landmere Quay was a retiring little landmark for visitors to point at. "Imagine! Doctor to the great Queen herself!" etc, etc. In 1871 Dr. Gull cured the Prince of Wales of typhoid fever.

"An eminent bloke, to be sure," I said with admiration.

I'd actually known all these details but was careful to express awe when Jill went on about him. To please her, I casually mentioned that I might visit St. Michael's churchyard just for interest. With a wry smile, she insisted that she accompany me. "I've something to show you," she said. As if in celebration, we made enthusiastic love on her somewhat battered couch.

Occasional Ripper nuts—fans, addicts, whatever— still photograph Gull's cottage site, to the annoyance of local villagers. There is no actual mystery about his grave. It is ornate, certainly a cut above the others at St. Michael's. Nor is there any riddle about Dr. Gull's death, for his career was exemplary and his demise seemly. In short, I was a bit disappointed, yet kept on hoping, for hadn't Jill said that she *alone* knew where the Ripper lay? Yet Dr. Gull's name is there for all to see, and there are better Ripper candidates than the reputable Sir W. W. Gull, M.D. We stood there. Jill linked my arm with hers and read the headstone's inscription aloud.

"*What doth the Lord require of thee, but to do justly and to love mercy, and to walk humbly with thy God?* His favorite quotation," she observed. "Recognize it?"

I shrugged. I'm no scriptural scholar. "The grave's quite a size."

"Twelve by nine—far too big for two persons!"

The odd thing was that I did vaguely recall the phrases from somewhere. She saw my frown and explained.

"It was the inscription above the Working Lads Institute in Victorian Whitechapel." We walked on among the gravestones. "Where—"

"Where the first two Ripper inquests were held!" I exclaimed.

"Exactly!" She hesitated, then came to a resolve. "This way, Jonathan."

She drew me to a headstone a hundred yards across the churchyard path, away from consecrated ground. I read it.

"I see you don't do crosswords, darling!"

And finally I understood. The letters on this headstone didn't spell Gull's name but formed a perfect anagram, with three letters—R.I.P—added. I was thunderstruck.

"You're the only person I've ever told," she said simply. It was a drab day, nobody about. "My grandfather was lord of the manor in those days and deleted the burial record. He had the right, you see, to allow Dr. Gull to be buried here in unconsecrated ground away from the parish pious. Leaving the Gull family grave there for propriety's sake and to decoy souvenir hunters."

"Isn't it in the church registers?"

"No. The page is missing, of course." She spoke as if explaining to a child. "Only you and I now know the truth. Of course, Dr. Gull knew Mary Kelly very well indeed. Did you know that?"

"No." For I hadn't.

Mary Kelly was slain by the Ripper. I'd taken detailed notes on her grotesque murder. Looking at Jill's face, smiling at me with adoration, I realized that her sharing the secret with me was some sort of love gift. And a tremendous one it was. Only the *two* of us! Which immediately suggested that two minus one leaves one.

Alone, so to speak, and in possession. I honestly think I must be forgiven for the rather unfortunate consequences, truly I do. Life sometimes introduces obligations when they're most irksome. That being so, could I be blamed if solutions come with the same spontaneity? I don't think so.

Maybe I ought to have cooled my synthetic ardor a little more gradually, but I was too impatient now I knew that Dr. Gull, aka Saucy Jack the Ripper, wasn't buried in his marked grave but nearby in unconsecrated ground and the headstone inscribed with an anagrammatic name. My treatise—I began it that very night—on Saucy Jack was going to be voluminous. I already had mounds of data and a complete filing system (but coded—I wasn't as naive as Jill!). Modern DNA matching with Scotland Yard's bloodstained notes would be all the confirmation I'd need to prove Dr. Gull's claim—and mine—to immortality. My spectacular treatise would be the crime world's sole messenger! Naturally, when Jill rang asking where we were to meet next day, I cried off. Too busy.

Twice during the next fortnight she cornered me into having supper, and I slept with her. It was however all rather unsatisfactory. I don't know about other people, but passion's the damndest thing to simulate. You have to feel it, or it simply isn't there. After these episodes, we began simply to drift. It happens, isn't that so? Anyhow, I'd never been a great believer in close acquaintanceships. She wrote me pained letters, one so embarrassingly personal and imploring that I thought it the height of presumption. I didn't bother to write back, for what can one say? There's a time and place for those kinds of emotions. My world had simply moved on.

A good two months later I was invited to talk to the Creative Writing Group at Greyfriars, a local adult education institute. The class leader apologized for the "unavoidable absence" of two of her people. Something in the way she said it prompted me to peruse the class list. Mrs. Jill Leanderton was enrolled but did not attend my lecture. Fair enough, she must have felt embarrassed. The other non-attender was a man. The class leader said, smiling with obliquity, "Mrs. Leanderton and her friend had an appointment." And the whole class exchanged meaningful glances. The implication was plain. Jill had taken up with someone else.

This caused me profound anxiety. I couldn't sleep that night. Priceless information that proved a love gift to me might well seem a worthy gift to a subsequent lover. Jill was, I well knew, sentimental. Most sickening of all, her new bloke was a wannabe writer. Why else was he attending scribbling sessions, doubtless fawning over Jill? Sweating, I could see Jill revealing the secret, the gravestone's clue, the Ripper's real grave. And could imagine her new lover writing some lunatic idiot thesis and making an utter pig's ear of it. I'll be frank. Rage consumed me, for whose secret was it? It was mine, mine by fervor, mine by right. Jill was wealthy. What if she paid some vanity publisher to rush out a nonsensical tome co-authored by herself and her lover?

Thinking about it almost made me ill. This is what I meant about consequences and solutions. They cannot be avoided this side of madness or the grave. Instantly I saw that I had a duty to protect the—*my*—precious gem of history about Jack. I simply couldn't let it be basely handled by some nerk in, Jesus, a *creative writing class*. It would be so unjust. I was forced to act.

The following week I used the old tennis-ball trick to steal an elderly motor from outside the Welcome Sailor, a pub convenient for Greyfriars. (In case you're new to car crime, press half a tennis ball onto the lock. Release it swiftly, the lock springs. Warm-wire the ignition. Drive off.) I waited for Jill to emerge from Greyfriars. He wasn't with her. Maybe she was on her way to meet him? It was dark, proving that heaven was on my side. She always parked on East Hill, which is usually pretty deserted in the lantern hours, and I'd seen her car there. I judged it perfectly, accelerated into her just as she stooped to unlock the door, driver's side. A bus had just passed on its way into town, otherwise nothing moved. I saw no pedestrians.

Murder, I discovered to my astonishment in that moment, conveys a certain serenity if properly planned. I can't honestly say I even remember the actual impact. When my motor car struck Jill in the gloaming, it caused more of a shudder than a slam and certainly created none of those dreadful images of the kind you see in television dramas of the victim's horrified face against the windscreen. But then we writers have this terrific power of concentration, to focus the mind at vital sublime moments. It's a gift.

I returned the motor unobserved—it was the pub's darts night and the place was heaving. I was distressed by the simplicity of the whole thing—after all, *should* murder be so easy? My sense of propriety has always been meticulous, even stoic. I've often thought of joining the Polite Society—yes, one actually exists but never quite receives the attention it deserves. My actions against poor Jill? Consequences and solutions again, and that's all. And I'm quite certain she would have been glad to have served her purpose. It is the English way, and Jill was quintessentially English, by which I mean tidy, proper, most of all *responsible*. Like me, I suppose.

For a brief spell there was the usual fuss in the local papers—out-of-town late-night drunks were blamed. People these days regard traffic accidents as little more than troublesome weather. Some deaths do occur, sure, but they are accorded the same status as minor floods in Argentina. "Poor people, what rotten luck," one says, then life goes on.

From the deep respect I felt for Jill, I didn't attend her funeral. This doesn't mean I neglected her in my prayers, certainly not, for I'm not without a writer's inherent sensitivity. Staying away was simply the sort of compassionate touch I'm sure Saucy Jack would have approved of. I'll bet he too refrained from watching the funerals of the women he removed—I can't quite see them as *victims*, not now that I've actually participated in a similar act. Well, not *similar* as such, because I was clearly forced into it, whereas Jack's efforts had more spontaneity.

One possible spin-off, though: if my definitive treatise on Saucy Jack proves a runaway best-seller, as will surely prove to be the case, I might well use the publisher's advance to have his anagram headstone replaced and so keep the mystery going. Knowledge can be something of a heavy burden, the question of its perpetuity a moral minefield for the possessor.

In the ten weeks since Jill's actions irrevocably led to my having to murder her, I've kept watch on St. Michael's churchyard. If Jill did tell her lover, sooner or later he'll feel bound to turn up and take notes, snoop about. I know it. I have his name and address from Greyfriars, of course. Dealing with the illiterate lout will prove elementary, because the Gull family grave is certainly big enough for at least one undetected extra.

As I write this, it dawns on me that a crime writer's work is never really done. It demands an absolute lifetime of loyalty to the cause.

Jonathan Gash is well known as the creator of Lovejoy, rogue antiques dealer and subject of an A&E television series starring Ian McShane. Gash, who lives in En-

gland, has struck out in a new direction in a series of mysteries with Dr. Clare Burtonall, reflecting Gash's own medical background. His most recent title is Different Women Dancing.

V-2

Edward D. Hoch

Lisa Barrister had never consulted a private investigator before, and in the autumn of 1944 with the war still raging she was uncertain if there'd be one available in all of London. Seated now across the desk from this aging man named Matthew Javage, in a dingy Victorian office building on Moorgate in the heart of the City, she wondered if this was what she really wanted. The building's exterior was virtually covered in faded pink terracotta, which should have been a clue as to what she would find inside.

"I'd expected a younger man," she found herself saying, and immediately regretted the words.

Matthew Javage smiled, showing tobacco-stained teeth that somehow went with the cigarette burns on the desk. "My son is a younger man, but he's serving with the RAF. In time of war you take what you can get."

"I noticed the name on the door. *Javage & Son.*"

"That's a surprise for when he gets back. It's all me right now. Me and the missus."

Lisa remembered the receptionist in the outer office. "Oh! Is that your wife?"

Javage nodded. "My Sarah. We're keeping things going. Now, what can I do for you, Mrs. Barrister?"

"It's Miss Barrister," she corrected.

"I'm sorry. In this business I often deal with marital problems of one sort or another."

"No, this is something quite different. As you must know, the area where I live has been a prime target for German bombs and especially for the V-2 rockets that started hitting us last month. Whole blocks have been leveled."

The private detective nodded sympathetically. "The City has been hit hard." The square mile of the City of London, surrounded by its neighborhoods and environs, ruled by a Lord Mayor who took precedence over everyone except the sovereign, was the heart of London's business and financial life.

"I think something strange has been happening with these bombings," Lisa said, now reaching the part of her story that always raised doubts among her listeners. "I think someone on the ground is planting explosives and setting them off during the bombings."

Matthew Javage frowned. "Why in the world would anyone do that?"

"Did you ever read the Chesterton story about the murdered man hidden on a battlefield? Where else to hide a blown-up building than in an air raid?" Seeing his dubious expression, she hurried on. "Look, the Germans are on their last legs. A year or two from now we'll be at peace. These ruined areas are going to be valuable to someone. I want to know if they're being bought up now and by whom."

"Might I ask what caused you to have these suspicions in the first place?"

"I've seen V-2 rockets explode, Mr. Javage, several

times during the past month. Usually from a safe distance, I'm happy to say. Last week, during a V-2 attack near our neighborhood, the house right across the street blew up while I was watching. An old woman who lived alone on the top floor was killed. The house itself was badly damaged, but a V-2 would have left nothing but a crater in the earth. I pointed out my suspicions to our firewarden and to the police, but no one would listen.''

The detective pursed his lips, thought about it, and finally said, ''Your suspicions are far-fetched at best. But if you're willing to pay for it, I can look into the matter.''

''How much will it cost?''

''Three guineas for our consultation today, then three guineas a day plus expenses. I think you'll find those terms are quite reasonable.''

She handed over the first day's payment. ''Can I phone you?''

He handed her his card. ''When the phones are working. Come, I'll introduce you to my wife.''

She was a bit dumpy and slightly overweight, wearing thick glasses and a haggard look. The Blitz had done that to some people. She glanced up from her typewriter as her husband appeared. ''Sarah, this is Miss Lisa Barrister, our newest client. I'm going to be examining some records of real-estate transactions for her.''

''Pleased to meet you,'' the woman said without changing expression.

Lisa shook hands with Mr. Javage at the door and hurried downstairs to the street.

Honey Mason, Lisa's neighbor in the row of semi-detached houses a few blocks south of St. Giles Cripplegate Church, came over to see her as soon as she arrived back home. Honey was a big, jolly woman approaching sixty, who'd buried two husbands but was always willing to try for a third. Lisa had lost her teaching job at a girls' private school when the students were evacuated out of London during the early days of the Blitz. Luckily a family inheritance had supplied enough money for her to live on. She had no doubt she could resume her teaching career once the smaller schools re-opened. In the meantime she did volunteer work for the Red Cross and other worthy projects and got to know neighbors like Honey Mason.

"I was worried about you," Honey told her. "Where've you been? I've got some news."

"I went to see that detective I mentioned. I've hired him, Honey."

"Well, it's your money. I don't know why one more bombed house interests you so much. Maybe it was a V-2. Maybe it was a gas explosion. What difference does it make?"

Her mood was not unlike Lisa's own. It had been different with the V-1 missiles. They would fly overhead like a small plane until they ran out of fuel and the engine cut off. Then they would plunge to earth and explode. With the V-1 you could tell by the sound when the danger was greatest. With the V-2, a giant rocket fired from the European mainland and aimed to hit London, there was virtually no warning. Since they traveled at supersonic speeds, there was no defense against them. Did it really matter if a V-2 or something else had destroyed the house across the street?

Yes, it mattered to Lisa. "What's your news?" she asked Honey.

"They're holding a meeting at the Guildhall Library tonight to discuss all the damage our area has received. I thought you might want to go with me."

"I certainly do! What time?"

"It starts at seven, so they'll finish early. Dr. Ellis will be there, and Peter Starling, the liveryman." The

City of London's Lord Mayor and its sheriffs were elected each year by the aldermen, who represented the various districts or wards. They'd lost much of the power they possessed in the Middle Ages but still served as a line of communication between the people and the Lord Mayor.

"I doubt if it will mean much," Lisa said. "Starling can veto any resolution that we might pass. But I'll go with you. I know Dr. Ellis will speak for our side." He was Lisa's dentist, a sturdy, intelligent man who could hold his own among the politicians. "But let's take another look at number 29."

That was the house across the street, still standing, though its upper floor was gone. They crossed over, and Honey used her strong arms to pull open the makeshift door that had been nailed across the entrance. They went inside, avoiding the charred timbers and the dead rat that had been there since their last visit.

"Nothing's changed," Honey said.

Lisa shook her head. "This was no V-2. Why don't they see that?"

"Come on, let's close it up again."

After Honey went back to her house, Lisa put in a call to Matthew Javage's office. His wife answered the phone. "Sarah, this is Lisa Barrister, your new client. Is Mr. Javage available?"

"He's gone out. Can I give him a message?"

"Yes, please tell him there's a meeting at the Guild-hall Library tonight at seven, regarding the destruction in our area."

"I'll tell him," she said and hung up.

Honey and Lisa set off for the library at six forty-five, walking quickly through the blacked-out streets. They hadn't gone far when a fire warden with a flashlight stopped them. It was Lisa's friend Henry McGruder.

"And where might you ladies be going on such a night?" he asked, putting on his fake Irish brogue. He was a handsome young man in his early thirties, wearing helmet and armband, who walked with a slight limp from a wound suffered at Dunkirk.

"There's a meeting at the Guildhall Library," Honey told him. "We won't be out late."

But Lisa knew his eyes beneath the steel helmet were focused on her, not Honey. "Is this more about that crazy theory of yours?"

"It's not so crazy, Henry."

He gave a sigh. "Be careful, and go right home."

The meeting room at the library was already filled with more than a score of people from the area. On the stage at the front, five local spokesmen and political leaders sat behind a long conference table. She recognized Peter Starling at the center, with Dr. Ellis to his left and a man named Green on the right. Exactly at seven o'clock the meeting began. Starling introduced himself and the others at the table and called upon Dr. Ellis to speak first.

Lisa's dentist was a graying, distinguished man who knew what he wanted to say. After going over some statistics on the number of demolished homes and buildings in the district, he told them, "The Blitz has torn the social fabric of London. We have already suffered the worst damage since the Great Fire of 1666. No longer is London one great city but rather a collection of small towns. There is no time to visit friends in distant neighborhoods between the sirens. In Clapham, where day raids are frequent, the people have a hunted look about them. They fare better in Westminster. The night raids are heavier, but the deep shelters in the Underground offer more protection. Here, especially since the coming of the V-2s last month, we have suffered day and night. Some among us believe the destruction is so vast that it might be partly caused by Nazi sympathizers on the ground.''

"I never said they were Nazi sympathizers!" Lisa whispered in Honey's ear. She became aware of a newcomer just behind them and turned to see her detective, Matthew Javage. "I'm glad you could come," she whispered, and he nodded.

After the other three had spoken briefly, Dr. Ellis made a motion that a message of concern regarding the amount of destruction in the district be conveyed to the Lord Mayor. The suggestion was raised that an additional fire truck and crew be stationed at one end of Lisa's street near St. Giles.

Then the liveryman, Peter Starling, took over. He started speaking without being called on. "I sympathize with all the torment you feel for your neighborhood and for London. But fully two-thirds of the city is in ruins. Other areas have suffered as much or more than we have. This is war, ladies and gentlemen, and until our advancing armies can overrun and destroy the V-2 launch sites, there is very little we can do. Let me tell you something of this weapon we face. The V-2 is a liquid fuel rocket with a one-ton warhead. It is fired to an altitude of fifty miles at its peak and then curves down to its target." He cleared his throat. "I must also point out, of course, that St. Giles Church is technically outside the one-square-mile limits of the City of London. Damage done in that immediate area is the concern of others.''

Before it was taken, Lisa knew what the vote on the proposal would be. Starling's veto sent it down to defeat, and the session ended on a sour note. People filed out quickly, anxious to get home.

"I wanted you to see what I'm up against," Lisa told Javage when they were outside. She introduced Honey, and they walked together for a time.

"This house that concerned you—"

"Number 29," Lisa said, "directly across the street from my place."

He nodded. "I should examine it tomorrow. There may be something the police missed."

For once there were no rockets in the night to awaken her, and Lisa slept until after eight. She breakfasted and dressed quickly, planning to put in some extra time at the army hospital. But as she was leaving the house shortly after ten, she noticed something unusual about the bombed-out house across the street. The front door, which had been held closed by nails, was now ajar. Either Honey hadn't properly closed it following their visit or someone had been snooping around.

She crossed the street and went up to the door. From inside there came a low groan, barely audible. Lisa carefully opened the door and stepped across the threshold.

Matthew Javage lay there gasping for breath. There was a bloody wound in his chest and more blood was coming from his mouth. He stared up at her beseechingly and managed to gasp, "V-2!"

She dropped to her knees beside him. "Who did this? Who?"

Again he gasped, "V-2!" Then he was dead.

The detective in charge was a man named Ambrose, who questioned Lisa at length regarding her business relationship with the murdered man. "You say he was a private detective employed by you, but your reason for hiring him still isn't clear to me, Miss Barrister."

Lisa went over it again, stressing her suspicions about some of the district's bomb-damaged buildings. "You must see it yourself, Detective. A house like this should have been blown away by a V-2 rocket. Instead, only the roof and second floor are gone."

"Are you trying to tell me someone other than the Germans is doing this?"

"Some of it, I think. That's what I hired Javage to find out."

He consulted his notes. "This knife found by the body is the apparent murder weapon. Did you ever see it before?"

"No."

"And you saw no one over here this morning?"

"No. You might ask my neighbor, Honey Mason. She's usually up before me."

Honey was already among the crowd in the street, attracted by the police cars. Ambrose brought her in, but she could add nothing to Lisa's account. "Our kitchens are all at the back of the house," she pointed out. "We're not usually looking out the front windows first thing in the morning."

He showed her the bloody knife, but it meant nothing to Honey. "His last words were *V-2, V-2.* Mean anything to you?"

Honey glanced uneasily at Lisa. "I suppose he was trying to say the building had been hit with a V-2 rocket."

Lisa had to admit it was the likeliest explanation. "But that doesn't explain why he was killed."

"These ruined houses sometimes attract the homeless, especially young boys suddenly on their own. Javage may have stumbled on someone who'd spent the night here and got killed for it."

Lisa glanced around. "Did you find evidence of anyone living here? Food, blankets, a flashlight, or candles?"

"No," Ambrose admitted, "but it seems a likely explanation."

Lisa walked Honey back across the street, then decided there was someone she had to see. "I'll be back later," she told her neighbor.

"Be careful!" Honey warned. "If the rockets don't get you, the killer might."

Lisa set off in the direction of Javage's office. She wanted to break the news to the detective's wife, if the woman hadn't already heard it. The day was cool and clear, and the news from the European front was good. Soon, she told herself, the V-2 attacks would stop.

Henry McGruder came out of one of the buildings, wearing his helmet and armband. "Do you work night and day?" she asked as he fell into step by her side. His limp seemed less pronounced when the weather was good.

"Someone has to. What were the police doing up by your place this morning?"

She told him about the stabbing, and how she'd found the body. "His dying words were *V-2*."

"Maybe he was imagining another attack," the fire warden suggested. "There were no missiles yesterday, and I doubt if they'll go two days in a row without launching a few."

"I like to think they don't have any more."

McGruder shook his head. "The word we get from Intelligence is that the Nazis have manufactured more than twelve hundred V-2s. They've used a few on the battlefield, but most of them are aimed at London."

"If they ever launch that many, there'll be nothing left of the city." In that instant she thought it was a crazy idea that anyone could hope to profit from such human misery.

"I have to turn here," he said when they reached a corner. "Take care."

"You too."

Lisa continued to the building on Moorgate that was her destination. Climbing the stairs to the second-floor

office, she found the place to be unusually quiet. The
door to Javage & Son stood partly open, and Sarah Javage was seated at her desk. Lisa knew at once that she'd
already heard the news of her husband.

"Mrs. Javage—"

Her head jerked at the sound of her name, and she
looked up quickly. "We're closed," she said in a tone-
less voice.

"Mrs. Javage, I know about your husband. I'm the
one who found his body."

The tears rolled from her eyes then, though her crying
was more a series of silent sobs. "The police were just
here to tell me," she said, "but they didn't give many
details. What happened?"

Lisa told her what little she knew. "He'd been
stabbed. He died in front of my eyes. I'm sorry."

"He was in that house? The one that was bombed?"

"Yes. He must have been working on the case for
me."

Sarah Javage nodded. "He was going to check the
real-estate records today, but first he wanted to look at
that house to see if he agreed with what you said about
it."

"Did he talk to anyone else?" Lisa asked.

"I don't know about that."

"Thank you. Please send me a bill for whatever I
owe."

The woman stared up at her with empty eyes. "How
would I measure that?"

Lisa knew what she had to do next. She went to Dr.
Ellis's office and waited until it was time for his lunch
break. He came out to the waiting room smiling. "Tooth
trouble, Lisa?"

"Not this time." She told him what had happened.

He listened and shook his head. "That's terrible! Is there anything I can do?"

"There might be. Someone at that meeting last night might have seen me speaking with Javage. They might have guessed that I'd hired him to look into my theory about the demolished buildings. If they followed him this morning or came upon him at that house, they might have killed him."

"I'm a dentist, not a detective," he reminded her. "But how can I help?"

"Could you call another district meeting at the Guildhall Library for tonight? I'll help contact people if you need me. I don't know Starling well enough to ask for his help, and I think it's important that we get people together after this killing."

"I don't know if that'll get you anywhere. Starling will never approve a request to the Lord Mayor."

"Let me worry about that."

Dr. Ellis gave a sigh. "All right, if the phones are working, I should be able to get through to most of the people. Seven o'clock?"

She nodded. "Same time as last night."

Lisa spent the afternoon on the phone herself. First she called Honey next door, who agreed to accompany her to the meeting. Then she reached Sarah Javage, still at her husband's office.

"I have to make funeral arrangements tonight," the woman told her.

"It won't take long. I need you to arrive at the meeting just as your husband did last night, at exactly the same time. Wait in the back of the library meeting room, and I'll signal when I want you."

"I don't—"

"I think it'll help find your husband's killer, Sarah."

"All right," she agreed reluctantly.

"Be there at seven, but stay out of sight."

That evening, at just six forty-five, Lisa and Honey started out for the meeting. "I don't know what this is all about," her neighbor said.

"You don't need to know. I just want to run through last night's meeting to be sure I remember everything correctly."

"That detective wasn't killed at the meeting."

"I know."

Since they were going by the same route at the same time, Lisa wasn't surprised when she saw the beam of McGruder's flashlight waving at them. "Is this becoming a nightly ritual?" he asked when he recognized them.

"It's a good way to meet men," Honey insisted.

"A good way to get yourself killed if those missiles start flying."

"There's another meeting at the library," Lisa explained, "about the killing this morning."

"Be careful," he said, turning his eyes to the night sky. "They're overdue."

There was a smaller crowd than the previous night, and Peter Starling started off by announcing he could stay for only thirty minutes. Dr. Ellis and one of the others, the man named Green, were behind the table with him again, but the two remaining chairs were empty. At seven o'clock Lisa took the floor.

"I asked Dr. Ellis to call another meeting tonight because of the terrible killing which took place in one of the bombed-out houses this morning. I'm sure you've all heard about it. The victim, a private detective named Matthew Javage, was hired by me to investigate the bombings in our district which I believed had not been caused by the V-2 rockets. I won't keep us long, and I know some people are missing tonight, but I'd like to run through the conversations and speeches quickly in the order they occurred last night. You see, the murdered man was with us last evening. Mr. Javage entered this room shortly after the meeting began and sat right behind me.''

Her announcement caused the expected stir. When it subsided, Lisa added, ''The victim's widow will join us tonight, playing his part. She will enter on my signal, during Dr. Ellis's opening remarks.''

''Are all these theatrics really necessary?'' Peter Starling asked. ''Just what do you expect to prove?''

''Let's wait and see.''

Starling sighed and did his part, introducing himself and the others at the table, including those whose chairs were empty. Then Dr. Ellis spoke, giving an abbreviated version of his earlier remarks. Lisa signaled to Sarah Javage, and she entered the room to sit in the next row as instructed.

''Pay attention now,'' Lisa whispered to the woman.

The other man, Green, spoke his piece, and then Starling gave his rebuttal. The vote was taken, with the same results as on the previous night.

''So what does all this prove?'' Mr. Green asked.

Lisa turned to Mrs. Javage. ''Please tell us the names of the people at the table,'' she requested.

Sarah Javage looked blank. ''I can't. I never heard their names.''

''That's exactly what I wanted to prove. Your husband didn't hear them last night, either. He arrived after Mr. Starling had introduced everyone. The speakers simply spoke in turn without further introduction, and even Mr. Starling didn't wait to be called on. Javage didn't know any of their names, and that—''

Her words were interrupted by a shattering explosion that sounded quite near. The library windows rattled, and suddenly the night outside was lit by flames.

"Take cover, everyone!" Ellis yelled. "Down to the basement!"

Honey risked a closer look out the window. There seemed to be sirens everywhere. "It's down by the river!"

They all knew the sound of a V-2 explosion by now, and within seconds there were two more, both close by. Lisa and Honey guided Sarah Javage down the steps to the bomb shelter. The lights had gone out, and all was confusion. Dr. Ellis produced a flashlight and stood by the shelter door so the others could find it.

They heard another explosion a bit further away, and someone started lighting candles in the shelter. It was Peter Starling who was first to speak.

"Everyone calm down now! We should be safe from anything but a direct hit." He turned to Lisa. "I'm sorry for the interruption. Please continue, Miss Barrister."

"I feel foolish talking about this with missiles landing all around us."

"No, no!" he assured her. "You brought us here for a reason."

Lisa moistened her lips. "I had to run through all this just to be certain of my own memory. You see, I'd hired Mr. Javage yesterday to look into recent real-estate transactions in this area. As many of you know, I've been suspicious for some time that the V-2 attacks were being augmented by bombs exploded on the ground. I informed Javage of my theory, and he went this morning to have a look for himself. Only someone who saw him at the meeting last night was following him. They saw him enter the bombed house and feared he might find some evidence. Javage saw his killer and recognized him, but he didn't know his name."

"So he called him V-2?" Honey asked.

"A dying man with a mouthful of blood doesn't always speak clearly. I heard his dying words as *V-2*, but what he actually said was *veto*. The only thing he knew about his killer was that he'd vetoed last night's resolution."

Peter Starling grabbed for her then, catching her around the throat before anyone could move.

Then the room was bathed in light, and she heard Henry McGruder running down the stairs calling her name. "Lisa! Are you all right?"

Starling released his grip for just an instant and she jabbed her elbow hard into his stomach. "I'm here, Henry," she called out. "You're just in time. Get the police!"

The investigation into Peter Starling and his real-estate transactions dragged on for weeks while he sat in his cell charged with the murder of Matthew Javage. A duplicate of the knife used in the killing had been found in his home, along with quantities of explosives and detonators that could be triggered by a sudden loud sound. The exploding V-2s themselves had done the job, sometimes by chance killing more innocent people.

One day Starling must have had enough. On his way to the mess hall he'd leaped to his death over a third-floor railing before the guards could grab him.

"I suppose you saved my life that night," Lisa told McGruder later, one night after the Allied armies had overrun the V-2 launch sites.

"You saved your own life," he answered. "The war will be over soon now, and you'll be back to teaching."

"Maybe," she said. "How about you?"

"There's lots of rebuilding to be done by people like us, not Starling. I may go into politics, run for a seat in the Commons."

"If you do, I'd like to help with your campaign."

He smiled at that. "You know I'll be in touch."

One of the most accomplished short-story writers in mystery fiction, Edward D. Hoch is a regular contributor to Ellery Queen's Mystery Magazine *and won an Edgar award for his short story "The Oblong Room." His most recent title is* The Ripper of Storyville and Other Ben Snow Tales.

The Golden Rounds

Susan Holtzer

"Anneke, I *know* he stole them." The One Who Plants Tulips stamped her foot on the hard, rough surface, scattering crisp red-gold leaves. I jumped quickly to a higher branch, instinct-driven, although I knew the gesture wasn't meant for me. Directly in front of me I spied a small cluster of seedpods; I rose on my hind legs, spreading my tail for balance, and began to remove the seeds and stow them in my cheeks.

"Phyllis, I don't know what to say. Even if you're right, I don't see what I can do to help. I'm sure the police . . ." The One Who Feeds Peanuts, whose self-name is Anneke, swept the fan-shaped rake across the ground, gathering the leaves into a warm, deep pile. Later, foolishly, the humans would stuff them into bags and carry them away, but for a while they would remain. I promised myself a romp through the colorful mound, the fun of scattering the leaves back across the grass, at least once before they were gone.

"Oh, the police." The one whose self-name was Phyllis waved a hand. "Look, just let me tell you about it, okay?" She spoke quickly, quicker than most humans make sounds, not waiting for the Anneke to reply. She was smaller than the Anneke but wider, and the hair on her head was yellow, the color of the puffy Food called popcorn. "You knew Uncle Mitya, of course."

"Not really." The Anneke moved her head from side to side, a gesture of the negative among humans. "We haven't lived here that long."

"But you must have known who he was," the Phyllis insisted. "I mean, Dmitri Markovich was famous, after all."

"He was a classics professor, wasn't he?"

"Well, yes, but that was hardly all he was. Surely you saw *Our Ancestors, Ourselves* on PBS a few years ago? It was one of the highest-rated series ever done by public television. Uncle Mitya really brought the classical world alive for the masses."

"Something like Carl Sagan did with *Cosmos,* you mean?"

"Hack work." The Phyllis waved her hand again. "Uncle Mitya's show was *much* better. He didn't *pander*, if you know what I mean."

"Mmm." The Anneke made a noise in her throat.

"And of course," the Phyllis rushed on, "there were his books, too—*Our Ancestors, Ourselves* was a *New York Times* best-seller, and he wrote several of the definitive textbooks in classical studies. It was a real tragedy for the whole university when he got sick. And for me, too, of course. Not that it wasn't a lot of work, taking care of him, but it was the least I could do, after all."

"You moved in with him to take care of him?"

"Oh, no. I was living there with him for the last five years. He needed someone to take care of him—he was

brilliant, of course, but not very *practical*, you know?—
and when I divorced my husband, it seemed sensible for
me to be the one.''

''He didn't have any children, I take it?''

''No. Uncle Mitya never married—he devoted his entire life to his academic work. And of course his coin
collection was really part of that work. That's why those
coins are so important to me, you know, not because of
how much money they're worth. I wouldn't sell them
unless I really *needed* the money.''

''Those are the coins that are missing?''

''Yes. And my darling cousin Franklin stole them. *He*
doesn't care about their scholarly value. All he cares
about is the money they'll bring.''

The moving rake had uncovered a handsome clutch
of acorns from the tree next door. I skittered down the
side of the maple tree and stopped just above the roots,
head down. I twitched my tail and measured the distance
to the acorns. The Anneke was no threat, a Food-Giver,
but the Phyllis, I had cause to know, was a Hostile.

''Hi, Swannee.'' The Anneke greeted me by the Food-
Name she had assigned me. (My self-name, of course,
remains my own; I am always amazed at how easily
humans reveal theirs.) She bent down and picked up an
acorn, which she threw to me. I plucked it out of the air
and stuffed it into my cheek.

''Don't encourage them,'' the Phyllis said in a voice
full of sharp notes.

''Oh, that's Swannee,'' the Anneke replied. ''He's
kind of a pet.''

''You shouldn't feed them,'' the Phyllis insisted.
''They're pests. And besides, it's not good for them. It
not only makes them dependent, they get overfed—look
how fat he is.''

''He is, isn't he?'' The Anneke bent slightly and fixed
her eyes on me; I chittered and flicked my tail politely.

"I've always thought that meant a bad winter on the way. I remember a few years ago, the squirrels were all so fat by November that they looked like little furry beach balls, and it turned out to be one of the worst winters on record."

"They're pests," the Phyllis repeated. "They chew through the phone lines, they dig up my bulbs every spring, they claw through the attic screens, and I can't tell you how much time I spend trying to keep them away from my bird feeder. Uncle Mitya loved watching the birds. After he was bedridden, it was one of his few pleasures, except for his coin collection." The Phyllis jerked her head and glared at me.

"Anyway. The coins," she went on. "There were thirty-seven of them, all gold, all Greek or Roman. It wasn't a huge collection, but it was very fine—Uncle Mitya only collected the *best* pieces. The whole collection was worth more than a hundred thousand dollars. And I refuse to let Franklin get away with it."

"How can you be so sure it was Franklin who stole them?" the Anneke asked. I moved forward and then sideways and then forward again until I reached the scatter of acorns.

"Because he was the only one who could have." The Phyllis's voice rose, then fell. "Look, here's the way it happened. The coins were kept in two felt-lined boxes in a wall safe in Uncle Mitya's bedroom. Only four people had the combination to the safe—Uncle Mitya himself, me, Franklin, and Mel Washburn, Uncle Mitya's attorney. I don't know why Uncle Mitya gave Franklin the combination, but he did, and far be it for me to tell him what to do, even though I did suggest several times that it wasn't a good idea. But as I said, Uncle Mitya wasn't very *practical*.

"Anyway, he was sicker this week than he had been, drifting in and out of consciousness most of the time, and we were all preparing for the worst. But then on Thursday he seemed to improve for a while. He was much more alert, and around noon he asked me to call Mel Washburn. I asked him why, but all he said was that he wanted the company. Mel was his oldest and closest friend, although I never could understand what Uncle Mitya saw in him. He isn't a very ... *cultured* man.

"But of course I called him, and he came and sat with Uncle Mitya for a while, chatting about silly things like some television sitcom they both liked. And then Uncle Mitya asked Mel to bring out the coins, so he could have a look at them. When Mel opened the cases, Uncle Mitya actually picked up one or two of the coins and rubbed them between his fingers, a terrible thing to do to ancient coins, and I started to remonstrate with him, but Mel waved a hand at me, very rudely I can tell you. And since I didn't want to answer rudeness with rudeness, I just kept my mouth shut. And then after a while Uncle Mitya put the coins back in their slots, and Mel put the cases back in the safe.

"And then Franklin showed up. Just waltzed in as though he were welcome. And instead of demanding that he leave, Uncle Mitya actually held out a hand and said how glad he was to see him."

The Phyllis took in a breath and let it out, her lips pursed together. "I hate to make a public display of family unpleasantness, but you do have to know about Franklin. He's what's called an academic bum. You must know the type, there are so many of them around Ann Arbor—a couple of degrees, half a dozen programs started and stopped, always jumping from one field to another. He's thirty-one years old and still trying to 'find himself.' " She took in another noisy breath. "His parents—Uncle Mitya's brother and his wife—died when Franklin was a teenager, and Uncle Mitya supported him completely after that. He paid all Franklin's tuition, too, for years and years, but Franklin was always after him for more money. And then one day he asked—no, *demanded*—that Uncle Mitya finance a year at the Sorbonne for him. At least, he said he wanted to study at the Sorbonne, but all he was really after was an all-expense-paid year in Paris where he could run wild on Uncle Mitya's money. This time Uncle Mitya finally had the sense to refuse, and Franklin had an absolute screaming fit. He called Uncle Mitya the most awful names, and finally he stormed out of the house swearing he'd never set foot in it again. That was nearly a year ago, and the two of them never spoke to each other again—although that didn't stop Franklin from cashing the tuition checks that Uncle Mitya continued to send every month.''

I had filled my cheeks full of acorns and was burying several of them under the azalea bush at the corner of the house when I heard the call. ''Chtkchtkchtk!'' The challenge came from the edge of the grass, where the hard black surface runs toward the back of the house.

''Chkkkchkkk!'' I called a warning. I had marked this territory as my own, of course, but sometimes a newcomer will test my resolve.

This one was a youngling, foolishly attempting to expand his own territory. He took two jumps forward; I advanced to meet him, chirruping a last warning; he leaped at me, and we rolled over and over, caroming through the leaf pile, hind legs kicking out, claws digging at each other.

It was over in seconds, as such battles usually are. He yielded, of course, and raced away; I pursued far enough to make my point before leaping back to my tree and caroling a triumphant call from a high branch. I am still big enough and strong enough to defend what is mine.

The Anneke was making a low, chuckling sound of

appreciation, her lips pulled back from her teeth, but the Phyllis had her mouth pressed tight.

"So when Franklin showed up, I expected Uncle Mitya to send him away." The Phyllis went on talking as though the fine battle hadn't even occurred. "But oh, no. Instead, he sent *me* away." She squeezed her hands into fists. "Not only that, he sent Mel out of the room also—said he wanted to talk to Franklin alone. I didn't trust Franklin, of course, but what could I do? So Mel and I went downstairs and waited in the kitchen while I made Uncle Mitya some tea—at least I could remind him who'd been taking care of him all this time." She stopped talking for a minute, providing welcome silence.

"And then Franklin came downstairs and told us Uncle Mitya was dead.

"I raced upstairs, of course. Mel was right behind me, and so was Franklin. Uncle Mitya was lying on his side with his mouth open, and I could tell he was dead even before I touched him.

"All three of us stayed there while the doctor came, and the undertaker's men. And when they were all finally gone, Mel said that since he was Uncle Mitya's executor, he was going to take the coins and put them in a safe deposit box. Only when he opened the safe, the coin cases were empty." The Phyllis opened her eyes wide and fixed them on the Anneke, who, to my displeasure, lowered her own, thus losing the dominance contest. "So you see, Franklin was the only one who *could* have taken the coins."

"Did your uncle leave them to you in his will?" the Anneke asked.

"Not specifically. Unfortunately, Uncle Mitya was a strong believer in family. He left me the house, I'll say that for him, which is only fair since I've spent years living there and taking care of him when I could have been out making something of my own life. But everything else is split equally between Franklin and me. And the coins are by far the most valuable part of his estate.''

"Are you suggesting that Franklin killed your uncle?''

"N-o-o, apparently not.'' The Phyllis moved her head from side to side slowly. "They did an autopsy, and they *say* he died of natural causes. But I know Franklin stole those coins.'' Her voice rose unpleasantly. "Only what did he *do* with them? And why can't the police find them?''

"It's not that I want to help Phyllis Markovich particularly,'' the Anneke said. "She's actually a pretty nasty piece of work. But she does live right across the street. I can't very well tell a neighbor that she's a greedy, self-important twit. Besides . . .''

". . . there's a puzzle to solve.'' The Large One, whose self-name is Karl, spoke in his rumbling voice. "Believe me, you won't offend the department if you find those coins—in fact, you'll earn the undying gratitude of every cop on the force. The woman is driving us crazy.''

The two humans were inside their house, sitting down and taking Food. They had slid up one of the wall openings and set a small pile of peanuts on the ledge. There was a Food machine nearby, but that held only small seeds, and this early in the morning I left it for the sparrows and the occasional robin. Later I might explore it for the larger sunflower seeds. I enjoy the acrobatic challenge of the Food machines, especially the ones that require me to hang upside down by my hind legs.

"Hmm.'' The Anneke made a throaty sound. "You're morally certain that the nephew—Franklin—did take the coins?''

"Oh, he took them, all right. He's hardly bothering to deny it—just sits there and smirks at us.'' The Karl moved his head sideways and pressed his lips together. "Mel Washburn confirmed that the coins were in the safe when he and Phyllis left Franklin there and gone when he went back upstairs. No one else *could* have taken them."

"But then, how could he hope to get away with it?"

"Because he didn't know they'd just been looking at the coins. The cases were put away before Franklin arrived; for all he knew, the coins hadn't been out of the safe for days."

"All right, then." The Anneke raised a shallow container of liquid to her mouth, drinking in the clumsy way that humans take fluids. "I assume there was a full-scale search?" The Karl moved his head up and down again. "To start with, why don't you tell me where you're sure the coins *aren't*."

"Well, to begin with, they weren't on Franklin's person or on his clothing—he himself insisted on a complete strip search as soon as Mel raised the alarm. Second, they're not in the house; not only did the police do a thorough search, but Mel brought in an expert security team to do a full-scale treasure hunt, complete with electronic sensing devices."

"Well, if they're not in the house, then they have to be outside it," the Anneke said. "Could he have just opened the window and tossed them outside, figuring he'd retrieve them later?"

"Nope. The yard was searched just like the house. In fact, each of the adjoining properties was also searched, just in case he threw them beyond the Markovich property. Nothing was found."

"No; I didn't really expect it to be that easy." The Anneke broke off a piece of Food with her hand and put it in her mouth. "How about an accomplice? He could have tossed the coins out the window to someone else, couldn't he?"

"An interesting thought, but highly improbable, I'm afraid. The problem is that Franklin couldn't have known his uncle would die at that moment, and before you ask"—the Karl held up one hand, a hand larger than my entire tail—"Dmitri Markovich really did die naturally. Believe me, when we found out about the coins, we did the most extensive autopsy possible. Pending the results of one or two exotic analyses, there was no murder. No, this seems to have been a wholly opportunistic theft."

"Damn. All right, can you be positive that Phyllis herself didn't take them?"

"Absolutely. She and Mel swear they were together from the moment they left Franklin in the bedroom to the moment the theft was discovered."

"Could the two of them have been in it together?"

"In fact, that's exactly what Franklin is claiming happened. And it's true that we only have their word for it that the coins were there when Franklin arrived." The Karl used a metal implement to bring Food to his mouth. "But why would they? Or more to the point, why would Mel? Mel Washburn is sixty-seven years old, a widower with no children, and a millionaire several times over. Aside from the fact that his reputation is impeccable, I can't begin to imagine what motive he could have."

"Could he have been having an affair with Phyllis and done it for her?"

"Mel Washburn?" The Karl threw back his head and made a loud sound, his lips parted in a wide rictus. "Even if I could believe that—and I can't—why not just marry her? Or give her money, if that's what she wanted? Or even just buy the damn coins for her—he'd be well able to afford it. For him to put himself at this kind of risk . . . He'd have to be insane." He moved his head. "No, Franklin took them, all right. Now all we have to do is *find* them."

"Karl, what if they're not even still there? Wherever 'there' is. Couldn't Franklin have retrieved them by now?"

"No." The Karl moved his head from side to side. "We held him for forty-eight hours on suspicion of theft, and when we had to release him, Mel's detective agency put him under twenty-four-hour surveillance. What's more, he knows it. No, whatever he did with the coins, they're still there."

The Time of Red Leaves is my busy season, of course. Collecting and storing Food for the Time of Cold and preparing a warm, deep lining for the nest occupies most of my time. Still, I allow myself time to play.

The cold rounds of metal that humans occasionally drop on the ground are normally of no interest to me. But it is rare to come across a large pile of them, especially ones so large and heavy. Besides, these were in my way.

I picked up one of them and dropped it, and when it hit the hard surface below, it made an interesting clanking sound. I scampered down, retrieved it, raced back up, and repeated the maneuver. This time it landed on end and rolled a fair distance. I leaped after it, and it led me a satisfying chase before yielding.

I played the game several more times before stuffing the round of metal into my cheek. Then I made my way back up to the roof, where I took to the wires and on across the street to my own turf. Then over the brown-colored roof and down the rear of the house, where a flowering cherry tree produces small, hard fruits that keep well throughout the Cold.

The Anneke was visible behind one of the transparent wall openings in a space filled with large white objects. I jumped to the ledge and rapped with my claws on the hard, invisible surface; when she turned to face me, I chirruped and flicked my tail, and she slid up the covering and showed her teeth. (This does not seem to mean challenge among humans, although it can be disconcerting.)

"Hello, Swannee," she greeted me. "Come for dinner?"

I have trained her to bring me peanuts when I come to the wall opening, a not-trivial accomplishment considering that she seems unable to comprehend tail-flick. But she is still clumsy; instead of placing the peanuts on the ledge for me to pick up, she persists in tossing them in such a way that I have to scoop them out of the air. Well, she does the best she can.

"Here you go, you greedy thing." She tossed me a peanut and then another, both of which I stowed away in my cheeks. I did the same with two more, but there was no room for the next. Well, the metal round was less important than Food. I removed it from my cheek and let it drop to the ledge, standing erect to catch the next peanut.

"Just one more," the Anneke said, but then her arm froze in midair. "Is that—Swannee! Where did you get that?" She dropped the peanut on the ledge and grabbed the shiny metal. "Karl!" she called loudly. "Karl, quick, in the kitchen!"

"What is it?" The Karl appeared behind her.

"Look at this!" She handed him the metal piece.

"Where did you get this?"

"You're not going to believe me when I tell you," she said.

"But where on earth did he find it?" The humans were standing on the wooden platform at the front of the house, peering across the street.

"I don't know," the Karl said, raising and lowering his shoulders.

"Well, at least it tells us that the coins are still around somewhere," the Anneke said.

"Not necessarily. This could be one that got dropped or misplaced accidentally when the rest of them were taken."

"I suppose." The Anneke stared intently at the house belonging to the Phyllis. It was large and white and far too humanized, with close-cropped grass that was difficult to dig through and sparse, low-clipped bushes along its sides. Only the big northern pine at one side made it at all tolerable—that and the patch of succulent bulbs at the back, which provide welcome nourishment in the Time of Burgeoning.

"Still," the Anneke spoke, "assuming the coins are still there, where are they?" She turned her head upward, to where I perched on my maple tree. "Dammit, Swannee, I wish you could talk."

"I wish he were Lassie," the Karl rumbled. "Then he could just bark and lead us there."

"Very funny." The Anneke tilted her head. "Let's think about squirrels for a minute. What do squirrels do?"

"Eat," the Karl replied immediately.

"They gather food . . . and they *bury* it." She turned to face him. "He could have dug it up."

"From where? And how did it get buried?" The Karl spread his hands. "There's no way Franklin had a chance to bury the coins. He was with someone from the moment the theft was discovered until we completed our search."

"But . . . Damn. All right, then, what else do squirrels do?"

"Let's try it from a different perspective," the Karl said. "Where do squirrels go?"

"The short answer is, anywhere they want." The humans made their low chuckling sound. "Underneath, around, through, on top of . . . On top of." She paused. "I don't suppose Franklin could have climbed down that pine tree, could he? No, of course not. Those branches can barely support a squirrel. Well, then, what about the roof? Or the rain gutters? Could Franklin have reached *up* from that bedroom window?"

"Nope." The Karl pointed toward the house. "It's a high roofline, because of the attic. No dormers or anything like that, either, just flat siding all the way up."

"It's not one of the more interesting Burns Park houses, is it? Awfully flat and blank. What about that attic? Phyllis did mention that squirrels had chewed through the attic screens. I assume the attic was given the same full search as the rest of the house?"

"I'm afraid so."

"Damn." She continued to peer at the house. "Karl, is it a finished attic?"

"I don't know. I wasn't involved in the search. Why?"

"It must be finished." She gnawed her lower lip. "Those sliding aluminum windows obviously weren't original."

"And?" He turned to look at her.

"Look up there, *above* the attic' window." She pointed. "See that metal vent? That means that when they remodeled the attic, they dropped the ceiling across the peak in the middle and created a kind of crawlspace above it. That's why there's a vent—to prevent moisture buildup. The thing is, there isn't a squirrel worth his acorns who couldn't get in there. Did anyone search up there?"

"I have no idea." The Karl moved his head from side to side. "It's certainly worth a phone call to find out."

"There's been a squirrel up there, all right." The One With No Hair dropped a shiny black bag on the grass—a bag filled with *my* acorns. I clung to the metal gutter along the edge of the roof, chittering my outrage.

"But no coins, I take it," the Karl said.

"Nope," the One Who Sneezes said, sneezing. "Just a lot of dirt, leaves, droppings, and moldy acorns." He sneezed again.

"Damn." The Anneke held up the round of yellow metal. "Where *did* he get it?"

"What's the normal range of a squirrel?" the Karl asked.

"Beats me." The One With No Hair kicked the black bag at his feet. "I hate the damn things anyway. Rats with tails."

"Besides," the One Who Sneezes said, "the Markovich kid couldn't've gotten them off the property anyway." He sneezed.

"Maybe the squirrel stole the whole batch of them," the One With No Hair said.

"Naah. Why would he?"

"Who knows? Squirrels are nuts. No telling why they do anything they do." The One With No Hair kicked the bag again hard.

Months of hard work were in that bag, months of collecting and storing, months of sustenance for the Time of Cold. I knew what that shiny black bag meant. Like the warm leaves, my store would be taken away, never to be seen again.

Maddened, I leaped from the gutter to the pine tree, then dropped to the smooth, slick surface of the Food machine. Hooking my hind claws into a narrow groove along its edge, I hung head-down and scrabbled inside. For once, it wasn't Food I was after. The One With No Hair was directly below me.

"Ouch!" I had scored a direct hit on the smooth pink scalp. "What the hell was that?" He looked up, rubbing the top of his head. "It's that damn squirrel."

I chittered and flicked my tail, and before he could flee, I acted once more, swiftly, targeting the very center of his upturned face.

"Hey!" He ducked—too late!—and backed away hastily. Too hastily. Down he went, tripping over a tree root and landing heavily on his back end.

"Chkthkchkthk!" I warbled in triumph, but I could hardly hear myself over the babble of sound from the humans. The Anneke was making her chuckling sound, lips drawn back. The Karl was standing over the rounds of metal, looking from them up to me and back again. They all seemed to be talking at once.

"My God." The Anneke's voice rose, and she pointed. All eyes were now fixed on me, where I still hung, head down, from the top of the Food machine. "The bird feeder! See? In among the branches. *That's* where he hid the coins!"

They continued to stare, even the One With No Hair, who had resumed his erect stance. "That's impossible," he said. "I'm telling you, we *looked* out that window, Lieutenant. You can't reach that bird feeder from the bedroom. Hell, you can't even *see* it from there."

"Yes, you can," the Anneke said. "You wouldn't be able to see it if you looked straight out the window, but Dmitri Markovich was bedridden, remember? I'll bet you'll find that the bird feeder is on a clear visual line *from the bed*."

"And Franklin was upstairs alone after Markovich died," the Karl said. "The bird feeder is right outside the window of the room next door. All he had to do was nip down the hall into the next room, open the window, and drop the coins into the feeder."

"But wouldn't Phyllis have found them when she re-filled the thing?" the One Who Sneezes asked.

"No." The Anneke moved her head back and forth. "You don't open that kind of bird feeder; you just pour the seeds in through the top.'' She looked upward. "Right where Swannee is now. There isn't a bird feeder made that will keep out a really determined squirrel, is there, Swannee?''

"Chkkchkkchtk!'' I warbled in agreement.

In 1992, Susan Holtzer won the St. Martin's Press/Malice Domestic Contest for Best First Traditional Mystery with her novel Something to Kill For. *Holtzer has since followed up this early success with four novels, including* The Silly Season.

Just Only One Little Mystery-Pistery

H. R. F. Keating

Inspector Ghote heard what they were saying. Inspector Harbhajan Singh, seniormost Crime Branch detective, was standing in the open doorway of Additional Commissioner Dhasal's cabin. So, emerging onto the upper veranda at Bombay Police Headquarters to apply for two days' Casual Leave, Ghote could not help registering every word of their conversation.

"It is one of those murder cases any local subinspector can handle," Mr. Dhasal was saying. "But number one suspect, who is inheriting fat proceeds of the life insurance, is some British lady. So it is becoming Crime Branch business, and last thing I am wanting is trouble-bubble from foreign diplomats. So someone should be off there, as of today."

"You are thinking I must go?" the big Sikh inspector's voice had in it as much incredulity as respect for his senior would permit.

"No, no, no. No need for any top-notch officer. But who to send?"

"One answer only." Harbhajan Singh blared out a cheerful laugh. "Fellow who is always sent if it is some can-carry business."

"Inspector Ghote. Yes, of course. Why didn't I think of Ghote? Very man for what, after all, is just only one little mystery-pistery."

Step by step Ghote lowered himself backwards down the spiral stone stairs.

Not anybody so deaf, he said to himself, as he who would not hear. Sometimes, indeed, he thought, it would be a pleasure to be altogether deaf. To live in a world of one's own. No longer a police officer always being called for duty, no longer a husband always having to listen to a wife, no longer a father always and always being asked for money. To be cut off, and content.

But, no, my hearing is one hundred percent normal. Better than normal itself. As a boy how many times did my father say, *Never needs oil to clean his ears, little Ganesh?*

With a sigh he started up the steps again, banging down his shoes as hard as he could and reflecting sadly that he was unlikely now to get his Casual Leave. He knocked on the Additional Commissioner's still just-open door.

"Come."

He entered, giving Harbhajan Singh a quick nod as they passed on his way out.

"Ah, Ghote. Just the man. Murder inquiry for you. Needs Crime Branch supervision. Out at a place called McClenahanganj. Heard of it?"

"Oh, yes, sir." *At least I am able to show first-class knowledge, even if I am a can-carry officer fit for just only one little mystery-pistery.* "McClenahanganj is up in the Ghats. Settlement in the cool of the hills for

Anglo-Indians, founded in 1930s by one Dr. Mc-
Clenahan. But almost closed down now. On a branch
line from Nasik.''

"Quite right, Inspector. Been there, have you?''

"No, sir, no. I am just only reading about this place
in some magazine.''

"Well, now's your chance to see it. Case sounds
straightforward, but local sub-inspector may be going to
charge-sheet a British lady. I want to be damn sure his
investigation is tip-top, start to finish. So keep your eyes
fully peeled, yes?''

"Yes, sir.''

Well, Ghote thought, locating among the row of de-
caying tin-roofed bungalows along the dusty road the
one called Dunroamin, *at least this shack is in somewhat
of a more decent state than the others. But all the same
I would not have thought a British lady would be staying
in such a place, even if in U.K. she had been sharing
house with this Anglo-Indian woman, now deceased.*

But true enough, unlike The Nest, The Retreat,
Sweethome and The Hermitage passed on his way, Dunroamin had evidently recently been put in order. The
bamboo fence outside was spick-and-span. The ground
behind it had been dug over. Some attempt, too, had
been made to remove the layers of differently colored
paints applied to the woodwork over the years since the
distant days of the British Raj, although no one as yet
had covered them with some new color.

That all fitted in with what Sub-Inspector Thakur,
heavy of body, sullen of face, solidly chewing at a paan,
its sharp odor of lime paste assaulting the nostrils, had
told him earlier in McClenahanganj's run-down police
thana. Mrs. Bessie Kichenchand, Anglo-Indian widow of
a Gujarati businessman who had made good in England,
and the lady she had shared her house with there, Miss

Ryder, had apparently decided a little over a year ago to retire to McClenahanganj where their joint incomes would give them a better life than in increasingly costly England. And having acquired Dunroamin, they had spent some money on making it more comfortable.

But, Ghote thought, this much was probably the full extent of Thakur's accurate information. A fellow more used to beating a confession out of the handiest suspect than to conducting any sort of pukka investigation. And at a check now because even he had realized that Mrs. Bessie Kichenchand's British companion who would now acquire the hundred-thousand-pound insurance pay-out—how many lakhs of rupees was that?—was not a person you forced a confession out of at the end of a hard-swung lathi. Not even if all the signs were that someone had inexpertly contrived to fake a break-in.

He walked up the beaten-earth path and knocked at the bungalow's door.

In a moment it was opened by a person who could be none other than the British Miss Ryder.

Good name for her, was Ghote's instant reaction. She looked, to his eyes at least, like someone who had spent her life riding some big English horse, tall in its saddle, long legs encased in boots and britches, face tanned from days and days chasing many-many foxes. Here in McClenahanganj, though, he saw, she seemed to make her claim to superior status simply by letting her fingernails grow and painting them bright red. Well, perhaps that might impress the aged Anglo-Indian ladies in their bright cotton frocks he had seen carefully keeping out of the sun as he had walked up.

He introduced himself as coming from Crime Branch in Bombay. For an instant then he thought he heard a tiny indrawn gasp from this tall, hard-faced woman. But however much he prided himself on the sharpness of his hearing, he could not be sure. Had he heard a sign of fear from someone who, just two nights before, had smothered to death her Anglo-Indian companion? A sudden dread that a first-class investigator would do better than dull Sub-Inspector Thakur at finding evidence to convict her? Or had it been something else altogether that had caused his dart of suspicion?

But perhaps there had been nothing. Perhaps he had heard no more than a chance intake of breath. So was this tall, elderly, but tough Englishwoman guiltless after all? Had Bessie Kichenchand actually been smothered to death by the totally deaf twelve-year-old tribal servant-boy the two women had acquired when they first came to McClenahanganj, now nowhere to be found? Thakur had shown signs, too, of liking him as a suspect. Nothing easier than to obtain a confession there. Once you had located the boy and, of course, penetrated his dome of deafness—just like, he thought, the comforting impenetrable blanket he had wished for himself outside Additional Commissioner Dhasal's door.

Or was the murder really committed by some tribal thief, coming sneaking out of the surrounding jungle looking for things to steal? Or by the young man Thakur had also spoken about, Bessie Kichenchand's cousin-nephew, Albert Shiner, the youngster she had never met before, summoned from Bombay to see her here in this remote, run-down settlement?

But—coming back to the beginning again—had it been Albert Shiner's very arrival just two days ago, perhaps soon to be left a large share of insurance money, that had made Miss Ryder decide to take action? Certainly she looked like someone who, if they had decided action should be taken, would not hesitate to act.

She led him now into the bungalow's single living room, still full of the sagging chairs and leaning cane teapoy tables that must have come with the place, but marked out, too, by some new acquisitions. There was a bright and shiny TV set. There was a miniature Swiss cottage with VIDEOS HOME painted across its front. There were two rows of glossy gold-framed photographs. He peered at the nearest of these: Miss Ryder and presumably her now dead friend, a little shrunken creature, in the doorway of what must have been their house in England.

"Poor Bessie's photos," Miss Ryder boomed. "Tried to make her leave them behind when we left Home. Now, God knows why, I find I want to keep them."

"Yes, yes," Ghote murmured, not a little embarrassed. "It must be most disheartening for you to lose your lifetime friend."

"Speak up, man," Miss Ryder commanded abruptly. "Little deaf nowadays. Blasted nuisance."

Ghote gulped and repeated his words of condolence in a voice he felt to be unnaturally loud.

"Yes, well, there it is. Now, can I get you a drink, Inspector? There's still some rum, poor Bessie's favorite. Or the local guava wine. Not exactly French, but not too bad."

"No, no. I am here to see scene of crime only."

"What's that? Scene of what?" Miss Ryder cocked her head at him.

Ghote bit his underlip.

"The scene of the most sad event," he pronounced in ringing tones.

"Ah, yes. Bessie's room. Well, suppose you must."

"Thank you. But first may I ask if this house has been broken into before?"

"No. Can't say it has. Not while we've been here. But always has to be a first time, you know."

"Other troubles from tribals, yes?"

"No, the tribals haven't worried us. Have to put a ring of carbolic down round our beds at night, though. Snakes."

A few more routine questions, and then he repeated his request to see the dead woman's room.

"Right, then. Follow me."

There were, he found, just two bedrooms at the back of the little house. With a scarlet-clawed hand, Miss Ryder thrust open the door of the one on the left.

Ghote took in the bare room where the returned Anglo-Indian widow had spent her few last months. The smell of snake-defying carbolic was still strong in the air. Through the half-open leaning doors of an old almirah he saw a few boldly colored flowered dresses forlornly hanging. On a narrow chest of drawers there was an ancient horn-backed hairbrush, beside it a comb still sprouting a cluster of gray hairs and at one corner a vase holding a bunch of withering ferns.

As he looked, a gecko shot out from behind its cover and snapped up a fly.

"You can see where that thief got in," Miss Ryder said, jerking her head towards the room's single glassless, barred window.

And yes, one of the bars had been pulled from the rotten wood at its foot and wrenched aside. A lithe tribal could, just possibly, have squeezed through. But in principle he had to agree with what Thakur had said: all the signs of being faked.

Who, then, had done the faking? It should have been Miss Ryder. But could she have wrenched away that bar and kept her long, painted fingernails intact? Probably not. Probably not. So who had crept in here, pulled the pillow from under the sleeping woman's head and pressed it down and down onto her face? The mattress, a thin, miserable affair, still retained the deep impress of that thrust-down head. He looked at it for a long moment more, sighed and turned away.

"Thank you," he said to Miss Ryder, remembering

to speak as loudly as she seemed to require. "That is all I am needing to see."

It was not, of course. What he had wanted to see, to see and to hear, was Sub-Inspector Thakur's prime suspect. And having seen her, he found he was in two minds. Yes, there could be no doubt that this hardy Englishwoman, even though she must be seventy years of age or more, would be easily capable of holding a pillow over her shrunken companion's face. And she was the one with most to gain from the old Anglo-Indian woman's death. With lakhs and lakhs of rupees to gain.

But equally, her straightforwardness—was it typically British?—had impressed him. The whole time he had been in the house, she had shown no signs of inward guilt and she had, too, been plainly much distressed, in an unexpressive English way, at the sudden death of her friend.

But who else could be responsible for that death? It was almost certainly not some sneaking tribal. It would have had to have been a very small man to have managed to squeeze in at that window, and nothing in the house had been stolen either. So was it the absconding deaf twelve-year-old boy? Possible, but hardly likely, though it was plain that seeing the dead woman, his first thought would have been to run off. Then what about the young man who had come up from Bombay to see this distant, not yet met relative?

Had he, finding the old lady so frail and believing she had already put him in her will, been swept by sudden greed for his share of her life-insurance money? So then had he come creeping up in the darkness from the retiring room at the railway station, where, Thakur had said, he had slept that night? In the dark and the silence, with only the never-ending squeaking of a million crickets, so much present as to go somehow unheard, had he come creeping up to the house? Tried the barred window? And when only one bar came away, had he gone round to the flimsy door and pushed that open? And then brought his feeble old auntie's life to a quick and easy end?

Whether this was what had happened or not, one thing was clear. If Miss Ryder was arrested, the case against her would by no means be watertight. And that would mean trouble from above. British High Commission-wallahs poking in their noses. Just what Additional Commissioner Dhasal did not want.

So find that young man, Albert Shiner. And do my level best to see if, after all, he may be the murderer.

He located Albert Shiner at the almost deserted railway station. He was sitting on a rusted iron bench in the shade, with a battered old metal loudspeaker dangling by a single wire above him, relic of the days when McClenahanganj Station had been part of the pride of Indian Railways. A cigarette was drooping from his thickish lips. He was looking with bored vacancy at a half-mad woman fruit-seller bickering or flirting with a pair of semi-naked tribals round an old oildrum, where they seemed to be busy brewing country liquor. There could be no doubt this was the boy he needed to see. No one else in this remote backwater would be wearing smart, narrow-legged blue jeans and a T-shirt with the title of the latest Bollywood Hindi movie printed across it.

He went over and sat beside him.

"You must be guessing who I am," he said.

"Policewallah."

"Just so. From Crawford Market H.Q. itself."

"Don't care where you are coming from. I got nothing to worry."

"No? So what were you doing the first night you were here in McClenahanganj?"

"What there is to do, a place like this?"

"Going up to see your long-lost auntie late, late at night? Finding same in bed? In one flash thinking that if she was not just only sleeping but dead also, you would have more of money in your pocket than you were ever having in your life till now?"

The boy rounded on him.

"Listen to me, you damn policewallah. I know your trick ways. You are wanting to pin that murder on me, just because I am Anglo-Indian and you think I am a child's play."

Ghote sat there.

"Well, if you were not doing that by night, tell me what-all was happening when you were going there by day, yes?"

Albert Shiner gave him a mistrustful glance.

"All right, you want to know. I am telling. One month ago getting letter from Bessie auntie, saying she here in India, McClenahanganj. And I am her one and only relative, so she leaving me something from her life insurance in U.K. And wanting me to go see her. Okay, she send me money for rail ticket, I come."

He gave Ghote a sly glance.

"Matter of fact, I travel W.T. and keep the money. So you want to charge-sheet me?"

"No," Ghote said. "Travelling paying or Without Ticket makes no difference to me. What I am wanting to know is what-all you were doing when you came here."

"Going to see the old lady, what else?"

"And . . . ?"

"And there she was, little old hunch-up lady with deaf aid stuck in her ear like they do. She one of us with slight tint only."

One of us, an Anglo-Indian. Ghote, knowing how important it was to Anglo-Indians not to be too dark, absorbed this.

"But when she did see her lost cousin-nephew," Albert Shiner continued, "she had damn little to say. Sitting and sitting there listening to some old-times film on the video, paying me no damn attention, while that angrezi woman she stays with was feeding me plum cake and tea. Merle Oberon, you ever hear of Merle Oberon?"

"No," Ghote said.

The boy's vacant face lit up momentarily.

"Merle Oberon, man, she big-big film star long ago. In Hollywood itself. And she Anglo-Indian, man. Just damn-damn beautiful. You know what Bessie auntie was watching on that video brought from U.K.? Merle Oberon and Laurence Olivier. Some damn film call *Withered Height*, something like that. But she top-notch star in it. Anglo-Indian."

"One credit to your community," Ghote said.

But he saw at once that flattery was getting him nowhere. He tried again.

"And your auntie what was she saying to you? Must be something. Was she saying she would change her will and testament because you were one fine upstanding boy?"

"No. Never said nothing. Well, one thing ..."

"Yes?"

"No, it's stupid."

"No. You tell me each and every thing that was happening. Or I will take you along to my friend Sub-Inspector Thakur, who is very-very good at making witness talk."

A flicker of fear on the face that had fallen back into vacancy once the subject of Merle Oberon had been dropped. It faintly reminded Ghote of something. But he dared not lose momentum.

"So what it was your auntie said? Tell."

"Was when that big angrezi woman was going out to tell their damn deaf servant to make tea."

"Yes?"

"Auntie been sitting there, deaf aid thing stuck in her ear, leaning forward whole time looking at this video—and it was just only black-and-white, man, I telling you—and taking not one damn bit of notice of me when I had come all the way out to this dead-alive hole to please."

"But when Miss Ryder was out of the room, she did say something, yes?"

"Yes. Funny. That film going quietly on and on and sudden she lean over and whisper."

"What whisper?"

"She say—funny, but I can't forget it, every damn word. She say, *Don't go away. Stay the night. Don't go.* But then Ryder Memsahib coming back, and Bessie auntie don't say one thing more."

"So did you stay the night? Was that why you were inside when your auntie was smothered to death?"

"Nah, man. I couldn't stay. They got no room, that Ryder Memsahib saying. Just only one bedroom each, and that deaf boy sleeping on floor in living room. So I tell her I'm spending one night in railway retiring room, then coming to see Auntie first thing, when maybe she's ready to talk a bit more. After that off I go."

"So you went up to Dunroamin in the morning?"

"And found Auntie dead. Some tribal got in, smother her. That what Ryder Memsahib say."

"She was saying that itself? She was telling you that?"

"Yeah. Why not? Was what happen, yes?"

But that was a question Ghote was not going to answer. He recognized, however, that Miss Ryder's insistence on pointing to a tribal as the murderer was something more that told against her.

And then came another thing.

"Giving me bit of advice, too," Albert Shiner added. "Wish I'd been quicker to take it."

"Yes? And what advices was she giving?"

"Told me to get back to Bombay fast as I could. Said they might think I killed old auntie if I guessed she'd put me down already for my share."

So, Ghote thought, *here is someone setting up yet another person to take the blame.* First a tribal who never existed. And now this Anglo-Indian antisocial. And this at last convinced him that Thakur must have been right all along. The British lady had smothered her feeble Anglo-Indian friend, whose insurance money she had intended to inherit.

But, he said to himself, *what of decent proof is there? Not enough,* he answered. *Not anything like enough.*

Suddenly from above his head there came a horrendously loud sound. He looked up in sheer fright. And realized that it was coming from the old loudspeaker he had thought long, long disused. He was even, then, able to make out that someone somewhere was announcing the arrival of that day's train to Bombay.

Was Albert Shiner going to take it when it arrived? Traveling with or without ticket? And if so, should he still stop him departing? Arrest him as a suspect, just in case?

But then—the idea came to him simultaneously as a sudden flash of knowledge and as a slowly unweaving trail of thoughts and facts—he realized there was no need to keep Albert Shiner in McClenahanganj. He was not the murderer of his aunt.

Nor was the tall, booming-voiced, scarlet-nailed British Miss Ryder. And it was certainly neither a wandering tribal nor the stone-deaf servant boy.

No.

He could not resist turning to Albert Shiner, now that

the loudspeaker had ceased to vomit out its noise, and telling him what had really happened two nights before in the shack called Dunroamin and why it had really been a flicker of fear he had seen when he had announced himself as a Crime Branch officer from Bombay.

"I am happy to tell," he said to the young man, "that your auntie is not at all dead. On the other hand, I must inform also that she is to be charge-sheeted under Section 302, Indian Penal Code, Murder."

"What—What you saying?"

Albert Shiner looked totally bewildered.

"I am saying your auntie, Mrs. Bessie Kichenchand, must have been finding after death of her late husband that she was having altogether too little of income. So she was deciding first, to come here to McClenahanganj, where no one was knowing her, and then to bully and persuade her companion, very-very feeble Miss Ryder, to pretend to be herself, Bessie. And then, when she had called you to see her so that you could be a nice-nice suspect, she was smothering the poor old British lady to death. Yes, the British lady. No wonder you were saying and stating she had slight tint only. She was as English as Queen Elizabeth itself."

"But—But how you knowing this, man?"

Ghote allowed himself a smile.

"Very, very simple. You were telling what I was just now realizing I was needing to know. You were saying, yes, that your auntie was listening, deaf aid in ear, to that Merle Somebody film playing quietly, quietly on video."

"She was. I told you, didn't I?"

"And then you were saying she was whispering, *Stay the night. Don't go.* Well, now, if a person is deaf and using deaf aid, she would be thinking video is playing at some good volume, yes?"

"Okay. But I don't see what you getting at."

"No? Kindly think. If someone is whispering when they should be believing TV is on loud, that must be meaning they are knowing-knowing TV is not loud. So they are not at all deaf. They have been bully-bullied only into pretending to be deaf Bessie auntie when they are in truth not-deaf Miss Ryder."

It began to dawn on the boy.

"Bessie auntie swapped over, so when someone dies called Mrs. Bessie Kichenchand, due to leave all that insurance, one Miss Ryder, who is all along Mrs. Kichenchand, is acquiring same. You know, Inspector, when they are saying all Anglo-Indians stupid, they damn wrong. My Bessie auntie very damn clever."

"But not altogether enough of clever, yes?"

"Well, yes. Yes, that right. But how you going to prove?"

"Yes, in the end if we are asking Scotland Yard wallahs to give us two descriptions, all will become clear. But, you know, I think I can expose Mrs. Bessie Kichenchand before even we are getting reply from London."

Albert Shiner was prepared now to believe Ghote could do almost anything.

"So how, Inspector?"

"She is all the time wearing bright-bright red nail varnish, yes? I was thinking when I was first seeing that this was somehow not altogether right. So you know what I am going to do? If some painterwallah was stripping old paint from woodworks of Dunroamin, then somewhere there you would find paint stripper, and—"

"Yes. Yes. You going to strip varnish off Bessie auntie's nails. And then you would see"—the Anglo-Indian boy glanced at his own nails—"that bluish tint that is always showing when some Indian blood is there, yes?"

"Yes. Just that. And then there would be no one so deaf they would not understand just exactly what is answer to this little mystery-pistery."

The resume of British mystery writer, editor, and critic H. R. F. Keating is a long and distinguished one, including his term as president of the famed Detection Club and author of the Inspector Ghote mysteries set in Bombay. His most recent book featuring the shy inspector is Asking Questions.

Aunt Agatha Leaving

Susan Kenney

"What's that?" Roz Howard asked, pointing to the crumbling remains of two tall chimneys looming on the headland as she and Aunt Jessie True rounded the northernmost tip of Fox Island. They had been out for a lingering early September daysail in Aunt Jessie's sloop *Verorum* and were now on a final starboard tack that would take them straight back to the mooring at Bayside and the promise of a warm fire. The setting sun had momentarily blazed golden off the brick, picking out the ruined stacks and throwing them into glowing relief against the trees. That was what had caught her eye.

Aunt Jessie was at the helm with her back to the island, so had to twist around to see what Roz was talking about. "Why, landsakes!" she exclaimed. "That's the old Randolph estate—I didn't realize you could still see anything after all these years, what with the trees and puckerbrush growing up all around and everything let go since the tragedy."

"Randolphs? What Randolphs?" In her own peregrinations around the upper reaches of Penobscot Bay Roz had encountered most of the legendary names attached to great family estates—Pingree, Rockefeller, Watson, Cabot, Onterdonck—but this was the first she'd heard of any Randolphs, let alone a long-ago tragedy.

"Why, the Beacon Hill Randolphs, of course. A brother and three sisters, Archie, Alice, Ada, and Agatha. He made a fortune in oil and land speculation right after the war, put up scads of fancy hotels and such, Randolph Arms this and Randolph Court that—who do you think invented Quadruple A?" She looked vigilantly to windward for a moment, readjusted the tiller slightly, then turned back to Roz.

"So sad. They owned this whole end of the island. Rich as stink, for all the good it did them. That was the main house; it burned right to the ground some fifty-odd years ago with everyone in it. Well, all except Agatha in point of fact, but that hardly mattered since she was gone within the week. Wiped 'em all out in one fell swoop. Such a pity. But mind the jib now; we're coming into that squirrelly bit just off the gong. I'll tell you all about it when we get back to port."

Some hours later, the old sloop now safely bobbing on her mooring, Aunt Jessie and Roz settled down in front of the fire with steaming bowls of beef stew that had been simmering away on the old cookstove along with a pot of mulled cider while they sailed around the bay.

"As I said," Aunt Jessie began, "there were just the four of them, all in their late fifties or early sixties; not a one of them had ever married. Your uncle Lou was the family lawyer; he'd inherited the job from his father, who was Uncle Archie's roommate at Williams. We called them all aunt and uncle, courtesy titles of course, but that's how close the families were. They lived right around the corner from each other near Louisburg Square, and in the summers we all headed up to Maine together. Lou's dad claimed he built this place on the bluff just so he could keep a lookout and get a running start on Archie if he ever had to. That Archie was a pistol; he had everyone else coming and going six ways to Sunday.''

''What about the sisters? What did they do?''

Aunt Jessie chuckled. ''Other than spend Archie's money for him, as he used to say? Well, I'll tell you, they were quite a colorful bunch. Archie had all the money, but he saw to it that his sisters were well taken care of; they lived in style—adjacent townhouses, cars, traveling allowances, the whole ball of wax. Aunt Alice's forte was golf and tennis; some said she was the model for May What'shername in that Edith Wharton novel—the title escapes me, *House of Innocence* or something. I always had my doubts about that; she may have been a terror on the links, but she wasn't any lissome beauty by a long shot, built like a fireplug with a face like a Boston terrier, just like the rest of them. All I know is, Archie had a tennis court and a nine-hole golf course built out there on the island just for her. Alice was the one who kept house for him in the summer; they liked to 'rough it' when they were in residence, meaning no live-in staff to speak of other than a secretary. They'd just hire in day help from the locals when they needed it; it was their way of helping out the island economy.

''Now Aunt Ada was active in the art world; she painted some, but mainly she liked to buy things; she was a regular whiz at acquisition. When she filled up one house, she'd go and buy another, all of which Archie anted-up for, naturally. Then there was Aunt Agatha, the world traveler, roaming the earth searching for adventure and recording it all with her trusty movie camera. She was my favorite.'' Aunt Jessie paused for a moment, a pensive expression on her face.

''In a lot of ways, she was the most tragic. She was the youngest and by far the most independent, but even so, no one expected her to break ranks with the others, especially when she reached the ripe old age of thirty-five. But lo and behold, she got herself engaged to marry a young man in the diplomatic corps, the date set, and the linens bought. Then her fiancé went down with the *Lusitania*. When she recovered from the shock, she took up filmmaking. Her first trip abroad after the war she brought back movie footage that would break your heart. She and her fiancé had planned to have a family, and she wanted to adopt some war orphans, but Archie and the rest of the family put their foot down; all for one and one for all, and no outsiders need apply.

''But I think the disappointment made her restless; it always seemed that wherever she was, she was forever leaving to go somewhere else. She just kept on traveling around the world and shooting her blessed movies everywhere she went. She had her own darkroom and processing laboratory with all the latest equipment to edit them, splicers and titlers and whatnot; all very professional. Whenever your uncle Lou and I went out to the island to visit, she'd show her latest—Venice, Constantinople, Baghdad, New York—they were quite good, too. In fact, at the time, some folks wondered if that's how the fire got started, some of that old highly flammable film stock she'd left there igniting spontaneously somehow. But no one ever knew for sure, since there was almost nothing left of the place. They couldn't even identify the bodies, only that they were the four that had been in the house together—Archie, Ada, Alice, and that poor young woman.''

''Wait a minute, Aunt Jessie! Who was the young

woman? And if Aunt Agatha wasn't in the house, where was she? How—''

"Now, Rosamund, just hold on a minute; you're worse than a six-year-old with your whos and wheres and hows! I'm getting to that. Here, sit back with your cider and be quiet, and I'll tell you the whole story."

"It would have been right around this time, Labor Day weekend back in '38. I remember it as if it were yesterday," Aunt Jessie mused. "The four Randolphs were all gathered out on the island as usual for their end-of-the-summer bash. Archie and Alice and Ada had been here for most of the summer, and Agatha, who'd been off in Timbuktu or someplace exotic like that, had come in on the mailboat a day or so earlier. It was a regular house party, all kinds of people popping in and out, Alice with her golf and tennis tournaments, Ada with her latest tent art show, Agatha with that old movie camera cranking away the whole time, recording it all for posterity—folks in their summer whites, croquet on the lawn, strolls on the beach, antics in the pool, all that happy prewar nonsense. We were there, of course, as friends of the family, but also because Uncle Archie had asked Lou to help him draw up a new will.

"Under the terms of the old will, everything went to the surviving siblings, and if none of them or other issue survived him blah blah blah and so forth and so on, it was to go to charity, plain and simple—what your Uncle Lou used to call bachelor boilerplate. But that was way back before Archie'd made his bundle and they were all past the point of having any 'issue.' It seems he wanted to set up a foundation, so that when he passed away, all the money would go into a trust, with his sisters provided for in their lifetimes. When the last of them died, the whole shebang—property, artwork, money, the lot—was to go to endow the Randolph Family Fox Island

Foundation, with the house and grounds to be used as a public library and museum and enough left over to build a school. He thought it would be a fitting memorial to their long and happy life together on the island. When the islanders got wind of this, they were ecstatic.

"Alice and Ada were all for it. The problem was, they couldn't get Agatha to sign off. Some years earlier, she'd taken this young man under her wing, some sort of distant cousin on the mother's side, but she referred to him as her nephew, and she wanted him in the will, too. Archie would have none of it. So that weekend they spent hours haggling over the terms in the library, while the guests cavorted all over and that poor young secretary, who'd only just been hired and was new to the job in the first place, had to play hostess to everyone.

"Well, finally the weekend was over, the rest of the guests had dispersed, and Lou and I had to get back, with still no sign of a new will. 'I'll talk to you in a few days,' Archie told Lou. 'I'm sure Aggie will come around.'

"No one ever quite knew what happened after that. Tuesday morning we all woke up to find the Randolph place burned right to the foundation with everyone in it. Only the garage was left standing. We could see the smoke from here." Aunt Jessie paused and took a long swig of her now lukewarm cider.

"But you said it wiped them all out," Roz ventured. "What about Aunt Agatha?"

"I was getting to that part. It seems that after their family set-to, Agatha up and decided to leg it back to Beacon Hill and had left on the last mailboat that afternoon. The nephew, who'd accompanied her abroad, was staying at her townhouse. He was the one who took the call the next morning and broke the news to Aunt Agatha, who'd gotten in late the night before.

"Well, of course, she went to pieces, prostrate with

grief. So the nephew drove up the day after and went with Lou to identify the bodies, which was a formality, of course, since they were burned past all recognition. It was pretty much a matter of counting up on your fingers who was and wasn't there. As far as anyone could tell, the four of them had been watching a bunch of Agatha's movies in the library; it was a cool night, and they had the coal heater running. It must have malfunctioned, and with all that film lying around—well, the place went up like an incinerator.

"Agatha immediately went into seclusion; when Lou tried to speak to her by phone, she couldn't even talk. She was last seen later that week getting into her car in Boston to drive up here to make the funeral arrangements. But she never arrived. They found her car parked by the Penobscot River Bridge, with a note saying she'd gone to join the others. Evidently she'd walked out onto the bridge and jumped. Her body was never found. Now, isn't that a sad story?"

They sat in silence for some time, staring into the fire. Finally Roz spoke. "What happened to all the money?"

"Funny you should ask. After the shock wore off, that's what everyone wanted to know, especially the islanders. Well, to their dismay, the nephew wound up with the whole bundle. Since Agatha had survived Archie, even if it was only for a few days, under the terms of the current will, she was deemed to have inherited. And he was next of kin, even if he was only a first cousin once removed. Their father's sister's daughter's son, if I remember rightly—name of Holden, Edward Holden.

"Once the will was probated, that was that. Lou talked him into donating the estate to the island with a few thousand over, which was not too popular with the locals, since it barely covered the loss of the tax revenue and the town ended up barely breaking even. Then before we knew it, he'd sold up the Boston property lock, stock, and barrel, and gone to Europe. We pretty much lost touch with him after that. I do know he served in the army over there and ended up with a British war bride, but what became of them after that, I have no idea.''

"Hmm," said Roz. "Sounds pretty suspicious to me, Aunt Jessie. *Cui bono* and all that. Take the money and run.''

Aunt Jessie spluttered into her mug of cider. "As I live and breathe, if you aren't just a caution, Roz Howard! You're not going to start playing detective on me, are you? I thought you were on vacation!"

"Come on, Aunt Jessie," Roz countered, laughing. "You love a good mystery as much as I do! It's a classic—a disputed inheritance, Aunt Agatha leaving in a huff and miraculously surviving the others, only to do herself in a few days later? And the distant cousin cops the lot just in the nick of time before the will gets changed? Didn't anyone think that was a little fishy? Was there anyone other than the so-called nephew who actually saw Aunt Agatha after the fire? For that matter, did anyone see Aunt Agatha get on the boat? Did anybody think of that?"

"Why, of course they did!" Aunt Jessie sputtered. "We weren't born yesterday, you know. There was a proper inquest; your uncle Lou and I even gave testimony. Besides, they had it all on film.''

Roz sat forward. "Film, what film?"

"The movie!" Aunt Jessie said in an exasperated voice. "The one I told you they were all busy shooting that weekend! The one that showed Aunt Agatha leaving! The one that's still downstairs in the basement with all the other stuff Lou saved from that time, if you want to see for yourself, little Miss Marple!"

*　　*　　*

It took the two of them a while to locate the can of film, packed in a fireproof metal box that smelled of mothballs. Then Aunt Jessie had to ferret out the old 16mm projector and the screen, the workings of which Roz luckily was familiar with from her summers here as a child. Still, by the time everything was set up and running, it was past ten.

"Are you sure you want to do this now, Aunt Jessie?" Roz asked. "It's late. We can do it another time, you know." In fact, she was dying to see the old movie footage, to put faces to all these names whose long-ago history had taken over, at least for the moment, her inquisitive imagination.

"Don't be silly, girl, I can tell you're champing at the bit. Anyway, it won't take long—the whole thing runs just under four minutes. There was just the one reel that survived; it was still in the camera they found in the ruins. The coroner had it developed, and they ran it at the inquest. But don't get your hopes up. It's quite rough, all kinds of stops and starts, what with the camera changing hands and such; I swear Agatha had everyone but the dog shooting at some point. If she'd lived, she'd no doubt have made something of it, but—you'll see what I mean."

"Why, look, Aunt Jessie, it's you and Uncle Lou! Don't you look handsome in your starched whites!"

It was the best Roz could do in terms of commentary under the circumstances. Aunt Jessie had not exaggerated the poor quality of the movie footage; it was for the most part fuzzy, full of blips and jerks, jumping from scene to scene and person to person in a flurry of senseless motion. The film had come on in a series of fits and starts, panning the lawn and gardens in a psychedelic blur, wobbling down the path to the private dock, then inexplicably cutting to a round, gnomish face peering roguishly into the camera upside down.

"That's Aunt Agatha," Aunt Jessie explained. "Such a clown she was and full of tricks. She takes the camera here; you'll be able to tell. Someone else who didn't know much about movie cameras had been filming up to now, probably Archie's secretary, Helen Trent. I think Agatha was trying to coach her a bit here, and a good thing, too, since she ended up doing most of the honors that last day while Agatha was inside closeted with the others."

Sure enough, the film smoothed out at that point and proceeded with some continuity and grace into scenes taken throughout the day: couples playing tennis; people strolling through the garden, lounging around watching a short, stocky older man with a familiar gnomish grin diving repeatedly and acrobatically off the board into a round swimming pool ("Uncle Archie showing off as usual," was Aunt Jessie's acerbic comment); Alice vanquishing all comers on the putting green, Ada showing off the latest art moderne; people standing for their photos, waving good-bye, and trooping down the path toward the dock. A touchingly young Aunt Jessie and Uncle Lou proudly rowing out in their dinghy to a spanking new *Verorum*, casting off, and sailing away, waving hats and hankies in a parody of farewell. The three older Randolphs and the pretty young secretary comically wiping their brows, staggering about, leaning together in a comic huddle, then waving at the camera. Come with us, come with us, the lips mouthed silently, the beckoning hands urged. Helen, the secretary, coming forward, the film jiggling as the camera changed hands, then the four Randolphs together, arm in arm, a quartet of amiable trolls dancing a comic cancan into the house.

Another break in continuity, and Aunt Jessie's voice

in the darkness. "Now watch here. This is the part you wanted to see—Aunt Agatha leaving."

Roz sat forward attentively as the camera focused on the doorway. And sure enough, here came Agatha, backing out in her fashionable, absurdly large, fur-collared coat and her close-fitting city hat, valise in hand, her face turned inward, talking to someone. Head nodding, yes, yes, yes. Still backing away, then turning, catching sight of the camera, walking toward it with an oddly awkward gait, then—what? Waving it aside? It was difficult to tell. If this was Aunt Agatha leaving in a huff, she didn't look particularly upset; in fact, Roz noted, she was still smiling, laughing even. But perhaps that was for the camera's benefit.

Cut to the dock. Aunt Agatha, still smiling and waving, always the ham, moving away from the camera along the dock to the waiting mailboat, handing down her valise to the cabin boy, climbing down the ladder and, still facing the camera, mouthing her farewells. Like a cowboy wielding a lasso, the boy unloops the lines from the stanchions, the mailboat begins to churn forward away from the dock, Aunt Agatha standing at the rail, waving good-bye. The boat heads outward, with a wide sweep turns into the channel, and chugs out of the frame.

"See?" Aunt Jessie said triumphantly. "What did I tell you? Proof positive. Aunt Agatha leaving."

Roz nodded absently as she reached for the light switch. Sure enough, going, going, gone. So that was that. End of story.

"Hey, not so fast," Aunt Jessie protested. "Don't you want to see the rest?"

Startled, Roz looked at the film reel revolving slowly on the projector, then at the screen, still filled with dappled images. The film was barely past the midpoint.

"But Aunt Jessie, I don't get it. How can there be more footage when—"

"Tsk. And you the noted detective. There's more footage because Agatha left the camera behind. And," she prodded, "Agatha left the camera behind *because*—"

"Oh, I see—*because* there was still a lot of film yet to go. She left it with them so that they could finish the the reel."

"That's right. Family motto: Waste not, want not. That's how the rich stay that way. Anyway, there's still nearly two minutes' worth, nearly half the reel. Now, pay attention; this is the most interesting part. You'll get to see the inside of the house."

Roz focused on the screen. Here were the three remaining Randolphs, once again stationed right where they'd been on the front terrace, laughing and talking, beckoning and gesticulating, addressing the camera: come hither, join us, join us. Roz wished she could read lips to know exactly what they were saying. Something white fluttered off to the side, the camera jiggled—then, poof! the three had vanished, magically plucked away, the house front deserted. The secretary's inexperienced hand at work, no doubt.

Then suddenly she was inside the sprawling, dark-shingled house, moving down the light-struck hallway, panning from doorway to doorway. Roz watched, fascinated, as the camera wound through the dining room, the kitchen, the formal living room. And here were the Randolphs three discovered relaxing in their overstuffed chairs in the library, feet up, newspapers everywhere, nodding and smiling at the camera.

Amazing, Roz thought, the details of the interior quite sharp, only a little fogged by the light streaming in through the large-paned windows. She shivered a bit at the sight of the filmy curtains lifting eerily in a long-ago ocean breeze blowing gently through rooms that no longer existed.

Was that a telephone on the big old partners' desk? Yes, and as she watched, three heads swiveled toward it expectantly, then Archie moved to pick up the handset and stood there chatting amiably, nodding in staccato rhythm, hand in his pocket, jingling change. Roz listened, mesmerized. *I'm losing my mind,* she thought. *I can actually hear the breeze whispering, the waves slapping against the rocks.*

But it was only the film coming to an end, slipping off and flapping around the take-up reel. Roz reached over, shut off the projector light, and set the film to rewind, then sat for a while in silence, lost in thought.

"You know, Aunt Jessie," she said finally. "There's something strange about that movie. I can't quite put my finger on it, but—"

Aunt Jessie didn't answer. The dear old woman was sound asleep.

"Well," remarked Aunt Jessie the next morning. "You've certainly got a bee in your bonnet about this old Randolph business, haven't you? Well, now you can just sit there and rummage to your heart's content. Though I can't imagine you're going to come up with anything to prove that cockamamy theory of yours after all this time. I'm going up to town to do some marketing, so you just make yourself at home."

Last night, after Roz had seen a very sleepy Aunt Jessie up to bed, she had rerun the film several times, stopping and starting in a number of places, even watching it backward. An idea had come to her, but when she had tried it out on Aunt Jessie over breakfast, the older woman had pooh-poohed it in no uncertain terms.

"Why, Roz Howard, that's the most far-fetched notion I've ever heard! If it were even remotely possible, don't you think someone would have thought of it back then? Your uncle Lou wasn't exactly a babe in the woods, you know, and neither was that feller who conducted the inquest.''

But Roz had kept after her with various questions until finally Aunt Jessie had stomped off downstairs to the storage room and come back with a box of dusty file folders, which she set down on the kitchen table in front of Roz.

''There!'' she said. ''It's all in there. Lou kept all the records right up till the bitter end. He even talked them into giving him that old film reel when the county coroner's office was ready to chuck it out with all the other evidence when the case was closed. That's how we came to have it, since you didn't ask. Lou told them it had great sentimental value, moving pictures of him and his two best girls—me and the boat.'' Aunt Jessie paused briefly in the doorway, a wistful expression on her face. ''That old rascal could talk the mud out of a puddle and the wallpaper off the wall. Hmm, ahem!'' She made a great show of turning away and rearranging her canvas carryall. ''But you know that,'' she said briskly over her shoulder to Roz. ''See you later. Bye.'' And with that she was out the door and away, chugging down the lane in her beloved old Woodie.

Roz worked quickly down through the pile of folders, most of them carefully labeled in Uncle Lou's fine, upright (if somewhat faded) Spencerian hand, ''Randolph: Legal Papers.'' Copies of wills, deeds, financial transactions, a typed draft of Archie's unsigned will, a record of the will that had actually been probated, all of it just as Aunt Jessie had described.

She paused briefly over the four death certificates and then went on to a file that held mainly newspaper clippings carefully sorted and arranged by subject and date. Here were several accounts of the fire, with banner head-

lines, from various local and regional newspapers—
PROMINENT CITIZENS DEAD IN EARLY MORNING FIRE—
with follow-up stories detailing the investigation and
conclusions of the authorities at the inquest. An article
from the *Globe* detailing Agatha's demise, a summary
of the text of the note, the second inquest rendering a
verdict of Missing, Presumed Dead, a victim of suicide
while the balance of her mind was disturbed. Lavish
obituaries for all four Randolphs, and one brief notice
for "Miss Helen Trent, 23, formerly of Dorchester, trag-
ically, Tuesday, September 5, 1938, in a fire that also
took the lives of" etc., etc. "Miss Trent leaves no sur-
vivors." How profoundly sad, Roz thought; the poor girl
had been an orphan, with no one to remember her. The
Randolphs—judging by the film footage at least—were
probably the closest thing to family she had.

What else? So far she had found nothing strikingly
amiss, nothing to cast doubt on the official version of
events. Just two more clippings, dated some years apart.
RANDOLPH ESTATE SETTLED; Roz raised her eyebrows at
the amount. Granted, Edward Holden had had to wait a
few years until Agatha was officially declared dead, but
even so, he had ended up an extremely rich young man.

The last clipping was newer. HEIR TO RANDOLPH FOR-
TUNE DEAD AT 78; Edward Holden's obituary. So he had
lived to a ripe old age, enjoying his good fortune in
every sense of the word. Roz was about to read it
through when her eye was caught by an envelope, much
smudged, with Uncle Lou's name written across it in
faded ink: "Louis Fairbrother True, Esq." A small,
nearly illegible tag on it identified it as "Case 38-456
Exhibit B."

Roz opened the flap and slid out the piece of paper,
folded into thirds, a good bit narrower than the envelope
was long. She unfolded it carefully.

Dear Lou—(the handwritten message read):
I cannot come to terms with the others—leaving. I
hope to rejoin them shortly—even though it is all
my fault. But I cannot accept being left out—I trust
you'll do your best to take care of the matter.

Fondly—
Agatha Randolph

What's this, Roz thought, *a suicide note in the style of Emily Dickinson?* Odd, distinctly odd, and it wasn't just the dashes and idiosyncratic diction, either. She held first the notepaper then the envelope up to the light. The watermarks matched, even if the sizes didn't. She stared for a long time at the handwriting, with its distinctive curls and dashes, flowing headlong from one edge of the narrow sheet of notepaper to the other, with virtually no regard for margins. Obviously written in haste and distress.

Or was it?

Roz took a sheet of paper from the pad she had been using to take notes, creased it down the middle, smoothed it out, and began to copy the note exactly as it appeared, but with the entire text to the left of the center line. She was still at it, surrounded by wadded-up sheets of paper, when Aunt Jessie walked in the door an hour later, bag of groceries in hand.

Which she nearly dropped all over the floor when Roz announced to her in no uncertain terms: "Aunt Jessie, it's just as I suspected. Aunt Agatha never committed suicide. In fact, she never left the island at all. That film of yours was doctored, and not only that, I'm willing to bet this note is bogus, too. If you'll just bear with me, I'll show you what I mean."

* * *

Roz stopped the projector and sat back in the old wicker chair she had perched in while she demonstrated her version of events to a skeptical Aunt Jessie. "See the direction the mailboat takes as it leaves the dock, Aunt Jessie? It's heading off to the right. But the channel markers indicate the channel is to the left. Either the boat is going in the wrong direction or—"

"The channel is to the left. Always was. It shoals up into mudflats not twenty yards off that dock. That's why the mailboat always backed in, so it'd have enough purchase heading out that the rising tide wouldn't push it right off the swamp. But I still don't see—"

"Just wait. You will."

Aunt Jessie watched in silence while Roz ran the segment backward. The mailboat stopped in midchannel, emitted a puff of smoke, reversed, and proceeded to back up to the dock. The cabin boy looped the docking lines around the pilings, and a grinning Aunt Agatha emerged, valise in hand, waving and gesturing. "And here's what everyone missed before. Supposedly this is the late-afternoon boat, but there are no shadows. This was filmed at noon. So you see, Aunt Jessie, that's not Aunt Agatha leaving at all. It's Aunt Agatha arriving the day before. Now watch this."

Roz ran the film forward to the scene with the three Randolphs waving and cavorting in front of the house. "Now, here we presume, since all the guests were long gone and Agatha too was seen leaving, that there were only the three Randolphs left, and the camera was in the hands of Helen Trent. But look here." Roz stopped the film again and pointed to the flash of white at the edge of the frame. "This is the hem of someone's dress flapping, and there's a shoeheel to go with it. See the footprint in the gravel? There was a fifth person here, just out of sight."

"But . . . but who is it?"

"None other than Helen Trent, coming to take the camera from Aunt Agatha—"

"Who never left." Aunt Jessie sat quietly for a moment, her hands folded in her lap. "So," she said at last. "She died in the fire, too. They all died together." Suddenly she turned to Roz, her face a mask of agitation. "Then what happened to Helen Trent? Did she—was she—?"

"A murderer?" Roz finished. "I don't know, Aunt Jessie. All I know at this point is what we can gather from the film and the faked suicide note. I have an idea of what must have happened and that it involves Edward Holden, but it's only speculation at this point."

"So," Aunt Jessie murmured sadly. "I guess that means we'll never know."

"Not necessarily." Roz picked up the copy of Edward Holden's obituary notice. "Listen to this. 'Mr. Holden, a world traveler who later made his home in Newport, Rhode Island, is survived by his wife, also of that city.' I need to do a little checking first, but after that—how would you like to take a quick trip south?"

The Holden mansion was not particularly ostentatious by Newport standards; it wasn't even on the ocean, but tucked away behind great gnarled hedges along a quiet sidestreet. Roz had found the address through the simple expedient of looking up the name of Mrs. Edward Holden in the Newport phonebook. The plate on the stone pillar guarding the driveway said simply: "Foray."

"Why, as I live and breathe!" exclaimed Aunt Jessie. "This place looks just like the old Randolph place on Fox Island. They went and built themselves a replica!"

"Pretty creepy, but at least they were grateful," Roz commented as they drove into the circular drive and around to the porte cochere. They were expected. A liveried valet helped them out of the car and ushered them inside, where a butler greeted them. "Ladies. Mrs. Holden is in the solarium. Please follow me."

She was standing at the far end, staring out the tall window at the gardens beyond, the apparent steadiness of her tall, upright figure belied by the walker that stood off to one side.

"Miss Rosamund Howard and Mrs. Louis True, madam," the butler announced. "From Maine." He bowed, then excused himself, backing out the door and pulling it shut in front of him like a cuckoo in a clock, so comical in his precision, Roz nearly laughed. But this was serious business.

The woman turned and looked at them, impassive, hands clasped in front just at her waist.

Aunt Jessie True spoke first. "Hello, Helen," she said.

Helen Trent Holden put a hand out to steady herself on the walker, took a deep breath, and sighed. When she spoke, her voice quavered ever so slightly. "So someone's worked it out at last."

"Though you may think otherwise, it was in fact an accident, a tragic accident," the woman who had once been Helen Trent told her two guests, now seated across from her in a grouping of bamboo lounge chairs set in a corner away from the bright sun. A maid had brought in tea, lemonade, and a plate of tiny sandwiches.

"That night I went to bed as usual in my apartment over the garage. I couldn't sleep, and finally I got up and went into the main house to fix myself some hot milk. The lights were all blazing away, but there wasn't a sound, except for this flap, flap, flap noise coming from the library. I was already beginning to feel dizzy and sick, but I rushed in and . . . there they were, sprawled in their chairs as if they were sleeping. At first I couldn't believe it, their faces all rosy, and it seemed they must be still breathing, but—''

She paused, blinked several times. ''Please excuse me. It was quite awful. I still find it hard to . . . recall the details. But I saw immediately what had happened. It had gotten quite chilly that evening. All the windows had been shut tight, and they had the coal heater going full blast. The room was like an oven. The four of them had been overcome by carbon monoxide. I threw open all the windows and doors, but it was too late. I didn't know what to do. In a panic I called Edward; we were in love and had decided to get married. He was stunned. He adored Agatha—she was like a mother to him. In fact, she had gone to the island that weekend expressly to make sure that Archie made provision for Edward in his will. But that hadn't happened, and now they were all dead, and Edward would be disinherited. It seemed such a waste, and Edward so deserving . . .''

''So you decided to fake your death in place of Agatha's, so Edward would inherit after all,'' Roz said gently. ''There was the movie camera with the film still in it, and you grabbed it up, along with Agatha's valise and all the other evidence of her presence. Then you set the unwound reels of old film on fire, and as soon as the whole place went up, you simply walked away. No one noticed you on the mailboat, since you boarded at the public landing with so many others of the morning crowd.''

''That's right,'' the old woman said with just a trace of bitterness. ''No one would have recognized me anyway; I was just another nameless, faceless minion in the Randolph household.''

Roz continued. ''The place went up like tinder, the firefighters had no chance, and by midday the fire had consumed everything. By then you were well on your way to Boston, film in hand, where Edward was waiting.

But what gave you the idea to fake the film?''

"It was Agatha herself. I had been sent down to the dock to film her arrival with the new camera Archie had bought her as a surprise. She saw me and started laughing and waving and acting odd, walking backward and the like, and when she got to the house, she told me I'd been holding the camera upside down the whole time, that it was a trick filmmakers used to make things go in reverse and it would be terribly funny once she spliced it into the finished movie. 'We'll have me coming and going!' is what she said.

"Edward knew all about developing and editing from his travels with Agatha. We worked all that night in her photo lab, cutting and splicing, then projecting it over and over to make sure we had something that would work as proof of her leaving—''

"And then you refilmed the result, leaving it undeveloped in the camera, which Edward took back with him and surreptitiously planted at the scene when he drove up to identify the bodies. Meanwhile, you stayed at Beacon Hill posing as Aunt Agatha in a state of grief, black veil and mourning garb, speechless with tears, until you could fake her death as well. But the note was sheer luck, wasn't it?''

Mrs. Holden nodded. "She'd written it earlier that day and left it on my desk to type. It was a letter to the family lawyer—your husband, Mrs. True—about the disagreement over the will. When I read it over, I realized that if I cut it in half, what was left made it sound like a suicide note. It was perfect; frosting on the cake. Of course, that wasn't what it said at all. I can't remember now exactly how it went, but she had refused to sign until she got her terms and Edward was included in the will. She was going to leave the island and come back only when the rest of them stopped blaming her for holding everything up and agreed to include Edward. So you see, all we did, really, was to see that Agatha got her wish.''

Mrs. Holden paused briefly, a distant look in her eyes. Then she cleared her throat and went on in the same precise, even tone.

''Edward and I never had any children. But we had a good life together, and when he died, he left everything to me. You may be interested to know my will establishes a foundation to benefit Fox Island—the Holden-Randolph Family Bequest. It's been some years, but the islanders will get their money after all. With the proviso that this house be pulled down and rebuilt on the estate to replace the one that burned.''

With that, Mrs. Edward Holden pulled the walker over to the side of her chair, pushed herself upright, and stood, her figure regal, her face inexpressibly sad. ''Thank you for coming. I find it, oddly enough, something of a relief to speak of it at last. Willis will see you to the door.''

''Do you really believe it was an accident?'' Roz asked Aunt Jessie as they headed north.

Aunt Jessie thought for a moment. ''If it was, that was certainly some very inspired extemporizing on the part of those two young people—with a little help from the dear, departed Aunt Agatha, of course—to make sure they got what they wanted and thought they deserved. But I'm not sure it matters.''

''Why not?''

''That was one of the saddest faces I've ever seen on a woman, the kind you earn only over the course of a lifetime. Her whole life was a lie. She erased herself; the woman who was Helen Trent ceased to exist. Somehow I don't think either one of them got much joy from their riches, however they justified it. In the end, they only had each other and the memory of what they'd done.''

"Well, at least it comes out right in the end.''

"That's so. The folks on Fox Island are in for some rare good news, and very shortly, if I don't miss my guess.'' Aunt Jessie turned to Roz with a twinkle in her eye. "Say, shall we tell them?''

"Oh, I think not, Aunt Jessie. Let them be surprised.''

After a short hiatus from fiction writing, it's a pleasure to welcome back Susan Kenney with a story featuring sleuthing academic Roz Howard, who appeared in Garden of Malice, Graves in Academe, *and* One Fell Sloop. *Kenney is Dana Professor of Creative Writing at Colby College in Maine.*

The Deadly Glen

Alanna Knight

Only in my darkest dreams did I walk in Glen Corbie. Ugly splinters from the past were quickly smoothed away by the life I had enjoyed since reinventing myself, moving to California and marrying Rob.

Emily's murder was safely locked away under the debris of more than three decades, but ironically, it was Rob who reopened the door and let the past back in again.

Like many Americans, he was proud of his Scottish ancestry. His folks came from the Highlands, he loved to tell everyone.

Somewhat misty-eyed, he'd continue: "Some day I'm going there, back to search for my roots."

I humored him. It seemed safe enough, since every other person we met in the West could make a similar claim.

On the very day he retired and sold his partnership in the business that had kept us rich fat cats for more than thirty years, I was in the swimming pool. The pool was my refuge from heat and boredom, and I wondered how Rob would cope with inactivity.

It was an unpleasantly humid day, which made our palm trees hang limply against the smog-thickened sky as if they were having a bad hair day. And as Rob walked towards me flourishing a drink, I was remembering the facts of later life as related by female friends.

"You must be prepared, Ann. When husbands retire, they can turn very difficult to deal with," they added darkly, leaving difficulties unspecified to those lacking imagination.

Rob sat on the edge of the pool and smiled down at me, waving what looked like airline tickets.

"Honey, guess what—I've done it. Pack your bags— we're going on a trip."

"Another trip?" I tried to sound pleased as I struggled out of the pool. We were just back from Hawaii, and Rob's international business trips were no big deal. They were just a way of life with us. I'd been bored in most of the world's exotic locations.

"Where do you think we're going, hon?" Rob asked. I shook my head.

"Scotland, of course," he said triumphantly. "I've been doing a little research and I think I've found the exact spot where my folks came from."

I didn't argue. I was still safe. No need to panic. There was an awful lot of Scotland besides the Glen of the Corbies. When we looked at the map together, I averted my eyes from the curve where it lay, remembering the tiny loch, the twisting back road to the clachan that had been a heap of moldering stones since the Clearances.

Two weeks later we were in Edinburgh, listening to a pipe band on Princes Street, in the shadow of the Castle perched on its rock high above us. I sighed. How stupid to have worried. It really was good to be back, for down there in the New Town with its Georgian houses were my own roots.

I still believed that was my main attraction for Rob. Given his ancestry, a Highland lass for wife would have been preferable, but Lowland Scots was better than nothing, a forgivable shortcoming.

The hired car took us to Gleneagles, where Rob fulfilled another ambition—he played golf on the famous course—while I lay on the four-poster bed in our hotel suite, watching the rain and leafing through the portly, glossy mags.

I already knew that this romantic Scotland they depicted was yet another tourist trap almost as alien to me as the exotic lands of our worldwide travels. Beyond the hotel windows, those blue hills held the truth, the reality of a past history shaped by savagery and heartbreak, the bloodied pages of the Clearances that had paved the way for mass emigration.

I couldn't escape the past either. Like early-morning mist swirling across the golf course, it was already reaching out to touch me.

One day I saw, or thought I saw, Emily again, as we were driving through a village ten miles from the glen.

It couldn't be Emily, I told myself. She had been dead for more than thirty years. Murdered—

And then Fate took over the wheel of our hired car. Negotiating a narrow corner too sharply, we hit a large stone.

Rob sprang out, cursed. "It's the exhaust. Dammit. We'll have to get it fixed. Where do we find a gas station?"

I suggested we turn back.

"On this road? Not a chance. Hey, there's a signpost."

I guessed where the signpost was directing us. Five

minutes later we were limping along that old familiar road.

I held my breath as the twisting track unwound into the clachan. I need not have worried. Emily's croft, where it had all happened, was still there. Freely restored by later tenants, extra windows sprouting from the roof, the kitchen extended by a large conservatory.

Its origins swamped by modern additions, it was barely recognizable. Except for "W.B. 1842" carved above the front door, a reminder of the tacksman who had evicted the laird's tenants and brought death to the glen.

As we drove slowly past, I was curious about the TV aerial and satellite dish. Was their television set ever haunted? Had the present occupants ever switched on to find the solitary channel available was screening a tragedy in grainy black and white, a slaughter of women and children outside their elegant front door.

My own tragedy was nearer. Thirty years or a hundred and thirty meant little to these granite boulders, these hills that were older than time, the dark and secret waters of the loch.

We drove on. The tiny croft amid the clachan's ruins where I had lived with Adrian had vanished under a vast spread of glossy time-share apartments. But huddled in the car outside the petrol station at the entrance, I felt vulnerable, wishing we had never come.

Uneasily watching Rob and the garage man, I knew by the shaking of heads that it was too late for the repair that day. We'd have to stay over.

"It's all right, honey, He says the time-share has a motel."

And they had a room for us. Dear God. How awful, to have to spend one night on the exact site of the life I had buried so long ago. That ecstatic first love affair.

Sleep was impossible despite dinner and a bottle of

expensive wine. Listening to Rob snoring peacefully at my side, I stared at the ceiling and relived that other time.

Pretend that it never existed and it will go away had been Rob's philosophy. Happy to talk about my Edinburgh childhood, he was sensitive enough to skip other loves before him, willingly accepting my glossed-over version of the now-famous Adrian as a womanizer, unfaithful, etc., etc.

But I never told him or anyone else the real reason that I had walked out on Adrian that night here in the glen. How could I without admitting that by remaining silent, I was accessory to murder?

The awful thing was that I was genuinely fond of Emily. I was young, longing for Adrian's baby, certain that a baby would lead to thoughts of marriage, which had not yet occurred to him. Truth to tell, I was a little self-conscious about what was still called living in sin. In those days all well brought up girls were. It was a very bold move, which threw parents into shame and shrill despair.

As for Emily, she was sixty and childless. She told me once that Steve hated children and had made her have an abortion. Waiting each month for signs that I was pregnant, her revelation turned that aging matinee-idol husband of hers into a monster.

Adrian laughed and said, "Come on, Steve's all right. And he's a Member of Parliament, you know," he added primly, as if that gave him certain moral privileges over the rest of humanity.

I had a tingling awareness from our first meeting that Steve did not share his wife's glowing opinion of the young couple down the road. I was fairly certain he knew that we were just living together, that he was contemptuous and disapproving.

I made a shrewd guess that here was a man who chose

friends and acquaintances for what uses they might have for him.

Blinded by love and reading Adrian's mind (which I did very inexpertly as it turned out), I decided that poised on the threshold of his writing career, Adrian might benefit from Steve's influence. As for me, I was hardly worth cultivating, having left secretarial college at seventeen for a job at the local radio station.

My meeting there with Adrian was romantic enough. One day a beautiful young man, tall and blond, with blue eyes you could drown in, breezed through the swing doors and into my life.

Love was an easy game, and I saw marriage and happy ever after clearly written on the horizon. Adrian had started off as a radio engineer. Ambitious and inspired, he decided to try writing comedy scripts. It was a disappointment to discover that in common with many who make a living out of being professional funny men, there were few laughs in Adrian offstage.

I was eager enough to follow him to Glen Corbie, where he had a Highland series to write and had been offered a colleague's holiday croft. Besides my typing skills would be useful. It seemed like a great idea to him and seventh heaven to me. No disturbances, no intruders, just write all day and make love all night. No newspapers, a radio and an ancient television set. Reception was terrible in the glen, he told me. But our neighbors, Emily and Steve, were right up to date. They had color!

In no time at all, Adrian had established himself in their good graces. Emily was a TV addict. She had to be, since Steve went off to London each week, leaving her with nothing but a telly to watch to keep her from going crazy.

At least that was how it looked. And the fact that Adrian had worked for the media meant only one thing to her.

Every time there was a blip on the only channel received by the area, our phone would ring. Could Adrian fix it?

Of course he could.

Hours later he would return. I never asked him how long the repairs took, but a couple of hours did seem excessive.

Telling myself that to a young man a woman of sixty read as an old lady, I put behind me thoughts that maybe she fancied him and had a neglectful husband.

On the day it all began to go wrong, Steve had offered Adrian a lift to the train station for a research trip to Inverness among old newspapers.

"You'll be gone for three days," I cried.

It seemed like an eternity for me. I was particularly miserable, having awoken to unmistakable evidence that once again I wasn't pregnant.

As we walked down the lane towards Emily's croft, I held Adrian's hand as if we were to be parted forever while he whistled happily, quite utterly unaware of my distress. Babies meant nothing to him, but I told myself that it would be different when we had one of our own.

I tried to feel carefree, to match his mood. This baby I yearned for, this proof of our love, would be conceived when he returned.

On beautiful days life's like that. It can be very persuasive, make you believe anything. There's boundless faith provided by a sky infinitely blue, a drowsy hill and hedges buzzing with an unseen insect-army on a perfect summer morning.

Tall hedgerows concealed our approach to Emily's croft, but we could hear Steve shouting. His voice was loud at the best of times, and he sounded angry. Really angry.

His general manner with Emily suggested ill-concealed contempt, and this row doubtless followed the pattern of long-term irritation. Such marital disagreements don't usually lead to murder, but I was tempted to walk past quickly and hope they didn't see us.

"It's all in your imagination," he was shouting. "How could anyone but a fool be afraid of whatever it was you thought you saw. God, as if I hadn't troubles enough. The way things are going in this damned country, I'll be lucky to keep my seat in the election."

Emily was murmuring about being sorry, but he went on, "Just remember while you're busy seeing things that we could have had that cosy flat at Westminster. The choice of the glen was yours."

And seizing his briefcase, he marched across the garden to where the Bentley waited, elegant and incongruous in the narrow lane.

Emily trailed after him.

"You should be counting your blessings. I wish I could just sit and relax and do absolutely nothing all day. I have to see my agent, the telly people. Pity electioneering isn't your scene. You could be some help to me—for once."

We watched him lean over to deposit the bored husband's good-bye kiss, sexless and dry, upon her lips. I realized it meant nothing to either of them.

Turning, he saw us. "Good! Jump in, Adrian." And to Emily, "See you Friday as usual. Chin up, now, for God's sake. And stop imagining things. Try to enjoy yourself."

Winding down the window, he winked at me.

"As for you, young lady—your friend here has started seeing things. Perhaps you can put some sense into her head."

As they drove off, I felt embarrassed. I didn't know Emily all that well, but I could hardly walk away.

I smiled at her unhappily as shading her eyes, she looked fearfully across at the hill.

Strange that I hadn't noticed before the monstrous black crows—corbies they called them—hovering over its summit. Now for the first time I decided the hill looked faintly sinister in the morning shadow, hugging the stillness as if it lay in wait. There were white dots moving, the shapes of distant sheep, their distressed cries echoing faintly through the clear air.

Emily gripped my arm. "Will you come with me, please. It's just a little way. Oh, please."

As we walked up the hill, she said breathlessly that she had been walking there, as she did each morning. She had looked down and seen the glen as it was before the Clearances. There were people in the clachan that was now a heap of lichen-covered stones.

"A kind of Brigadoon," I said.

"Yes, yes. You see, my family came from here. Have you noticed the date carved above our door? 1842. WB. Those were my great-grandfather's initials. He was a simple peasant who became the laird's tacksman. He worked hard, became powerful, and amassed riches among the poor crofter tenants. And when the glen was cleared and the land turned over to sheep, the laird rewarded him well. He went south to to England and founded our woollen mills," she added proudly.

"And you actually saw into the past?" I was intrigued, having recently read Dunne's *Theory of Time*.

"Yes. I know I did." But Emily was baffled and afraid, kept repeating, "Nothing like this has ever happened to me before."

I could believe it. She was a big-boned, heavy woman with a big-boned heavy face. Solid and earthbound, never at any time in her life could she have been even a remote match for Steve's good looks.

Back at their cottage, her large hands shook as she served the coffee, while I murmured consolingly that I had heard that most of us have in our lifetime one experience of the supernatural for which there is no explanation.

For Emily, however, her ghostly glen became a regular visitor during the following week.

She was so distraught that I offered to get up early and go with her to the glen. Of course, I saw nothing. The glen had no cause to haunt me. I hadn't an ancestor who was responsible for its death. I guessed that was what she was afraid of. That those evicted crofters were taking their revenge on one of the hated tacksman's descendants.

Adrian laughed. "Not without reason. The Highland Clearances were an ugly episode in Scottish history and the brutality of landlords and tacksmen alike as cruel as anything ever recorded in the Middle Ages."

It was after these strange happenings, however, that I noticed a subtle change in the atmosphere. Steve became kinder. When the television went wrong, he had a new one sent up immediately.

Emily was delighted, but even this new luxury toy failed to soothe her poor jangled nerves. She no longer went up the hill each morning for fear of what she would see below. After that first time she never asked me to go with her again.

We both knew that the past was recreated for her alone.

As for Steve, he thought she was off her rocker and came over to suggest I should take her to Inverness for the day.

"Do a bit of shopping. Buy yourselves something nice." He grinned at me. "Have a good lunch. And spare no expense."

I winced a bit at that. Both Adrian and I guessed that Steve had married Emily for her money. The sale of her woollen mills in Yorkshire had greased the way for the vast electioneering campaign that had persuaded voters that this English ex-actor with the good Scots name was the right man to represent them in Parliament.

He ran us to the train station and he was in a very good mood. Great to be at home for a change, time to tackle some long overdue repainting of the rusted guttering while the weather held.

"Do take care, dear," said Emily. He promised to do so, and she said nervously, "You're not good on ladders, you know."

He roared with mirth at that. "My dear, young Adrian will give me a hand if I ask him nicely. Won't he?" he said to me.

If he's not too busy tinkering away in the barn, I thought. When he wasn't writing, Adrian was fascinated by anything mechanical. Motorcycles, radio and TV sets. Mr. Fixit himself.

It was fun to be among people again, and the sales were exciting. For the first time I decided I would be glad when Adrian had finished his Highland script. The lease of our croft expired in three months, and there would be nothing to keep us here. Flat-hunting in Glasgow or London suddenly seemed very desirable indeed.

Especially if the pilot for the series did well and Adrian achieved fame at last.

As for Emily, afterwards I was to be very glad that she had a happy, exciting day. A day that was to be the last in her life.

When we returned, the ladder was still propped up against the gutters, heavily daubed with spilt paint to indicate that men had been at work. Inside they were preparing supper for us.

I can't remember what we ate, but there was an air of jollity, of suppressed excitement about the occasion. There was wine, too, and we all drank—or seemed to drink—a lot more than usual.

The next morning I heard the Bentley roar past the

door and waved to Steve, who blew me a kiss.

Things are improving, I thought. *Maybe I've been wrong about him and Emily.* A sense of caution is advisable regarding married friends. However they appear together in public, nagging and disagreeable or glossy and hospitable across the dinner table, you have no way of knowing what goes on behind that closed bedroom door.

I remember that Adrian wasn't quite himself that morning. He spoke sharply when I made some inconsequential remark. A memorable hangover, I guessed, and he seemed anxious, waiting for something. A reply from the script editor, perhaps.

The phone rang. He leaped to it.

"It's Emily," he said. I could hear her shrill voice. He listened in silence and turned to me. "You take it. I can't understand a word. She's hysterical."

"Ann? Something terrible's happened," she said. "There's a dreadful old film, black and white, on telly. It should be the schools programme, but I'm sure it's our glen. It's awful, Ann. I shall write and complain. No children should have to see this—"

"Why don't you switch it off if it's so upsetting," I said gently.

"That's just it. It won't switch off. There are soldiers with muskets—listen!"

I could hear the voices, the screams and shots. It must have been deafening for her in that small, low-ceilinged room.

"Oh, God, I've just seen the church—and the hill. With those damned crows—"

It wasn't making sense. Adrian was in the bedroom. "Switch on the telly," I called.

Emily was yelling now. "There are women with sticks hurling stones at the soldiers. Sheep are running everywhere. Crofters are trying to drive them back, struggling with the soldiers who are dragging their families and furniture out of the crofts. They've even put out an old woman who's dying. Dear God—they're bayonetting the women, setting fire to the crofts—

"They shouldn't allow such violence on television in schools time. God knows what it's like in color. Oh, oh—there's a woman with her face smashed in by a musket—oh, oh—"

I could hear the screams and felt my flesh crawling.

"The man—the tacksman—he's giving the orders—dear God, it's great-grandfather. I recognise him from photos—"

Adrian came to my side. "What's she on about now?"

"Some film that's on. About the Clearances."

Adrian cursed. "Dammit. They never told me. You realise what this means—someone's pinched my script."

The glen was served by only one channel. He switched on the television. A schools programme on Peru.

He snatched the phone from me. "What's going on there?" He listened. I could hear her sobbing. "Right, right. Switch it off and I'll come across."

I heard her scream, "I've told you. It won't switch off—"

"It must switch off," Adrian insisted. There was a moment's pause. "There's what?"

He covered the mouthpiece, turned to me. "She says there are crows on the roof attacking the TV aerial. No, Emily. No—leave it be. I'll come across."

He put down the phone. "She says she's going to get at them with a broom. She's gone crazy, Ann."

My heart was pounding. I felt sick with a terrible premonition that something awful was happening. Something over which I had no control.

As we ran down the lane, I looked towards the hill, thought of Emily's ghostly glen. Perhaps it had been real after all. There were crows circling the roof, their raucous cries filling the air.

We heard her cry out. We saw her with a broom, climbing the ladder. Then she disappeared from view.

"Emily," I called out.

When we ran into the garden, she was lying on the stone path, the two top rungs of the ladder on the grass.

And Emily was quite dead. As we tried to lift her, we knew from the unnatural angle that her neck had been broken by the fall.

The next minutes were nightmare. A time when you hope you'll wake up. When you can never imagine that anything in your life will ever be normal or pleasant or that you will ever laugh again.

We laid her on the sofa, and I saw to my horror that the film about the Clearances was still running. Women were running towards the camera, staring out of the screen, faces cut open, blood streaming, one with an eye missing. A mother with a dead baby in her arms.

Adrian rushed across to the set. While I was searching for the doctor's phone number, he managed somehow to switch it off.

"I'll have to phone Steve. Make some coffee, will you."

The next few hours remain a blur. The doctor came and pronounced Emily dead.

The local constable arrived and was taken out to the scene of the accident by Adrian. He came back, pocketing his notebook.

"A terrible accident, miss. A large lady on a wobbly ladder. Happens all the time. Fatal accidents always take place in the home," he added confidently.

At last Steve arrived, and the local minister said a few prayers, while we listened in embarrassed silence, and

Emily's body was removed to the mortuary.

Dazed by it all, Steve looked oddly helpless. Yes, he would be all right on his own. We could go back home. He remembered to thank us for all we had tried to do.

I told him about the Clearances film that couldn't be switched off. And the corbies we had seen circling the roof.

He listened, said pityingly, "Rubbish, Ann. She was going insane. I've seen it coming. She imagined it all."

"She didn't. I saw the film as we carried her in. So did Adrian."

I looked at Adrian for confirmation. He smiled, shook his head. "I didn't see anything, Ann."

I stared at him. *You did. You switched it off.* That's what I wanted to say, but some sense of caution took over and made me hold my tongue. Like an alarm bell ringing deep inside, I felt danger. Danger, inexplicable and terrible.

Suddenly Steve collapsed into a chair, sobbing noisily. I looked at him in surprise. I didn't know he had cared that much.

Adrian patted his shoulder, looked across at me. "I'll stay with him. It's shock, you know. You go home to bed, Ann. Don't wait up for me."

It was twilight of that long summer evening, still bright enough as I walked past the spot where Emily had died to see that the ladder was there again, propped back up against the wall.

I knew by the time I reached our croft what was bothering me. What I had seen was not the same paint-spattered ladder that had caused Emily's death.

Someone had substituted a newer, unbroken one.

And sickened, I guessed the reason. The two rungs had been deliberately sawn through with the certain knowledge that someone as heavy as Emily would fall backwards onto the concrete path with fatal consequences.

I had to tell Adrian. I couldn't wait till he came home.

Coldly I considered Steve. The "accident" had been carefully thought out by someone who wanted rid of Emily. Who but Steve?

My first thought was for Adrian alone with a murderer.

I ran back down the lane. And stopped. You don't rush in and accuse a man of murdering his wife. Not when he has a rifle hanging above the kitchen fireplace. He used it to shoot game.

What if he seized it, killed us both?

In the dying light I looked at the ladder again and realized that Steve could not possibly have replaced it. Unless he had never left the house that morning. But Adrian had phoned him.

I tiptoed to the window. And there was my answer. My Adrian and Steve. And this was no stiff-upper-lip manly comforting I was witnessing. They were clutched in a lovers' embrace. Steve was unbuttoning Adrian's shirt. Their hands were roving, fondling, urgent . . .

The window was slightly open.

"You did it—love," gasped Steve. "You got rid of the old bitch for me."

Adrian smiled and kissed him. Kissed him, stroked his face with such love and tenderness as he had never showed me.

"And now we're free, we're both free," he said.

"Ann?" asked Steve.

Adrian laughed softly. "You know she never meant anything to me, never could. Not after you. Not to worry, she'll be easy to move. She's a lovesick fool," he added contemptuously.

"I wouldn't be too so sure about that. I think she

suspected something,'' said Steve coldly. ''She might have to be silenced.''

Adrian laughed again, and I waited no longer. I ran back to the croft, packed a bag and skirted the hill across to the main road, where a couple gave me a lift into Inverness.

· Standing on the empty platform, I was terrified Steve and Adrian would appear before the next train south. But they obviously had better things to do, and as I waited, I had ample time to examine all the flaws in my life with Adrian. Intimate things I hadn't understood which were now so obvious.

But I still didn't know how they had tricked Emily with that film, and it wasn't until many years later, when I saw an old black and white film about the Clearances revived on television, that I realized this was the one Emily had seen. It had been shot in Glen Corbie and there were crows circling the croft.

And I guessed then how they had worked it. Adrian had been involved in the early experiments on the video that gave an added dimension to televiewing.

And somehow he had contrived to fix the Clearances film in Emily's set.

There is however still one mystery that remains unsolved. The haunted glen that Emily insisted she saw. And was that what gave them both the idea?

As we drove out of Glen Corbie next morning, Rob grumbled, ''Didn't sleep much last night.''

''You could have fooled me,'' I said not unkindly. Like all snorers, he stoutly maintained that he never slept a wink. And believed it too.

''Bad dreams,'' he said ''One about this place, all confused. You were in it.''

''How extraordinary.''

He increased speed. We drove past the signpost, and

I breathed a sigh of relief. I was safe again. We'd never return.

"Not one hell of a happy place, honey," said Rob. "Didn't care for it one little bit. What about you?"

But like Emily's haunting, her ghostly glen, there are some things in life for which there are no complete answers.

A resident of Edinburgh, Alanna Knight writes for television and the theater and is the author of more than forty books, including her Victorian crime series with Scottish inspector Jeremy Faro and a well-regarded biography of Robert Louis Stevenson. Her most recent novels are Angel Eyes *and* The Coffin Lane Murders.

Time Share

Janet Laurence

The gulp in the voice told me the bad news was really bad. Usually when I get called out at three o'clock in the morning, it's for rowdiness, drunks who won't let other holidaymakers enjoy themselves or start to beat each other up. That's a pain, but life as head of security at a Lanzarote time share usually went smoothly enough not to resent the occasional rough edge.

The ring of the telephone had dragged me out of a deep sleep. Beside me, Sarah only stirred as I answered it.

"Jake?"

"Mmmm?" My hand slipped round the smooth curve of Sarah's hip, and sleepily she pressed her hand on top of mine. It felt good.

"I'm sorry." There was the gulp that sloughed off sleep and brought me sitting up in bed. "There's, that is, we've got a death."

Depression hit me.

Death was the worst. Serious illness was bad enough, but death meant medical and legal formalities and dealing with grieving families or friends. Death is rarely welcome and never on holiday.

"OK," I groaned. "Which villa?" I slid out of bed and reached for my clothes.

"He's, he's—" Again that gulp. Peter, the night manager, was taking this badly.

"Well, he's in the sauna."

"The sauna?" It didn't make sense. The gymnasium area was locked up in the early evening. If anyone's heart had failed to take the strain, they'd have been discovered much earlier.

"Look, come over, will you?" Peter said agitatedly.

"I'm right there."

I'd been at the Firebird Beach Club for three years. It beats city policing in grimy, dank, dark and not so great Britain any day. Here I had sun all year and a constant turnover of lovelies in search of a good time. I was a middle-aged but ultra-fit ex-policeman. My wife had walked out on me when my career ended in a sleazy corruption charge nobody could make stick but was a grotesque shadow I couldn't shake. For me the Firebird was close to paradise.

I slipped on yesterday's shirt and automatically added a tie. The management makes all its staff wear ties. Picks us out from the holidaymakers.

"What's happening?" Sarah mumbled. I told her not to worry and left.

Peter was waiting for me in the reception hall. Everything was quiet. The nightclub had shut down long ago, even though Wednesday night it stayed open late, because Wednesday night was prize night. Celebration time for the winners of the shuffleboard tournament, the bowls tournament, the tennis and all the other tournaments the management arranges for the happy punters. Firebird really tries.

In the spacious reception area with its comfortable rattan chairs and plastic plants were a young couple.

The girl sported a bright-pink crew cut, a crepe top that just about covered the necessary and an ultra-short skirt that had given up the effort. She was crying. The young man had too-long hair, Levi's and a dark T-shirt. He looked as though he wished he'd never come on holiday.

Peter waved a hand in their direction. "They found him. They are staying in different villas, thought the sauna would be—well!" He came from Birmingham, but his shrug was almost Gallic.

Yes, those slatted shelves might leave their mark, but there were worse places for a bit of nooky.

"How long ago?"

"Ten, fifteen minutes? The girl screamed, I went to investigate, then called you." His eyes shifted from mine. There was something he wasn't telling me. I wondered exactly what I was going to find in the sauna.

I went over to the couple. "You've had an awful shock. I'm sorry." The girl scrubbed at her eyes; she couldn't have been more than sixteen or seventeen. "Peter will get you a drink while I go and see what's happened."

"Can't we go back to our villas?" whined the young man. He ran a hand through the lank hair.

"In a minute," I told him and went downstairs.

The Firebird Beach Club gymnasium had been state of the art when it was first built twelve years earlier. Now the equipment, including the sauna, was out of date and little used. Only when the sun failed to appear did the members want to spend time inside.

Bracing myself, I pushed open the sauna door and entered.

The corpse lay along the bottom shelf, flab bulging over his tight trunks. His face wore an expression of deep surprise; eyebrows arched, eyes wide open, mouth a rictus that could have been from pain or sheer astonishment. One hand trailed on the ground. A neatly folded towel sat on a higher shelf.

The heat was off but the light was on.

I didn't need to touch him to be sure he was dead, but I felt for a pulse anyway. Then I studied the body.

The torso was badly bruised, but the red and black marks were edged with a yellowish-green that said they'd been inflicted days earlier. Likewise a scab on the lip. I heaved the heavy torso up from the slatted shelf. There was no knife sticking in his ribs. No sign of a wound of any kind, in fact. I carefully lowered him back to his original position.

Then I noticed a tiny drop of blood on the shelf by his head. I looked more closely. It seemed to have come from his right ear. I searched around and found a fragment of wood on the floor. It didn't look like a splinter from the bench. I was now certain this was a case of murder. An awful sense of anticipation tingled in me. It was a long time since I'd been faced with anything like this.

His clothes were hanging outside the sauna. The shirtfront had a large stain that looked like drink. Probably sangria. The sauna keys were in a trouser pocket. I took a final look round, then locked up.

The couple were drinking brandy when I returned.

It didn't take long to get their story. They'd stayed in the nightclub until it closed. The girl was here with her parents and a sister in a one-bedroom villa, and the young man was with five other youngsters in similar accommodation. No room in either for sexual activity. So they'd wandered down to the sauna.

I could imagine them all too clearly, giggling with

desire about to be satisfied, hands everywhere, bodies throbbing with lust, stumbling into the small cabin, not even noticing it was occupied.

"I almost sat on him," squeaked the girl.

"I put the light on," added the boy. "As soon as I looked at him, I could see he was dead." Brandy had done wonders for his self-possession. By morning he'd be telling anyone who'd listen how it had been to discover a body.

"Who, who is it?" stammered the girl. "I think I've seen him around."

Yes, she would have. Peter had been too cowardly to tell me the dead man was a friend and colleague.

I took their names and villa numbers and let the youngsters go. Then I phoned the doctor and the police.

It was a long night.

By the time the boys in ties and the girls with jackets appeared at eight-thirty, ready for another day of high-pressure selling, we'd got the formalities over.

The inspector in charge was a small Spaniard by the name of Fernando Martinez with a lugubrious face and a well-honed sense of humor. We'd often shared a bottle of the local beer. I'd made it my business to get on terms with the island's police force as soon as I'd arrived.

"So, my friend, life here isn't always healthy, eh? You can tell me about this man, yes?" he asked after the body had at last been carted away.

The early-morning delivery of croissants had just arrived, so I liberated a few and took him off to my place for breakfast. I rang first to warn Sarah, but she'd obviously left, and when we got there, all was tidy. She'd even cleared up the debris from the delicious meal she'd cooked me the previous evening. I appreciated her tact.

I had to force myself to believe Adrian Ashby was

dead. I'd only known him for four months, but we'd got on from the moment he joined the sales team. Actually, it would be more accurate to say rejoined. He'd left his position as sales manager at Firebird to chase some well-heeled bit of charm back to Surrey a few years earlier, thinking his meal ticket had come up.

Women had always caused Adrian problems. Many years ago he'd married a widow with two kids. It hadn't turned out well. "Never take on stepchildren," was a piece of advice he was fond of handing out.

When he'd been made redundant from his job as a leather goods salesman (Adrian was the chap to take with you if you were thinking of choosing a bag from the many offered to bargain-hunting tourists), someone told him there was a good living to be found in Lanzarote. Plus, of course, sun, sand and sangria!

By the time he was on the way to becoming the highest-striking salesman on the Firebird team, he'd found a local girl who seemed everything a man could wish for—great ass, always smiling, and cooked a mean paella. Unfortunately, with Maria came Maria's mama. That was too much for Adrian.

Besides, he said, there was an inexhaustible supply of lithe and lissom girls arriving to relax in the sun. Adrian was happy to love 'em and let 'em leave, until Tina came along. She, I gathered, had been quite something. Older, yes, but still with a great figure and all the experience that comes with years, plus a generous income.

I heard all about life with Tina on one of our regular bar crawls. "The thing was, old boy"—Adrian had delusions of background, played up his minor public school education—"I'm like Oscar Wilde, can resist everything except temptation." He'd swirled his dry martini olive through the cocktail's oily depths.

"And she was temptation?" At that moment I was in danger of being tempted myself.

Some months earlier I'd been sitting by a swimming pool, downing some quite acceptable sangria and congratulating myself on Lanzarote's low crime rate, which made my job a doddle, when a class act went by, consulting the small club map that gets handed out to newcomers.

Tall, wearing tailored slacks and a silk shirt, she had long legs, full breasts and a nicely rounded behind. Honey-colored hair was clipped back from a strongly boned face graced with a sensual mouth.

I levered myself up. "Can I help?" I offered. "I'm part of the scene around here."

She removed her dark glasses. Tiger eyes of honey-gold streaked with bronze looked quizzically at me. "Are you?" She made the two words sound inviting, amusing and preposterous all at the same time.

I took the map from her and checked the villa number at the top right-hand corner. Then couldn't believe my luck. It was only just round the corner from my home. The management likes to have security in the thick of things, as they put it. "You're almost there," I said. "Why not join me for a drink while they sort your luggage out? It shouldn't take long."

Another look from those tiger eyes. I was sure she was going to refuse.

Wrong! Two minutes later she was on a lounger beside me and I was skillfully eliciting some background from her. She was a new member of Firebird, a restaurateur in the West Country.

"I work every hour God sends in the summer, then collapse in the winter," she said, smiling. "I took the membership off someone so a debt could be settled."

"Some debt," I riposted. For two weeks we had been selling her size of villa for over ten thousand pounds. But you could pick up an existing membership for maybe half that sum.

She shrugged. ''You know how it is.'' I didn't, but it didn't seem to matter.

Sarah stayed two weeks. She was cool, laid back and not inclined to mix, but seemed happy to spend time with me.

I had no quarrel with that. I took a day off and showed her around. We went to Timanfayo, the bleak-as-the-moon volcanic heart of the island, whose six-year eruption in the eighteenth century devastated a once fertile land. I'd heard NASA used Timanfayo for practising moon landings, and I could believe it.

Before the end of the first week, we'd slept together. Sarah in bed was a revelation. The woman-of-the-world exterior crumbled, and what I held in my arms was a young girl, unsure but touchingly eager to be led down love's soft paths to its flaming sunset (there was something about her that made me think in technicolor). I reckoned all she'd known so far were boors and macho types.

At the end of her stay I'd taken her to the airport on the pretence of unobtrusively checking the club's organization there. ''Till next year,'' I'd said.

''I may manage another week before the season starts,'' she'd told me, her young-girl face taking over for a moment.

''I'll count on that,'' I said.

I missed her more than I'd expected. When, therefore, Adrian appeared and I heard about Tina, you will understand my interest.

''Tina,'' he said musingly that night we ripped apart Costa Teguise. ''I staked everything on that woman!''

''How long had you known her?''

''A thousand years.'' He popped the olive into his mouth and sent his gaze roaming round the bar, lingering for a moment on a rather obvious twenty-something with everything she had to offer on display. "Tina was the Sphinx, the Tower of Pisa."

"The Venus de Milo, the Mona Lisa," I put in derisively. "Adrian, Cole Porter you are not!"

He gave me the easy grin that always got the punters and said, "She was a few years older than me, so what? I didn't mind being her toy boy." He looked down at his capacious belly. "In those days I didn't carry so much luggage, kept myself in good shape. And, no, she didn't fall for a younger man."

"So what went wrong?"

"The soft life became too soft. I mean, when you know that there's no struggle to pay the bills, that the tax man holds no fears, that you can go on the razzle but mustn't dazzle any stray piece of crumpet that may cross your path, well, existence somehow loses its zest. And have you any idea the amount of effort a woman who's said good-bye to fifty puts into trying to look thirty?" Adrian helped himself to some more salted almonds. "Christ, the more often she went to the gym, the masseuse"—he gave a wry twist to the world—"the hairdresser, the health farm, the more bored I became." He waved for another round of drinks.

I surveyed him curiously. "Toy boy" was not the term for Adrian. Forty-five if he was a day and, as I've said, overweight. But he had charm, a twinkle in the brown eyes, a creased face that looked trustworthy and a way of making anyone feel special. But I'd met Firebird members he'd sold their weeks to who would cheerfully have consigned him to a special purgatory reserved for salesmen who persuade clients beyond their best interests.

The thing with the Firebird Beach Club is that the costs don't end with buying your weeks. There are hefty maintenance charges to be met each year, whether you come or not, and they get regularly increased.

Still, you have your dream in the sun, the villas are stylish and well maintained, the facilities generous.

"I tell you, old boy," Adrian continued, "never allow yourself to be maneuvered into a position where one woman controls you."

"Even if she's well-heeled?"

"Especially if she's well-heeled." For once Adrian sounded bitter. "I don't know about you, chum, but leaping to do someone's bidding is not my style."

I could believe it. Adrian, when he wasn't talking to punters, had a short fuse. I could imagine Tina had found life more interesting than she'd bargained for. "So you came back here." The new drinks arrived, and Adrian started twirling another olive.

"You bet." He grinned widely.

"Leaving a desolate Tina?"

"She'll get over it, get to like not having a slob cluttering up her life."

I'll say this for Adrian, he was really sold on the whole Firebird concept. He'd left as the sales manager. When he returned, they couldn't even offer him a job as an ordinary salesman, so he'd gone to a complex in the south of the island. Then Firebird began construction of a whole new phase of super-luxury villas on an unprepossessing piece of land next to the existing club. Adrian was back on the team and he showed no resentment at working under someone who'd been his junior salesman. "Watch me," he'd said the first time we went out together. "In six months' time that snot nose won't know what's hit him."

To watch Adrian in action was an education. He'd been involved in working out the original sales strategy, emphasizing the worldwide exchange rights as well as the facilities of the Lanzarote resort until the bemused punter felt he was privileged to be offered such an opportunity. He made every couple he escorted around feel he was their best friend. But, as I may have mentioned, not everyone remained so happy with their purchase.

And now Adrian was dead and I was sure he'd been murdered.

Over the croissants and my famous black coffee laced with Irish whisky, I gave Fernando the gist of this, only omitting any mention of Sarah, who had turned up the previous Thursday for what she called a quickie. She hadn't let me know she was coming, but I'd seen her arrival on the reservation sheets. Once again her cool act had quickly melted, and we'd taken up where we'd left off.

"So," said Fernando, "you tell me the sauna is usually locked?"

While Fernando had organized his forces, I'd been doing some checking. "Charley, the manager of the gym area, says Adrian came down just before closing time, tipped him the wink, said he wanted a sauna and could he drop the key in at Reception when he'd finished."

Fernando made notes in a tiny, cramped hand. He could have a good stab at getting the Lord's Prayer on a postage stamp. "And this Charley, he agreed?"

"Lord, yes. Whatever else he was, Adrian was totally reliable over that sort of thing."

"So, your Charley gives this man the key and goes off, yes?"

"Yes," I agreed.

"The dead man didn't say to this Charley he was to meet someone in the sauna?"

"No," I said slowly. "But Adrian spent most of yesterday showing a young woman around. Apparently she was interested in membership."

"Ready to pop her cork," had been Adrian's aside to me as I'd come across them checking out the show villa.

He'd left her exclaiming over the jacuzzi bath in its marble surround and punched the top of my arm in self-congratulation at the fine job he was doing. I'd asked him why she was on her own. The rule was never to show one half of a couple around. A long day's work could be undone in a moment by an uninterested partner popping an ice cube of doubt into the other's enthusiastic cocktail.

"Single, old boy. Came here with some mates and loves it. Thinking of investing a small legacy she's just come into. Could be an interesting evening in sight!" He gave me a lewd wink and returned to his prospect, by now smoothing the polished chintz of the quilted bed-covering. I'd left them to it. The girl was in her mid-twenties with a roly-poly cuteness, and I could visualize her turning up annually with a different girl or boyfriend in tow. Whatever it did to their bank balance, single members found that possession of one of our time shares greatly increased the value of their friendship.

"Her name's Jenny Severn, and she's in BV15, that's Buena Vista," I added as Fernando wrote carefully. Villas at Firebird were arranged in sets of thirty around one of several swimming pools, each given a different Spanish name. "Five friends holidaying together. Not early risers." I'd already been along to BV15. Not a sign of anyone stirring. "However, they'll soon be up. They're due to leave today." Thursday was change-over day and checkout time was ten o'clock.

"Jenny Severn," Fernando repeated, checking what he'd written but getting the emphasis all wrong, "You think he have sauna with Jenny Severn?"

I opened my hands in a gesture of ignorance. "How can I tell?"

"I find out. Now, you have other thing to give me, yes?"

"Fernando, you have a true cop's nose for information.'' I grinned at him. I had a real peach of a lead that I hadn't even hinted at. But then, he'd seen the bruises on the body, just as I had.

Three, no, four days earlier a member had rung Reception to say that one bloke was trying his best to kill another.

I'd gone along to sort things out.

In a narrow passage by the laundry, a big chap was laying into Adrian. There'd been a touch of professionalism about the way he slugged one heavy fist after the other into the other man's body.

Adrian's face was gray with pain. If he'd tried to defend himself at the start, he'd long ago given up any resistance. He was a punch bag about to collapse.

I grabbed the assailant and dragged him away. It took all my strength and experience. The man had the power of an ox. Finally I forced him against a wall, got his name and told him to forget it.

''I'll kill that bastard if I see him again'' had issued through clenched teeth.

I'd given him a final word of caution, then had taken Adrian to my quarters, poured him some whisky and attended to his wounds. ''What was all that about?''

He'd ruefully fingered his lower lip where the skin had been split. ''Amazing the way some people can harbor a grudge,'' he'd said bitterly. ''Four years ago I sold buggins there his membership, almost my last deal before I left. I put him on the easy pay plan, and now he claims he can't keep up the payments and can't find the money for the maintenance. He blames me for all his financial troubles.''

''He found the fare to fly out here.''

Adrian sighed. ''And that's another grudge he's got against me. Apparently some woman offered to pay the fares so they could holiday together and now claims he's engaged to her. He's been looking for me ever since.

And to think I greeted him like a long-lost pal." He sounded aggrieved—punters weren't supposed to behave like that—then winced as I anointed his bruises. "I never should have left Bristol, old boy, could have got another job there if I'd looked."

"So why did you leave?"

He took a big swig of my precious The Macallan malt. The color was coming back into his face now. "Women, what else! Couldn't cope, old boy. Three of them! Two obese youngsters who weren't mine and were starting to cause trouble, one wife who wasn't up to it. Can't stand women who cry when things aren't going their way." He grimaced then winced as if the movement had hurt his cut lip. "Escaped by saying I'd send for her and the kids when I'd got things sorted." His outrageous, salesman's cheeky grin lit his face, cut or no cut. "But then things were too good to import old trouble."

I finished telling Fernando this.

He looked at his notes. "So there is a señorita who spend day with him and a matador who treated him like the bull. The matador has grudge, and maybe the señorita did not like advances, yes?"

Most girls didn't need to murder a man to send him about his business. Jenny Severn might, though, have had another motive. I decided to keep this to myself for the moment.

"This deserted wife, Tina? She is not here?"

"We'd have heard," I said. "No, you can count her out. But Martin Ewart wasn't at all chuffed at the way Adrian was overtaking his figures."

"Chuffed?"

"Pleased."

"And who is this Martin Ewart?" He had difficulty with the name, and I spelled it for him.

"He's the current sales manager." I explained about

Adrian having trained Martin and then left, finally returning to serve under him.

"But it must be dead man who has grievance, no?"

"No. Adrian was after Martin's job, reckoned he could topple him. And the way the figures were beginning to shape up, it looked as though it was only a matter of time before management found some excuse to say good-bye to Martin."

I thought of the young man's baby face, the fluffy hair that was rapidly receding from a brightly shining forehead. He had a wife and two children and was desperate to keep his job. He wasn't an inspirational type but he was sound, respected by the sales force and understood the scene. None of that would have stood a chance against Adrian once the numbers really started crunching.

"What did the doctor say?" I asked Fernando.

"The doctor?" He looked up, his gray eyes as alert as if he'd got out of bed half an hour ago instead of at four o'clock. I hoped I looked equally fresh but doubted it. "He say if sauna turned off at time of death, it be between five and seven o'clock. He have to wait for post mortem examination but he think he agree with you. Your friend killed by something sharp hammered into his brain through eardrum."

"Cocktail stick?"

"No. He think bigger, perhaps wooden. How you say?" He screwed up his face for a moment then produced, "skewer."

I was impressed with Fernando's vocabulary. I thought about the fragment of wood I'd found on the floor of the sauna. It could have been from a skewer rather than a cocktail stick. I wasn't that familiar with culinary implements.

"Come!" Fernando got up with a surge of energy. "We find this señorita and talk to her first, yes?"

Jenny Severn, in the middle of her packing, was tearful but adamant that she had said good-bye to Adrian at three o'clock. "I'd decided not to buy membership," she whispered. "I didn't like the idea of all that money just going, you know?" She picked up a big white bag and put it in the small case that was open on the living room's fold-down bed. Her friends' clothes were in untidy piles everywhere. What seemed to be Jenny's collection looked half the quantity the others had brought.

Outside I said to Fernando, "That's one strongminded lady. There aren't many can escape Adrian when he's in full flight. He must have been very disappointed."

"What he do when disappointed?"

I knew the answer to that one. "Find something to make him more cheerful."

Which wouldn't have included having a sauna with Paul Boxer, his amazingly well-named assailant of the other night. We found Paul in the beachside bar with his lady friend, both dressed for the plane and knocking back a last jug of sangria before the coach arrived to take them to the airport.

When he heard the news, he went deep purple, then the color drained away from beneath his tan. "Gawd almighty," he whispered.

"Paul!" his friend reprimanded crossly.

"Shut up," he snapped at her. "Don't you see, you silly cow, they think I did 'im in?"

At that she blanched as well and ran a hand down her shell suit. "They can't," she wailed. Then, quick as a flash, added, "You was with me all yesterday."

The look he threw her might have been grateful, but I doubt it. This was one sharp cookie, and he'd have a hard time escaping her clutches.

Fernando grilled them both, which was a mistake.

I'd have had them in separately, found discrepancies in their stories, As it was, they were able to concoct a fine farrago of sunbathing then—wink, wink—having a rest before going out to the Chinese restaurant just down the road. That fact, at least, was easy enough to check.

On our way to find Martin, we passed Sarah sitting on a lounger by one of the pools. She, too, was dressed and ready for the plane. Perhaps it was my imagination, but I thought she looked a touch desolate. Then she saw me and looked up with a smile. "Busy man, Jake!"

The smile faded as I told her what had happened. "I knew it must be something serious for you to just disappear, but that's awful!"

"Look, I'm going to be pretty wrapped up today. I probably won't be able to take you to the airport."

She smiled again. "No problem. I booked on the two o'clock coach just in case."

My gaze lingered on the tanned arms displayed by her short-sleeved silk blouse, then on the curves it so nicely emphasized. "Any chance of you sharing a bit more time over the next month or so? I could fix a villa easy as anything."

I was sorry she was wearing her dark glasses. I'd have liked to see the tiger eyes light up. But the smile was everything I could have hoped for. "That'd be nice," she said simply. "Ring me at the weekend?"

I nodded. Then Fernando and I went and found Martin Ewart. He was sitting silently in the membership room, twisting a pen around and around in his fingers. I reckoned I knew what his thoughts were. Guilt at feeling relieved his job was no longer in danger.

But he couldn't produce any sort of alibi for the period between five o'clock and seven o'clock. "I'd just lost a sale and was looking around the shops," he said with an air of hopelessness.

Fernando took him through an account of his window-shopping. He'd looked at all the usual—holiday clothes, embroidered tablecloths, leather goods, tacky souvenirs—then ended up at a windsurfing place. He hadn't bought anything, so no credit card slip to support his story, hadn't even talked to an assistant. "I felt too down," he said, as though that explained everything. Finally Fernando gave up. "My friend," he said to me, "I go to post mortem examination now. I come back later, yes?"

I saw him leave in his noisy little car then wandered back inside. By now it was past two o'clock. It was strange to think Adrian would never again come down the staircase that twisted round the central elevator, a smile on his creased face. I desperately needed to know who had dispatched him from life and why.

I went over to the reception desk and asked to see Jenny Severn's details. I looked at the address, a suburb of Manchester. That was a long way from Bristol. Jenny didn't have a Lancashire accent, though.

I found her sitting with her friends in a corner of the reception area, slumped in the rattan chairs and listening to Walkmans. Jenny lifted an earphone to listen to me, and an insistent, tinny beat floated onto the ether.

I took her to an empty part of the hall.

"Jenny, where's your home?"

She looked bewildered. "Home?"

"Where you grew up."

"Oh, that! We lived in Surrey."

Not what I wanted to hear. And her slight accent definitely didn't belong to the Home Counties. "Ever since you were born?"

"What is this?" She managed to sound injured and intrigued at the same time.

"Just routine," I said.

Big blue eyes looked doubtfully at me, but then she

seemed to decide there couldn't be any harm in the question. "We lived in Norfolk until I was about ten, then Dad got a job in London and we moved to Surrey. Will that do?" she asked perkily, dipping her head and giving me a look from under her eyelashes. A real flirt she could be. "Because if it won't, you'll have to drive me to the airport. The bus is here."

I let her check her luggage onto the two-thirty coach and went back to my quarters. I took out the grill pan to cook some sausages for a late lunch and felt grateful all over again to Sarah for cooking me supper and then clearing up.

As I watched the sausages, I went over Jenny's story again. There had to have been something I'd missed. I turned the sausages, then dropped their wrappings in the kitchen bin. With a name like Severn she ought to have come from Bristol.

Suddenly I was out of there faster than a Scud missile. Even as I ran for my car, I was yanking out my mobile phone. By the time I had started the engine, I was through and explaining what I could.

Thursdays are always a nightmare at the airport. Planes never stop landing, and by the time I arrived, the check-in hall resembled the anteroom to Hades, people milling everywhere. I scanned the overhead desk signs and soon found the right flight. I studied the two waiting queues. She was nearly at the check-in. Then Fernando came up to my elbow. "I have had to leave my deputy at the post mortem. I hope you know what is what." Fernando was proud of his grasp of idiom.

But I was already striding towards her.

She turned and saw me. She must have seen my expression, because her mouth opened slightly, her eyes closed and she swayed.

I grabbed her shoulder.

"How nice of you to come and see me off," she said

steadily, the tiger-gold eyes flickering. Her strong-boned face was set in rigid lines.

"Sarah Driver, I arrest you," started Fernando.

"For God's sake, wait until we get outside," I ground out, gripping Sarah's upper arm with one hand and taking charge of her luggage with the other.

At the police station Sarah made no attempt to deny the charge. "He deserved it," she said stonily. "He killed my mother."

It was as I'd suspected. Adrian's elder stepdaughter had come after her mother's errant husband. The tale she told was common enough, a stepfather who sexually abused his wife's daughters, then deserted the family.

"He was a no-good bastard," Sarah told us without emotion. "But she loved him. She had one letter that said where he was. She waited to be sent for and heard nothing. She was like a plant deprived of water, just wilted. Finally I dragged her to the doctor's. They said her cancer was treatable, no reason she shouldn't have a full life. She wrote and asked him to come and see her. He never replied, and she was dead within a year." There was an animal savagery in her voice, and the tiger eyes glowed fiercely. "The day she died, I swore I'd kill him."

A failed marriage later, Sarah met Mrs. Adrian Ashby, a recently separated wife recovering her self-worth at a health farm.

"She was very bitter about con men who went after a woman's bank account. It wasn't difficult to discover that Adrian had returned to Lanzarote. Tina said she was trying to sell her membership, she'd sold on her weeks for the last three years, but buyers were nonexistent. I told her I could be interested, and she practically had an orgasm. Then it was just a matter of coming out here and waiting for him to appear.''

"He didn't recognize you?" I asked.

"I'm three stone lighter and twelve years older than when he made our lives hell. I was called Sally then, and the last thing he expected was me to turn up," she retorted.

"You find him easy to join you in sauna?" Fernando enquired curiously.

She eyed him scornfully. "A supposedly accidental meeting after he'd been given the brush-off by a young punter? An attractive girl spills a drink down him, apologizes, then suggests they get to know each other in a sauna? Would you have hesitated?"

"It was too easy," I agreed. "All you had to do was say you'd meet him down there then make sure no one saw you. Not difficult, so few people use the gym. And the kebab skewer?" I saw the broken pieces of thin wood in my rubbish bin, tasted again the beef kebabs she'd grilled for our supper. They'd been loose on the plate when she'd put them before me, no sign of a skewer then.

"Half of one stashed in my bikini." She glanced down. "It was stupid of me to choose that for our meal. Trouble is, I'd had to buy a whole packet and I never like to let anything go to waste."

"How do you knock it in?" asked Fernando.

"My shoe," she said.

"And he calmly lay there while you bashed it down his ear?" I asked incredulously.

"I told him to face me, lie down on his side and close his eyes while I prepared a nice surprise." Sarah gave a short, grim laugh. "He was expecting me to take off my bikini! Instead, well, let's just say he won't time-share with anyone else!"

"No," I agreed bleakly.

She looked at me with understanding. "I'm sorry about us. We really had something going, didn't we?"

I'd thought so too, but who wants to share time with a girl who can bang a skewer down your ear?

Drawing on her culinary background, British author Janet Laurence features cook Darina Lisle in her mystery series. Her most recent novel is Appetite for Death.

Buffalo Gals, Won't You Come Out Tonight

Miriam Grace Monfredo

November, 1825

"This body needs identifying," said the Lockport village constable, who stood on the towpath beside a waterlogged corpse just hauled from the canal.

Peregrine Jeremy Peel IV barely registered this comment, being too preoccupied with his own body to give another's much thought. He gazed down at the icy gray water he straddled with one foot on the gunwale of a packet boat and the other on the edge of the canal wall. Which wouldn't have been a concern had the boat not suddenly swung away from the wall. And while it was true that Peel had long legs, at any moment they would not be long enough. Nor would it be the first time the Erie Canal had forced him into the posture of village idiot.

He supposed it would be considered unmanly if he

were to yell for help. But the alternative was to plunge into the frigid water, slam against the bottom of the partially drained canal, then splash round in search of a way to scale the concrete wall. Meanwhile, his toes curled inside his boots, Peel continued straining to drag the boat and the wall closer together. His legs continued splaying farther and farther apart. And now a ripping sound from the crotch seam of his trousers made further do-it-yourself measures insupportable.

"Excuse me!" Peel called to those gathered on the towpath. "Excuse me, but I seem to be having some difficulty . . ."

Simultaneously, the boat lurched sideways to bang against the wall, Peel leaped for solid footing, and a large dark object flew past his head. This was followed by more large dark objects hurtling past him, accompanied by an earsplitting, unrecognizable noise.

First things first, resolved Peel, as from the safety of the towpath he gave a quick glance at his trousers. Nothing crucial being revealed, he then quickly turned toward the source of the uproar. Several hundred yards beyond, feathers of brown and black and white swirled as if down-stuffed pillows had exploded. The maelstrom made it impossible to see anything that might have provoked such frenzy on the part of what Peel finally determined to be crazed Canada geese.

All at once a musket boomed. In a cloud the geese lifted, wings working like bellows, their honking strident as they became airborne. Shortly, all that remained was a slowly descending rain of feathers and one very large and bedraggled-looking goose.

Peel took a step toward the survivor. Out thrust a long black neck, the goose hissing a threat as it rose upon knobby legs. After which it abruptly toppled over and lay motionless on the gravel of the towpath.

From behind Peel came the voice of Constable Jamie

Stuart. "What in tarnation was all that racket about?" asked Jamie, his musket still smoking. "Commotion was loud enough to wake the dead." He glanced over his shoulder as if to assure himself that the corpse was still as lifeless as it had been minutes before.

Peel walked toward the prostrate goose. It hadn't moved a feather. A closer look, and Peel could guess why it had been attacked: the nearer he got to it, the larger it became. From the tip of its tail feathers to the tip of its conical bill must have measured well over four feet, and the white-feathered chinstrap that commonly ran up the head of Canada geese consisted, on this goose, of only a small white patch.

"Perhaps it's different enough from the others to make it an outcast," Peel said to no one in particular. "Especially if it was trying to mate."

He felt an unexpected sadness at this observation, but then a grunt from Jamie Stuart brought to mind why he and the constable had been summoned there.

"You an authority on geese, city boy?" asked Jamie, the chuckle in his voice not unkindly.

Peel shrugged. "In Boston they'd come through twice a year and stay for a week or so. There was a water hole nearby," he added. There seemed no point in explaining to his cousin Jamie that the water hole was, in reality, a man-made pond of considerable size. Formed at considerable expense on the Peels' Beacon Hill estate because of a whim on his mother's part; one that his father had indulged as he indulged all her whims. Even those European tours that took her away for months on end.

"Constable Stuart?" called a man from down the towpath. "What'd you want us to do with this here dead body? Take it to your office in the firehouse?"

"Now, why would you think I want it in my office?"

"So where *do* you want it?"

"In the icehouse!" the constable shouted, and motioned for Peel to follow him.

Peel had just turned back for a last look at the moribund bird when its wings began to flutter. Then, while Peel gaped in astonishment at a Lazarus-like revival, the goose reared its head and rocked itself to an upright position. After which it immediately settled back, nestling into the towpath gravel and gazing at Peel from uncommonly dark eyes that appeared to hold no lingering malice. Several bald patches among its thick breast feathers caught Peel's attention. Undoubtedly battle scars.

From behind Peel came the crunch of footsteps. He turned to find one of the men who had previously hoisted the corpse from the canal gripping a musket at his side. The man raised his arms. "Good dinner or two from a big gander like that," he said, taking careful aim.

Peel could not have explained what made him move to position himself between gun and goose. "I don't think you want to eat that bird," he said.

"Why not? Looks like good eatin' to me."

"Then take a look at its eyes. Extremely dark eyes like that," stated Peel with absolutely no basis in fact, "are the sure sign of a sick bird."

"That so?"

"Yes, indeed. It would almost certainly be fatal to eat that goose."

The other man lowered his musket. But a moment later, grinning as if a novel idea had struck him, he raised the gun again. "Reckon I'd best shoot it, then. So's nobody else eats it."

"No, I wouldn't think shooting it was the answer," said Peel rapidly. "Might be that the sickness, whatever it is, has been passed on to other geese. We don't know what we're dealing with here, so I think the smart thing would be to investigate—before anyone eats goose again.''

''You know a lot about sick geese?'' came the completely reasonable question.

''It happens that I do,'' said Peel, marveling at his mendacity. There had been a time, not so long ago, when he would have bitten his tongue before willfully misstating the truth. A few months in this western New York outpost had made him a liar. Or perhaps it was the truth that had changed its face.

''This bird needs a thorough examination,'' said Peel firmly. That seemed safe enough, as the man confronting him did not seem liable to question Peel's own susceptibility to the sickness. Besides which he, Peel, was known to most of the town as a lawyer, something the Lockport residents viewed as a fairly incomprehensible occupation. So probably nothing he could suggest would make them any more skeptical of him than they already were.

While the other man ambled off, Peel shot a look at the goose. The bird regarded him with a serene eye, as if the recent deceit had not proven this man to be untrustworthy.

Peel heard Jamie Stuart calling him. He turned and started down the towpath, tossing ''Better fly south!'' over his shoulder.

''As I said before,'' Jamie told Peel when they stood over the corpse, ''we need to identify this body. Find his kin and a place to get him properly buried.''

Thoughtfully, Peel studied the corpse: a small-framed man, likely as not under 150 pounds, the only truly distinguishing items about him being a shallow indentation on his forehead and some odd-looking marks or bruises around his wrists. When the constable lifted the man's linen shirttails to uncover a belt, then unbuckled and removed it, more bruises were visible.

"What do you suppose this is for?" he asked Peel, handing him the belt, from which hung several pouches filled with small, rounded, rather greasy-looking gray pebbles.

Some of the pebbles spilled out onto the towpath. Peel bent over to retrieve them, then tossed them in his hand and shook his head. "I have no idea. Unless . . . unless these were used as weights by someone wanting to make sure this man's body sank." Peel again hefted the small stones. "But they aren't heavy enough to insure that."

"You saying someone killed him?"

"There's a head wound . . ."

"C'mon now, Perry, don't get fanciful. He probably hit the canal wall when he fell in. It's a simple case of drowning—won't be the first or the last in this canal. Don't go making it complicated." He threw a blanket over the body.

Peel continued to stare at the stones.

"One way to identify him," Jamie added, "might be to find out how long he's been dead. Could help locate somebody who knew him. Doesn't look like he's been in the water long—I'll get the doc to guess at a time of death."

"No one's been reported missing around here," Peel said, although those who worked the canal usually came and went without leaving a trace. "Of course the eastern flow of the current could have carried him from anywhere west of here, even from as far as Buffalo."

The western reach of the canal extended to where Lake Erie flowed into it at Buffalo Harbor; Peel recalled that at the canal's opening ceremonies earlier in the year, this had been theatrically phrased as "the wedding of the waters." The completed man-made river ran 363 miles across New York State, through hills of stone, across swamps, around mountains, into valleys, and, in aqueduct form, over natural rivers and Iroquois streams.

It had been trial and error, Yankee ingenuity and Irish muscle, that had built the Erie Canal. A monumental feat of engineering which had been accomplished by a young nation without engineers.

Now the canal was being drained for the winter, and some unexpected debris had been uncovered: carriage wheels, several mule carcasses, wagon loads of whiskey bottles, even an empty steamer trunk. None of these, to be sure, was quite as unexpected as a dead man.

Peel, with the toe of his boot, lifted the blanket to confirm a sudden notion. "Look at his jacket, Jamie."

The constable gave the corpse a reluctant glance. "What about it?"

"Despite the water damage, you can see the jacket's not that of a laborer—notice the expensive buttons. I think this was a man of substance."

"So why hasn't someone reported him missing?"

"Maybe someone has," Peel said. "Why don't I send notices to towns along the canal from here to Buffalo? Just the circumstances and a general description."

"You may have something there. Once we get to my office . . ." Jamie's voice trailed off as his glance went past Peel's shoulder, then, "Well, I'll be damned!"

Peel turned to look. Five feet down the towpath stood the goose. It scooped up a few pieces of gravel before it turned a dark, steady gaze on Peel.

And as he and Jamie Stuart started for the firehouse, the goose trailed after them with a slow, rocking gait.

In early evening the wind picked up, and by the time Peel reached his cabin, dead leaves were scurrying across his path. He opened the cabin door, unhappily aware of the presence behind him.

"You know," he said, "you're taking a chance being here. It's going to snow any day now, and you need to head south—either that or risk becoming someone's *pâté de foie gras.*"

The goose nestled into the dirt of the path.

"Have it your way," Peel said as he crossed the cabin threshold. "But you'll regret it."

He closed the door behind him.

Several hours later the wind began to howl at the windows, and gusts down the chimney made flames in the fireplace dance. Peel, seated before the fire reading Boswell's *Life of Johnson*, heard sudden sharp pings at the windowpanes. Freezing rain, he thought. Another thought made him rise and go to the window beside the door. He peered out. It was still there, huddled against the driving sleet, its head tucked under a wing, with clearly no intention of flying south anytime soon.

Peel pulled at the door, intending to open it just a crack, but the wind tore it from his hands and sent it banging against the cabin wall. The head of the goose reared up and snaked out toward Peel. After which it stared at him through the curtain of sleet that was glazing its entire body.

Which meant that, even if it wanted to, the bird couldn't fly. Ice crystals dropped from its feathers as it rose unsteadily and swayed toward the cabin. If he had a brain in his head, Peel thought, he would shut the door in the face of this . . . this albatross. That he did not shut it he could only ascribe to an image of his father, Peel III, on the day he pointed a finger at his son and said, "You will leave Boston now, before you manage to disgrace irreparably the good name of Peel." This had come about because he, Peel IV, being bored nigh unto death, had slept through every course required by Harvard College. That he had not been booted out of Harvard did not mean he had met his father's expectations. Hence the banishment to the western New York outpost of his distant cousin, Jamie Stuart. A Scots name was apparently not susceptible to disgrace.

Peel held the door ajar while the goose waddled into the cabin with the aplomb of a star boarder who did this every night. And moments later, it had settled itself on a hooked rug a safe distance from the hearth.

When the gray of dawn came inching through the cabin windows, Peel was awakened by an insistent rapping sound. Assuming it was sleet, he rolled over. But since the irritating noise went on and on, he at last opened his eyes to see the goose tapping its beak sharply against the base of the cabin door.

Peel groaned, tossed off his blanket, and swung his feet to the floor. "What now, you wretched bird?" Then he saw why the goose had wanted out, but not before he nearly stepped in the heap just deposited in front of the door. Peel scowled as the goose now made its way back to the hooked rug, then he reached for his jacket. Grabbing a fireplace shovel, he took the gravelly dung outside, where he broke thorough a thin layer of ice beneath a bare-branched elm, and, too groggy to dig a hole, dumped and covered it with the season's first snow.

In the course of the next week, a fire at the Lockport Lumber Yard (which only an Indian summer rain and shallow water pumped from the Erie Canal had kept from setting the entire town ablaze) made Peel nearly forget the queries he'd sent out about the corpse. And in the meantime, Lockport's response to Peel's new situation had worn thin. The fact that he stood considerably taller than most men and that the crisp air of the country had filled out his hitherto thin frame had made the ridicule mercifully mild. Or at least covert. Peel himself could hardly lay blame on those who found his being shadowed by an oversize Canada goose a source of hilarity. But enough was enough. Besides, Peel was finding the bird superior to those animals considered more suitable companions. Unlike a dog, it did not bark incessantly or growl or bite; unlike a cat, it did not yowl or snarl or scratch. It did not smell, not much, nor did it require elaborate food or constant attention. The goose, simply, was there. Half the time Peel forgot about it altogether until a sly grin or a soft snicker reminded him that he did not walk alone.

It was on an unseasonably warm rainy morning that a response arrived from the Buffalo constable. "Yes, indeed," said the letter, "we have a man reported missing whose description tallies with yours."

Peel opened the door to Jamie Stuart's office in the rear of the firehouse to hear an odd, staccato voice. He entered to find the constable behind his desk, in front of which stood a short, buxom woman whose flat-brimmed, black straw hat rested on her head like a burned pancake.

"Peel!" said Jamie with obvious relief. When the woman jerked around to face Peel and then stared at him in rigid silence, he had the impression that he was confronting a doll with movable parts. Her face held little expression, and only the fluttering eyelashes above two perfectly round rouged spots on her cheeks indicated that she was mortal. Peel smiled, nodded at her, and looked questioningly over her head at Jamie Stuart.

"Peel!" said Jamie again, and again his relief was palpable. He raised his eyebrows as if conveying a significant message—one Peel could not begin to comprehend.

"We've got an answer to your inquiry," Jamie explained, before turning to the woman. "Allow me to introduce you, Mrs. Vandermeer, to my associate, attorney Peregrine Peel. Peel, this is Mrs. Joost Vandermeer."

The black pancake bobbed up and down mechanically and a tiny hand was thrust at Peel. "So glad . . . to meet you . . . Mr. Peel,'' came the spasmodic, high-pitched response.

Before Peel could respond, Jamie Stuart said, ''Mrs. Vandermeer is the wife—or, sadly, I should say is the *widow*—of the previously unknown deceased.''

''Are you from Buffalo?'' asked Peel. In response, he received a sudden torrent of tears from the widow.

''Oh, my poor Joost . . . to think . . . he just drifted . . . *all* that way by himself,'' the widow Vandermeer sobbed. ''I can't . . . can't bear to think . . .''

''Yes, ma'am, it's very upsetting, I'm sure,'' said Jamie with the evident weariness of having said this many, many times. He came around the desk to awkwardly pat the distraught widow's shoulder as she pulled a wet handkerchief from her purse. Over her head he mouthed at Peel, ''I'd just got her quieted down.''

Peel had seen that ''Buffalo?'' had indeed set off the widow Vandermeer, but the woman seemed to be recovering from the rigidity that made her resemble a wind-up toy.

A moment later, however, Mrs. Vandermeer pushed the handkerchief back into her purse and said to Jamie, ''Was there . . . anything besides . . . ah, other than . . . my Joost's body?''

Jamie looked confused. ''Other than?''

''Yes, I mean did he have any . . . well, for instance, was his . . . his money clip with him?'' she asked, more tears obviously held at bay only by strenuous effort.

''No, we didn't find any money clip, did we, Perry? But come to think of it,'' said Jamie, ''we did find—''

''Ah, Constable Stuart!'' interrupted Peel after failing to gain Jamie's attention, ''I think we need to have the widow identify her husband.''

The widow nodded and said, ''After that, Constable Stuart . . . you *will* sign the . . . the death certificate, so I . . . can take poor Joost home?''

"Of course, my dear lady. And we shall make arrangements to have your husband returned to Buffalo."

Peel, who had continued to try to gain his cousin's attention without success, murmured, "I'm not so sure you can do that, Jamie."

Jamie pointedly ignored this as he gently nudged the widow Vandermeer out through the doorway. Once outside, the woman unexpectedly shrieked, "My God, what is *that*? Oh, get it away from me! Get it away!"

"It's only a goose," Peel answered, although more interested in observing Mrs. Vandermeer's sudden liveliness than in explaining the bird. The goose had now moved directly into the widow's path and stood there with wings slowly moving up and down as if it might fly at the woman.

"Peel, would you get that damn bird out of here?" Jamie growled, patting Mrs. Vandermeer's small stiffened shoulder.

This proved unnecessary, as the town parson had just come around the corner of the firehouse, and the goose moved away on its own. While Jamie and the parson discussed plans for the deceased's journey to his final rest in Buffalo, Peel studied the widow. And when she and the parson had finally departed for the icehouse, Peel said again, "Jamie, I don't think you can sign a death certificate for Vandermeer."

"Why not? Man's dead."

"For one thing, it's a question of jurisdiction. *Where* did he die? For that matter, what did he die *of*? Yes, he was found in the canal, but we can't know for certain that he drowned. The Buffalo constable merely wrote that a man named Joost Vandermeer who fitted my description had been reported missing."

"Perry, are you *trying* to be difficult, or does it just come natural to you? It's obvious the man drowned—"

He broke off as toward them strode a tall, spare

woman of obvious determination, her arms swinging and her large jaw thrust forward. Marching up to the two men, she demanded, ''Which one of you is the constable here?''

''I am,'' Jamie said. ''Constable Stuart, ma'am. Can I help you?''

''I should hope so! I'm told my husband was recently found here in this town. Found dead.''

Peel exchanged a look with his cousin, after which each quickly looked away, as if to disclaim what the other might be thinking.

''Ma'am, I'm not sure what you mean. Who is—*was* your husband?'' Jamie ventured.

''The name's Vandermeer,'' said the woman. ''Joost Vandermeer. From Buffalo.''

Several frustrating hours later, Jamie Stuart sat slumped in his desk chair. ''Well, this is one helluva how-do-you-do! Two women claiming to be the grieving widow. What do you think, Perry?—which one of them is lying?''

Peel shook his head and stared at the ceiling of the firehouse. Both women had sworn up and down that they had been married for the past ten years to the deceased Joost Vandermeer.

Peel had thought it prudent to keep the women apart while he questioned them. Doll-like Mrs. Vandermeer Number One had identified the body in the icehouse as her late husband, then had gone to the rectory to weep on the parson's shoulder. Peel had escorted Mrs. Vandermeer Number Two to the icehouse, where she, her jaw jutting furiously, identified the body as *her* late husband, after which Peel escorted her to a nearby inn. She, too, asked if anything had been found on the body in the way of money. Peel had evaded her question.

In the past hour, he'd asked each if she had a marriage

certificate. Each said, "Of course I have one." But no certificate had been produced by either, and each said she couldn't remember where the certificate might be "after all these years."

Now Peel said, "Jamie, there's one other thing the Buffalo constable's letter mentioned. Vandermeer was—"

He broke off at a knock on the office door. He and Jamie scrambled to their feet when in walked a shapely young woman with hair the color of clover honey and eyes that matched exactly the turquoise blue of her cloak.

"Is either of you Constable Stuart?" she asked.

When Jamie nodded, she said, "I've just come from Buffalo. I understand you have found my father"—her lower lip trembled and her blue eyes filled—"my father, Joost Vandermeer."

Jamie hustled around his desk to clasp the young woman's hand. And to give Peel a knowing look that said they would now get to the bottom of this. "My dear lady," said Jamie, "my condolences. I suppose you know that your mother is already here."

"My mother?" said the daughter. "You must be mistaken, Constable Stuart. Some years ago, you see, my mother died."

Peel was already halfway out the door when Jamie yelped, "Where are you going?"

"To catch a stagecoach," replied Peel.

At his cabin he threw a few things into a valise, left the door slightly ajar for his feathered friend, and walked down the dirt path. The rain had ended and a few rays of sun were emerging when Peel spied, at the foot of the elm tree, a series of strange flashes. He walked over to peer down, then dropped to his knees. "Well, well!"

*   *   *

He returned two days later, shaken and sore from riding scores of miles over bumpy corduroy roads. But stagecoach was the fastest means of travel in the vast western New York wilderness that stretched between towns. Now, with his mind centered on what he had discovered, Peel went directly to the home of the village doctor. Then on to the constable's office.

"Where the devil have you been?" Jamie Stuart greeted him. "Fine time to run off and leave me with those women!"

"Where are they now?"

"Wife Number One is at the Blue Spruce Hotel. Wife Number Two is at McCormick's Inn. Daughter's staying at a boardinghouse on Church Street. I told them to keep their distance and stay put—I think they would have killed one another if I hadn't separated them."

"Possibly," Peel said, "although I believe only one is a murderess."

"*What?*" Jamie stared at him with skepticism. "There's no evidence of murder."

"Yes, there is," Peel said. "Those bruises around Vandermeer's wrists? The doctor says they probably were made by hemp rope. And there's more. Let's bring the women here to your office."

This proved to be an easier task than he'd imagined, as the two Mrs. Vandermeers agreed with alacrity. The daughter, however, had at first balked at the prospect of facing two women each claiming to be her mother and needed to be escorted to the office by the constable himself. When all were assembled, crowded close to one another in the confined space, Peel began.

"I've just returned from Buffalo," he said, watching the women's faces carefully, "where I had an enlightening conversation with the constable there."

Wife Number One's doll-like face gave nothing away. Wife Number Two hitched her jaw a notch higher and scowled. The honey-haired daughter sighed heavily and looked as if she was about to cry. Jamie Stuart stood leaning against his wooden file cabinet, then crossed his arms over his chest to regard Peel with a dubious gaze.

Peel addressed Wife Number One. "Your name, I understand, is Mrs. Colette Brown. And it is true you're a widow but not Joost Vandermeer's."

The woman's mouth opened, then quickly shut.

"Yes. I'm informed, though," Peel went on, "that you were a frequent companion of Vandermeer's. But you were not married to him. Nor were you," he said to Number Two. "Your last name is not Vandermeer but Taylor. And while Vandermeer was at one time married, it seems that his real wife died some years ago."

"As I told you," murmured the daughter, who now looked considerably less distressed. The other two women glared furiously at each other before they turned their anger on Peel. Colette Brown, with undoll-like intensity, snapped, "When he returned from his trip, Joost was going to marry me!"

"Oh, no, he wasn't," protested Miss Taylor. "He had decided to marry *me!*"

Colette Brown raised her large pocketbook as if to fling it at her enemy, and Jamie moved to position himself between the two women. "Let's just calm down here. Go on, Peel."

Peel nodded, then backed up against the office door, more to give himself some protection than to prevent an escape. "You both may be telling the truth about Vandermeer's intentions or at least may have believed what he told you," he said. "But when he disappeared, each of you saw an opportunity to feather your nest." Having said that, Peel abruptly realized that he had not seen the goose since he'd arrived back in Lockport.

"How dare you imply such a thing!" said Miss Taylor. "Joost wanted to provide for me."

Peel almost believed her sincerity. It was barely possible she had not known about the man's philandering. But unlikely. "Were you aware that Vandermeer was leaving Buffalo?" he asked her.

"I knew he was traveling to New York City," she retorted. "But he was coming back!"

"Yes, yes, he was," Colette Brown unexpectedly agreed. "He was only taking a short business trip."

"Did you know what kind of business?" Peel asked, although certain he had the answer.

The two women fell silent. The daughter, however, her eyes fixing him with an admiring gaze, sighed, "Mr. Peel, what a clever man you are. And I'm grateful that you've exposed these two for the scheming frauds they are. My poor, dear father—"

"It seems," Peel broke in, "that you were also planning to leave Buffalo, were you not? Leave permanently."

"Why, no," she said. "Whoever gave you that idea?"

"The owner of your boardinghouse there. She told me you had given her notice. That you were moving out."

"She's mistaken, Mr. Peel. I was simply leaving for a short trip with my father, that's all."

"I don't think so," said Peel. "The landlady showed me your room, and it was completely emptied of personal belongings. Whereas these other two . . . ladies . . . had tidy homes with everything in its place. Clearly they were not intending to go anywhere."

The blue eyes fluttered, and the young woman shook her head. "I can't imagine what you mean."

"I think you planned to leave Buffalo," Peel told her, "immediately after you killed Joost Vandermeer. Or had another boardinghouse resident—a man you'd frequently been seen with around town—help you to kill him."

"That's absurd!"

"No, the Buffalo constable and I questioned that man," Peel said honestly. "And he had quite a lot to say about you," he lied.

In truth the man had said little other than, "*She* did it!" But truth, Peel had been learning, was composed of many facets, much like the stones he fingered in his pocket.

The blue eyes blazed at Peel. "He's a liar if he said anything. Why would I want to kill my father?"

Jamie Stuart was staring at Peel incredulously. "Perry, I think you're out of your depth here. Why *would* she, or anyone, want to murder Vandermeer?"

"Because, as was fairly well known in Buffalo," said Peel, "Joost Vandermeer had of recent become a wealthy man. The Buffalo constable's reply to my initial inquiry stated that Vandermeer was a jeweler—you didn't give me a chance to tell you that, Jamie. And the constable and I, when we searched Vandermeer's shop, found a consignment agreement with a New York City importer. For a shipment originating in Brazil. I'd wager that's why Vandermeer planned to travel to New York City—either to return that part of the shipment he hadn't sold or to renegotiate the contract."

To those who were looking at him with bewildered expressions, Peel added, "These days, Brazil is where the best diamonds are found." He recalled a Brazilian diamond pendant belonging to his mother that had been the size of a robin's egg. "And it was the diamonds," he said, "that provided the motive for Vandermeer's murder."

"*What diamonds*?" came an immediate chorus from Jamie and the two bogus wives. The daughter remained tellingly silent.

"The rough, uncut diamonds Vandermeer had in a belt around his waist." Peel turned to the young woman.

"You didn't know where he kept those stones, but you'd heard that he might remarry and spend his money on someone other than yourself. When you discovered he was leaving town, you saw your opportunity. You assumed the diamonds were in his shop—when I went there with the constable, the shop showed the signs of being thoroughly ransacked. You killed Vandermeer or got your fellow boarder to kill him by knocking the man unconscious—hence the head wound—then binding his wrists and throwing him into the canal to drown.

"Of course you couldn't have known that the Erie Canal Commissioners had just decided the canal should be drained for the winter. You thought the body might never be found. But then you saw my inquiry that the Buffalo constable had posted outside his office. Which brought you here"—Peel turned to the other—"as it did you two women."

He was met by profound silence. Which surprised Peel. He wasn't accustomed to holding forth, much less having anyone listen. He reached into his pocket and withdrew a pouch, then poured its contents into the palm of his hand. A few of the stones flashed with inner fire. While the two older women and Jamie gawked at them, Peel watched the young woman. Her eyes had narrowed but not with surprise.

"It wasn't very foresighted of you," Peel said to her. "The only thing you accomplished was to kill the goose that was laying golden eggs."

"That was quite a performance of yours," said Jamie late that day, as they walked along the canal. "The best thing you did was to guarantee that the trial of the young murderess won't be here. It'll be in Buffalo."

Peel nodded absently as he searched the southern sky for the vanished goose.

"But how did you know those stones were diamonds?'' Jamie asked. ''They looked like greasy pebbles to me, at least they did when we pulled Vandermeer from the canal.''

''That's what diamonds look like before they're cut and polished. But the goose cleaned them,'' said Peel.

''What?''

''The bird must have scooped up some that dropped on the towpath that day. Since there's nothing harder than diamonds, they passed through its crop, getting ground against, and polished by, gravel it had eaten. The next morning I unwittingly buried them under snow. Didn't see what they were until rain washed away everything else.'' He turned from scanning the sky. ''Jamie, are you sure you haven't spotted it?''

''What? The *goose*? If it had any sense, it probably flew south. Look at that sky! We're due for a nor'easter for certain.''

Peel guessed it would be pointless to make more inquiries about the bird. If it had flown south . . . well, he supposed it was good riddance. He just hoped it hadn't tried to follow him to Buffalo or fallen victim to a musket.

When the storm gathered later that night, he lay awake in bed and listened to the wind howling and the snow beating against his windows. Then, from just outside, he heard something that made him sit bolt upright. It was a sharp, distinct rapping sound.

Peel grinned as he threw off his blankets and went to hold open the cabin door.

Miriam Grace Monfredo is a historian, former librarian, and author of the Seneca Falls historical mystery series,

which focuses on women's history in nineteenth-century America. The first book in the series, The Seneca Falls Inheritance, *was nominated for the Agatha Award for Best First Novel. The recent books in the series are* The Stalking Horse *and* Must the Maiden Die. *Continuing her interest in history, Monfredo also coedited (with Sharan Newman) two historical mystery anthologies,* Crime Through Time *and* Crime Through Time II.

Defender of the Faith

Sister Carol Anne O'Marie

Miss Lillian Hassett had been the housekeeper at Blessed Sacrament Rectory for as long as anyone could remember. "She came with the building," Lillian overheard that new whippersnapper of a pastor tell one of his priest friends.

That's what you know! Lillian thought, slamming the refrigerator door. *I came with Father Motherway.* Although "with" was not really the right word. Father Motherway was already pastor of Blessed Sacrament when Lillian was hired.

God's ways are mysterious, she thought, slipping on a fresh apron. She pushed a strand of her thinning gray hair off her forehead.

Years ago, after an especially fervent high school retreat, Lillian had thought that God wanted her to be a nun. Her own father had other ideas. "Over my dead body!" he shouted.

Poor Lillian cringed. She didn't know which way to

turn. She wanted to enter the convent, but certainly she didn't want her father to die. Of course, that was before she knew that there were things worse than death.

One Sunday when she read in the parish bulletin that Father Motherway needed help for his sister, Lillian thought that her prayers were answered. His sister, Miss Bridget Motherway, was also his housekeeper and was getting up in years. She needed someone for the heavier work.

Perfect! Lillian thought. She could obey her father, yet not stray too far from the convent. She applied for the job.

"You look like a strong, capable young woman," Father Motherway had said in that kind way of his. Lillian loved him immediately. The very next morning she packed an old suitcase and moved into a small room in the rectory off the laundry.

Just as she had every morning for nearly sixty years, Lillian hummed while she prepared breakfast for the priests. She began with a medley of hymns, the good old-fashioned ones like *"Panis Angelicus"* and "O Lord, I Am Not Worthy," not those fluffy things they play in Church now on the guitar!

Lillian glanced at the small, round portrait of Pope Pius XII in its place of honor on her kitchen wall. Right hand raised, the Pope smiled down from the papal blessing written in Latin, of course. Father Motherway had brought it back to her from Rome. Nowadays, both men, God rest them, must be rolling over in their graves.

Moving smoothly from one hymn to the next, Lillian kneaded the soda bread just as Miss Bridget had instructed her all those many years ago, although hers never had tasted quite as good. Pausing to give her arms a rest, she watched the crisp morning sun bathe her garden in its magical aura.

Actually, it was Miss Bridget who had taken Lillian

gently under her wing and taught her how to cook, how to make beds with square corners, how to keep a high polish on the rectory furniture, how to iron delicate chapel linens, and how to spot and press a black serge suit. In short, Miss Bridget Motherway had taught Lillian how to be the ideal priests' housekeeper.

And Miss Bridget was the essence of common sense, making sure that Lillian joined her every evening for a little glass of sherry or two. Christian Brothers, of course! "To help us relax and sleep," Miss Bridget had said. "Too long churning makes bad butter."

It was Miss Bridget who had made the young Lillian realize "doing for" God's chosen men was every bit as much a religious calling as being a nun. She had the sacred privilege of feeding, clothing, caring for *alter Christus,* other Christs, men whose dignity surpassed that of emperors and even of angels, because their words could change bread and wine into the Body and Blood of Christ. They could forgive sin. Miss Bridget said that it was their duty, as well as their privilege, to foster and to safeguard priestly vocations.

Slowly Lillian's desire to enter the convent had simply seeped away. How could she leave Father Motherway and Miss Bridget, she argued with herself, on the pretext of doing God's work? She was already doing God's work.

And to this day I've no regrets! Lillian thought, giving the soda bread a firm squeeze. *None at all! Especially when I see the nuns running around in slacks and mini-skirts without so much as a veil covering their heads, out until all hours of the night, doing whatever takes their fancy! No!* She shoved her fist into the dough. *I'm sure I did the right thing.*

She slid the rounded dough into the hot oven. Humming more softly, she listened for noises from the priest's bedroom overhead. She heard the strident ring of an alarm clock; then the young assistant's feet hit the floor. What was his name? Father Tom? Or was it Father Mike? So many assistants came through Blessed Sacrament, it was hard to remember. She still was not used to people calling priests by their baptismal names, even with the lovely title of ''Father.'' Somehow it just didn't seem respectful to her, and no matter what that young whippersnapper said, she'd never think it was!

Lillian felt her pudgy face flush. That was no way to think about the pastor. She took a deep breath and closed her eyes against the bright sunshine streaming into her kitchen. She must go to confession on Saturday afternoon and ask forgiveness. She'd be sure to stand in his line, not that there was much of a line these days. She'd confess to him that she'd called him a whippersnapper. Lillian suppressed a giggle. Afterwards he was forbidden to even let on that he knew who she was! *There's more than one way to skin a cat,* she thought, humming the first verse of ''Holy God, We Praise Thy Name.''

After Miss Bridget died, Lillian had taken over her rooms in the rectory. She missed Miss Bridget sorely and had planted a small herb garden in her memory. Father Motherway had blessed it. Over the years, her herbs flourished, and around the edges she added rose bushes and lavender and tall stalks of foxglove. The church janitor had built her a small wooden shrine in which Lillian enthroned a statue of Our Blessed Mother.

When her dear Father Motherway went home to God, Father Sullivan, who succeeded him, begged Lillian to stay on. With deference and a bit of trepidation, she agreed.

At first, everything seemed to be working out just fine. Father Sullivan was an easy man to do for. And where Father Motherway had enjoyed Lillian's cooking, Father Sullivan, an outgoing and gregarious man, enjoyed sharing her meals with as many other priests as possible until

Blessed Sacrament Rectory became *the* rectory to be invited to for dinner. Lillian's Blanquette de Veau, which was nothing more than an elaborate veal stew seasoned with some of her fresh herbs, was a tremendous hit. Blushing, Lillian prayed for humility when time and again she overheard priest guests call her Sullivan's Super Chef.

"You'd better be careful that some handsome man doesn't come in here and steal her away," one of Father's guests had remarked.

Handsome man, indeed! Even now Lillian's cheeks reddened at the very idea. Not that she hadn't been tempted once, years ago, by Henry Collins, the greengrocer. Then she saw only Henry's dancing blue eyes, his full head of dark curly hair, his obvious gentleness when he handled his apples and his tomatoes. When he asked her to the movies, the devil had almost made her forget her call to a life of single blessedness caring for God's chosen ones.

In the end, she had resisted both Henry and the Devil. Now when she went to the market she saw only an old man with faded eyes, a bald circle on his crown, and an enormous Adam's apple, who sniffled incessantly. Thank God his annoyingly cheerful wife was no longer there beside him. "Fertile Myrtle" Father Sullivan used to call her after she'd given birth to the seventh little Henry.

Lillian felt the familiar empty lurch in the pit of her stomach. No mind! She had chosen the better part. *Mercifully, God spared me,* she thought, savoring the quiet of her sunny kitchen. And to think, not one of those Collins boys became a priest, she sighed, pitying poor Myrtle Collins.

"Morning, Lillian." The pastor pushed open the swinging kitchen door.

Lillian hadn't heard the whippersnapper come in. Perspiration dripped from his face and formed damp spots all over his gray sweatsuit. He'd been out jogging. In her opinion, he'd have been better served saying his Divine Office.

"Good morning, Father," she answered respectfully, trying to remember the sacredness of his calling. "Your orange juice is freshly squeezed and on the table. The bread is just about ready to come out of the oven."

"Granola will be fine," he said before she had the chance to ask how he wanted his eggs.

She bit her lower lip and watched him rummage through her cupboards for the cereal box.

"This stuff is much better for your heart." He grinned, scattering flakes and nuts on her countertop.

Like a messy hamster, Lillian thought, avoiding his eyes. She reached for the coffeepot before he took it and dripped all over her waxed kitchen floor. Lillian hated coffee drops on her floor. In fact, Lillian hated anything messy or out of order.

"It is a reflection on the housekeeper," Miss Bridget, who firmly believed that cleanliness was next to godliness, if not just a step ahead of it, used to say.

It was Father Sullivan, God rest him, who first called her Tidy Paws. Father Sullivan was a joker, always teasing, although Lillian didn't think he was so funny when she heard him referring to dear old Father Motherway as Mother Fatherway.

Over the years, the priests had given her many nicknames, which they had no idea she overheard. Somehow, brilliant men that they were, it never occurred to them that their voices carried from the dining room table into her kitchen, even with the swinging door shut.

"Placid Miss Hassett" was one. "Lily of the Field" another. *Probably because of my spreading garden*, she thought. And "Diamond Lil." Lillian smiled. The nickname she liked best was, of course, "Defender of the Faith."

Father Clement, who succeeded Father Ford, who succeeded Father Sullivan had given her that title, an honor that only the Pope should bestow. Glancing up fondly at her papal blessing, Lillian sighed. And he would if he'd known, she thought, but for the present, only she, God, and His angels and saints knew just how staunchly she had lived up to her responsibility of safeguarding the faith and the immortal souls of the priests entrusted to her care.

And that Vatican Two Council had made it quite a challenge, Lillian fussed, watching her sink fill with swirling water and sunshine and deep-green spinach leaves. She could not imagine what that Pope John XXIII was thinking about when he opened those windows! In her opinion, he'd let a lot more than fresh air into the Church. And most of it was a scandal and a shame. She felt her face color with anger.

One long-ago evening while the priests had been eating that same fresh spinach salad, Lillian had overheard Father Sullivan suggesting that birth control may be a matter of conscience! Birth control! Pain shot through Lillian's body like a blast of icy water. She felt cold all over. She poured a small amount of cooking sherry into a coffee cup and took a sip to ward off the chill.

Why those two words should never even be on the tongue of a priest! Saying those words with the same lips that spoke the words of consecration! It was a sacrilege! Yet, she knew Father Sullivan was a dedicated man. It must be the devil's doing, corrupting one of God's chosen! Someone must save him.

In a daze, Lillian had stirred her stew. It would do no good for her to try to talk to Father Sullivan. He would just make a joke. Lillian knew that. This was no joking matter. It was her duty as well as her responsibility to act for the good of her pastor's immortal soul. The delicious aroma of meat bubbling in red wine, the bouquet of rosemary and marjoram filled her warm kitchen. What should she do? The bay leaf floating on the simmering broth in her Dutch oven gave her an idea.

The very next morning Lillian went into her herb garden. Her eyes slid to the tall stalk of foxglove towering above the daisies. She peered down the speckled throat of the poisonous purple bell-shaped flower, plucked several wrinkled leaves, and slipped them into her apron pocket.

Father Sullivan's sudden death was a surprise to everyone, well, almost everyone. It was common knowledge among the priests that he had a heart condition, but they all thought it was under control.

He woke up one morning complaining of blurred vision, then became violently sick to his stomach. When he began the tremors, Lillian called Dr. Slater. But poor Father was gone by the time the doctor arrived. The coroner found traces of digitalis, and all assumed that the priest must have experienced heart pains during the night and accidentally taken an overdose.

Father Sullivan's funeral was a grand affair. Lillian felt justifiably proud. Blessed Sacrament Church had standing room only, and Father looked so priestly she thought, for lack of a better word, laid out in his vestments with the archbishop presiding.

"What a shame for a good man to die so young," the housekeeper from St. Martin's had remarked to Lillian at the graveside.

There are things far worse for a good man than an early death, Lillian had thought, returning the sad smile.

His successor, Father Ford, was a lovely man—quiet, intelligent, with the appetite of a bird! Instead of the hordes of priests that Father Sullivan had to dinner, Father Ford invited only a few good friends. Father Dobkowski and Father Daniels were frequent guests at the rectory table, while Monsignor Moriarity, for all practical purposes, made Blessed Sacrament his second home.

Not that Lillian minded. She felt honored and awed to be serving a monsignor at her table. This was a man who was distinguished for his work and his zeal in promoting the welfare of the Church. Yet he was unpretentious and genuinely appreciative.

The monsignor must be a real saint, Lillian thought until one infamous evening.

"Married clergy." The words floated into her kitchen as clear and as unmistakable as if they were spoken into a microphone.

Surely, the reverend monsignor would have something to say on that topic! Married priests, indeed! Why, the priest's vow of celibacy was the glory of the Catholic Church. Anyone who tried to corrupt a priest was the devil's instrument. Lillian felt her face flush with indignation. Righteous indignation, she thought, moving closer to the kitchen's swinging door.

Holding her breath, Lillian listened, ready to remember every word of the monsignor's. Zealous, devout man that he was, he would set the whole table right.

"Maybe there's something to it," she heard the monsignor say. Pain, like a sudden blast of icy water, shot through her. Lillian shivered.

"But I ask you, gentlemen, at our age, who would have us?" The monsignor laughed. Lillian heard the other priests at the table join in.

The dignity and sacredness of the priesthood is no laughing matter, she thought, fury ballooning through her cold body. Lillian needed several sips of cooking sherry to warm herself.

Setting her thin lips in a resolute line, she added a touch of garnish to the monsignor's serving of her famous veal stew.

"Delicious," he said when she removed his clean plate. Lillian had difficulty hiding her pleased smile.

Following Monsignor Moriarity's sudden death, the archbishop sent out a directive to all the priests of the archdiocese. He urged them to get more exercise, to eat a healthier diet, and to have regular heart checkups. At least, that was what the housekeeper from St. Martin's told Lillian.

"They are all working themselves to an early grave," the housekeeper had said.

Better to die young than to live to old age if you are in danger of losing your immortal soul, Lillian had thought, nodding her head gravely.

It was no surprise to anyone when Father Ford decided to retire and move back to Ireland. The archbishop appointed Father Clement to replace him.

Now, Father Clement was Lillian's idea of a perfect pastor. He was a soft-spoken man, kind to the parishioners, visited the schoolchildren as well as the sick, and said his breviary in Latin. Every day after his lunch, Lillian watched him walk the perimeter of her garden, his black rosary beads in his hands.

Father Clement was always polite to her, calling her Miss Hassett, and appreciative of every small service. Before long, he even gave her a slight raise in salary and, to her delight, he always remembered to put his dirty underwear in the clothes hamper.

When Lillian overheard Father Clement call her Defender of the Faith, she had been tempted to tell him just how true it was. She wanted to pour out her anger over Mass being celebrated in English not Latin, with the priest facing the people. To tell him how cheated she felt when, after all her years of abstinence, it was no longer a mortal sin to eat meat on Friday. She wanted to rant that week after week she had struggled to work the priests' breakfasts around her own Sunday Mass attendance, only to be told that all along she could have gone on Saturday night instead. She wanted to protest because her lovely sterling silver St. Christopher medal no longer protected her when she rode the bus. How dared anyone unseat a saint? She wanted to tell him the rage, the grief, the fear she felt for the Church she had once known and faithfully served.

And she might have, too, if, like all good things, it hadn't come to an end. Father Clement was moved to the archdiocesan seminary to teach classical languages.

The whippersnapper had come into Blessed Sacrament like a tornado. Now the telephone rang off the hook. Barefoot women danced down the center aisle during the Holy Sacrifice of the Mass. Committees met at the rectory until all hours of the night. The Youth Group coordinator and his band of urchins tramped through her kitchen. The woman pastoral assistant who had taken over the small office in the front insisted on setting her hot coffee cup on the corner of the good oak desk.

These days Lillian never knew who might appear in the rectory dining room. Not that she minded feeding them. It was just that they were such a ragtag bunch to be seated at a priest's table: lay people, nuns wearing earrings, long-haired priests with beards, and once even a homeless man the pastor met while he was jogging.

Jogging! Lillian wrinkled her short nose. The very thought of picking up that smelly gray sweatsuit—what a perfect name for the thing—and dumping it in her spotless washing machine infuriated her.

She'd wait until "himself" got out of the shower, then add it to his towels, which would be in a clump in the corner of his bathroom where he never failed to leave them.

Lillian took a deep breath. What had Miss Bridget taught her years ago? "I will close my eyes to their faults and see in them only God's representative." Miss

Bridget was quoting some saint or other who undoubtedly had never been a priest's housekeeper, Lillian thought sardonically.

"Lillian?" The whippersnapper looked at her quizzically. She wondered how long he had been speaking before she heard him.

"Excuse me, Father," she straightened the bib of her apron. "What is it that you were saying?"

"You were miles away," the pastor said with a laugh.

Lillian's felt her face grow hot. *Only inches away,* she thought, clearing her throat with a nervous little cough.

"I was saying that tonight I've invited ten people in for dinner at about six o'clock," he paused as if he expected her to protest.

When she didn't, he moved toward the kitchen door. "Father Mike and I will be here, of course. Two of the guests are priests. The other eight are women." He threw the next words over his left shoulder as nonchalantly as one would grains of spilled salt. "Women who want to be priests. We are on a committee studying women's ordination," he said, leaving the door swinging in his wake.

Women's ordination! That icy blast of pain shot through Lillian's body. She felt her heart jolt, and her whole self went cold. She poured the remains of the cooking sherry into her coffee cup and drank it down.

She took several deep breaths, trying to calm herself. Women wanting to be priests! Why the Pope himself had clearly forbidden it. Surely Christ never intended that His other "alter" self be a woman. Again she felt the rage beginning to consume her. How could that young whippersnapper dare to endanger the dignity, the power, the holiness of the priestly vocation, the vocation that she had nurtured and safeguarded, cherished and served for all these years? Lillian pushed back the piece of gray hair hanging down on her forehead.

How did he dare to jeopardize the sanctity, the honor, the tradition of the Catholic priesthood for which she had given her life? Clearly there was only one reason he would do such a thing. He was not a priest at all. He was the devil incarnate! The pastor stuck his head back into the kitchen and gave her a crooked grin. "And Lillian," he said, "would it be possible for you to have that Blanquette de Veau you make? It's to die for!"

"Yes, Father, of course," she answered, returning a shy smile. "I'll be happy to make it for you and your guests." She slid a knowing glance toward the small portrait of Pius XII. Then, cheerfully humming the refrain from "Faith of Our Fathers," Miss Lillian Hassett resolutely walked out into her herb garden.

Sister Carol Anne O'Marie entered the Sisters of St. Joseph of Carondelet in 1951 and made her vows in 1954. She works with homeless women in Oakland, California, in addition to writing her mystery series featuring the enterprising Sister Mary Helen. Her most recent novel is Death Takes Up the Collection.

Just Stunning

Abigail Padgett and Douglas Dennis

"My daughter is about to begin her speech," Vivian McCall said brightly, punctuating the remark with an elbow to the ribs of the man beside her. As the clatter of hotel tableware subsided, she made small adjustments to a scarf at the neck of her well-cut red power suit and smiled expectantly at the speaker's table. The scarf, she acknowledged, wasn't *quite* up to the task of hiding an unfortunate sagginess at her throat. But it would have to do. At sixty-four she wasn't ready to purchase the ladder-back porch rocker and set of initialed julep glasses required of an Aging Southern Lady. Of those three words, she thought with a wry smile, only "Southern" might arguably apply to her.

"Unnhh," the gentleman at her side replied, belatedly moving a large forearm between her elbow and his Kevlar-padded rib cage. He'd considered the possibility of a physical assault during this conference. He'd even thought about bringing a bodyguard but scrapped the idea in favor of the slim vest beneath his monogrammed shirt. Body armor. This model was guaranteed to stop a .357 magnum slug. He'd expected trouble, just not in the form of Vivian McCall, who like her titian-haired daughter, had a reputation of being a handful.

"My dear Vivian," he said as polite applause ebbed beneath microphone feedback, "with all respect due your pride in Dusty's unprecedented accomplishments, may I beg that your physical exuberance stop somewhere short of fracturing my ribs?"

"I love it when you talk dirty," Vivian answered, batting feathery eyelashes. "Now, Henry, just hush and listen."

". . . thanks and gratitude to the United States Correctional Association for this honor," Dusty McCall began, raising shoulder-high a handsome plaque inscribed with her name and *Warden of the Year*. "But for two people, this moment would not have been possible. The first is our governor, Eddie Felsen, who, regrettably, could not attend today's luncheon. Governor Felsen had both the vision and the courage necessary to appoint a woman to the most macho job in the United States—warden of the country's largest maximum-security prison, the Louisiana State Penitentiary."

Good-natured laughter and a round of applause followed.

"And the second person responsible for my success is the Pulitzer-Prize-winning investigative journalist and former managing editor of the Baton Rouge *Daily Post*, a role model for working women everywhere and certainly for me. Many of you know her. My mother, Vivian McCall. Please stand up, Mom."

"She always does this to me," Vivian whispered crossly, half standing and quickly resuming her seat. "I'm just an observer, not a participant."

"Oh, I don't know," Henry said, squeezing her hand.

"Rearing Dusty alone after Matt died *while* winning a Pulitzer took more than a little 'participating.' "

Dusty's amplified voice, in the compelling tones of a practiced public speaker, bounced around the New Orleans Sheraton's banquet room. The overwhelmingly male audience pushed aside the remains of its chicken dijon and settled back to listen in earnest. Their world was changing, some of their jobs on the line. And this lady warden's job, too, each thought privately. Warden of the Year or not, did she think she'd still be running a state pen when government got out of the prison business and turned it over to private contractors?

". . . concern that in a race to protect the state's resources by privatizing prisons, the already unpopular concept of rehabilitation will be lost in a frenzy of cost-cutting," Dusty went on. "I don't have to tell most of you that illiteracy and lack of job skills underlie . . ."

Vivian leaned close to Henry's ear and whispered, "By the way, what brings *you* to this dismal gathering of bloated corrections bureaucrats and second-string state politicians? Not that I'm sorry to see your villainous old face again, my dear. It's been years, hasn't it?"

"Three, Viv. Don't you remember? We danced at the governor's inaugural ball," he answered, silver hair reflecting glints from overhead fluorescents. "I'm heading up a private prison firm now, and we're angling for a contract to build and manage two six-hundred-bed facilities for the state. Going private's cheaper, and there's a nice profit margin. Wave of the future. Prisons, schools, health care, even libraries—everything's going private."

Vivian scowled. "Last I heard you were a securities analyst. What in hell do you know about prisons, Henry?" she asked. "Closest you ever got to one was probably watching a rerun of *Dead Man Walking* on TV."

"Never saw it," he chuckled. "Too depressing. And I don't have to know anything, my love. We're subcontracting the construction and hiring retired corrections people to manage them. It's cost-effective, the governor likes it, and that puts us on the short list. All I have to do is nail down the penal pooh-bahs here, especially the guards from the Correctional Officers' Association, and we're looking at a $95 million contract. That's not kitty chow, Viv. Why don't I tell you all about it over dinner in the French Quarter tonight?"

Vivian nodded. "That would be lovely, Henry."

"Thank you," Dusty concluded over applause as she finished her speech. "And at this time I'd like to introduce the next and last speaker. I promise he won't bore you. The head of Armistad Associates and an old family friend, Henry Armistad."

"Time to go to work, Viv," he said, a twitching neck muscle the only sign of nerves. "Wish me luck."

"Break a leg," she said through a smile she was sure failed to mask her ambivalence.

Dusty had worked hard and made significant personal sacrifices to get where she was, Vivian thought. Prisons were the last bastion of a once male-dominated world and not receptive to the idea of women guards, much less wardens. But Dusty had proven her capability. Now she might lose everything she'd worked for as businessmen like Henry hired cut-rate "managers" for their cash-cow lockups.

And besides, Vivian thought, there was something *wrong* about turning the job of civic punishment over to private corporations. Maybe she'd just outlived her time. That's what the publisher's hotshot son had said, ever so candidly, when he urged her to step down from her job as managing editor. "New blood, that's what we need." More revenue is what he meant, at the cost of cutting reportorial staff and just printing copy off the wire services. She couldn't abide it, announced her retirement, and walked.

"Maybe the little hotshot was right," she thought as a long sigh disturbed the placement of the scarf at her neck. Retirement, exile really, had sapped her spirit.

Her reverie was interrupted when a freckle-faced man with an ash-blond crewcut and the torso of an oil drum leaped from one of the tables and stormed toward the speaker's table, where Henry Armistad, now frozen in midsentence, stood behind a podium. Vivian wondered why the man had chosen to wear a striped shirt with a plaid jacket. And what might account for the angled bulge barely visible in his left armpit. To her seasoned journalist's eye it was clear that the real story of the conference might just be shaping up.

"No more privatization, not while we have breath in our bodies!" he shouted, fists clenched. "Armistad, you build a fuckin' private prison and I'll burn it to the ground!"

"How rational," responded Henry. "And nicely put, too, whoever you are."

"Arnie Tripp. T-R-I-P-P," the man growled. "President of the Louisiana Correctional Officers' Association. We're trained professionals doing dangerous work, and we're not about to lose our jobs to some mangy outfit that comes up with the lowest bid and no benefits!"

"Well, Mr. Tripp," said Henry, the calm in his voice betrayed by the color rushing to his face, "I'm sure we can work out our differences—at a more appropriate time and place. We're all professionals—"

"You're no professional," Tripp barked, jabbing a sausagelike finger in Henry's face. "What you are is a bloodsucking leech, and you're not gonna get away with it!"

With that, Tripp spun toward the exit at the rear of the room.

"Remember what I said," he flung back over his shoulder. "All of you!"

Attention, however, had shifted to Henry as his face turned ashen and he slumped over the podium. Vivian saw it first and dashed toward the speaker's table, where Dusty had already lowered the older man to a chair. People leaped to their feet, voices rising in alarm. Someone rushed from the hall shouting, "I'll get a doctor!"

"Oh, Henry!" said Vivian, certain he was dying in her arms. "Hang on. Help is coming."

Eyes screwed shut, he gasped for air. Several hands laid him gently on the carpeted floor. Dusty loosened his tie and collar while Vivian clasped his hand to her breast and whispered, "Hang on, hang on," until she noticed color returning to his cheeks. Slowly his breathing normalized, and he looked up at the circle of faces.

"I'm okay," he insisted. "Just a little heart irregularity, but I've got a pacemaker. It's bringing the old pump back up to speed. No problem. I'll be all right soon."

"Of course you will, Henry." Vivian practically shouted in order to be heard over the crowd. "Pacemakers have improved so much since Dusty's father had one. Why, they're absolutely foolproof now!"

An Emergency Medical Services team carrying a stretcher, oxygen tank, and other lifesaving gear pushed through the crowd and elbowed Vivian aside. She stood, straightened her jacket and skirt, and found herself looking straight at Arnie Tripp. He towered above the others and wore what struck her as a most peculiar expression. Not hatred or anger. Certainly not concern. It was, she thought, more like the look on the face of a stalking cat. That cheerful concentration.

Later Vivian and Dusty strolled past the elevator bank toward the Sheraton's cluster of shops. They were on their way to the exhibition hall, and Vivian's mouth was set in a grim line.

"I don't approve of what Henry's doing with this private prison deal," she noted somberly, "but he's still a friend. He should be in a hospital, not just resting upstairs in his room. He could have another attack."

"You're being overly protective, Mom," replied Dusty, bending to drape an arm over her mother's shoulders. "The emergency medical people are sure it wasn't a heart attack. He'll be fine with a little rest." Then, with a probing glance, "You're afraid it'll be like Dad when his pacemaker failed, aren't you? Say, is there something I should know about you and good old Henry? I thought you two were just friends, but—"

"Don't be silly," Vivian sniffed, giving unnecessary attention to the collection of garish raffia handbags in a shop window. "Can you imagine going to lunch carrying a limegreen bag decorated with dead starfish and plastic crawdads?"

"We'll talk later," Dusty pronounced decisively.

At the front of the exhibition hall was an immense sign on a tripod easel.

JAIL SALE!
THE LATEST PRODUCTS FOR SAFE
AND SANE PRISON MANAGEMENT!
WELCOME!

A galaxy of vendor booths vied for their attention. Company reps hawked restraint chairs, stun guns and stun shields, razor fencing, leg irons and slash-proof vests, as well as toothpaste, corn chips and ice cream— evidence that mainstream corporations also coveted a slice of the lucrative prison pie.

"Toys for overgrown boys," Vivian humphed at a sales rep demonstrating a pair of hi-tech black hinged handcuffs.

A life-sized mannequin loomed in their path, clad

from neck to toe in a heavily padded jet-black bodysuit. The handcuffs, Vivian thought, would match. In addition, the figure wore steel-toed paratrooper boots, shin guards, knee guards, heavy leather gloves, forearm guards, a Kevlar vest, riot helmet with full-face transparent shield, and held a clear plastic stun shield in one hand and a stun gun in the other. Dusty and Vivian paused to examine the formidable figure. A sharp-eyed salesman immediately appeared beside them.

"The ultimate in protection for your tactical squad officers," he said, spotting the title "warden" on Dusty's name badge. "They can enter any confrontation situation confident of maintaining their bodily integrity, from cell extractions to full-blown riots. We guarantee it."

"What are the metal strips in that clear plastic thing for?" Vivian asked.

"This baby," replied the salesman, patting the stun shield, "delivers 58,000 volts from those strips. Guaranteed to get an offender's attention."

"Fry him like a chitlin, you mean," sniffed Vivian.

"No, ma'am. See, the amps are real low. It delivers a shock like when a person touches a bare wire at home, only more of it. Doesn't leave a mark. Customers have told me just the sight of one of these has turned uncooperative inmates into compliant ones. For the really stubborn, we have our low-cost, powerful Stunmaster stun gun. It fires two darts, just like you've seen in the movies and on cop shows. Puts 'em down and keeps 'em down. It could drop a rhino."

"Thank you," said Dusty. With Vivian beside her, she strode purposefully toward the back of the hall.

"Somehow all that stuff looks like something that dreadful man yelling at Henry during the luncheon would wear," Vivian said.

Dusty nodded. "Actually, Mom, he does," she replied. "Arnie Tripp heads up my Tactical Team, specially trained for serious problems like gang activity and riots. He and the other ultramacho types put on those Ninja Turtle suits and happily practice for the day they might get to use them. It keeps them out of the prison mainstream, where their shall we say authoritarian attitude causes problems. The Tactical Team is like a police officer's gun. I'll use it if I absolutely have to, but I'd rather arbitrate problems before they fester. The prison runs smoother that way."

They arrived at a booth featuring the Ionscan 400. "A Drug Buster That Works Like a Dust Buster—Identifies Twenty Narcotics." Dusty told the eager rep she had seen it advertised in the trades and was thinking of using it to screen prison visitors and low-level guards, ongoing sources for illicit drugs.

"It's more accurate than a drug-sniffing dog," the salesman beamed, "and never gets tired, needs food or exercise. Already potty-trained, too. I can let you have it for $55,000."

Dusty said she'd consider it and accepted a folder of promotional material.

Later, in Dusty's hotel room, Vivian sat on the bed nursing a bourbon from the minibar as Dusty showered and then got to work on her makeup. Ice cubes clinked, the central air hummed, and a stray shaft of amber sunlight pierced the gap between half-closed drapes.

"Now is as good a time as any, daughter dear," Vivian said, fluffing a pillow and leaning against the headboard. "What's going on in that pretty head?"

"Never could fool you, could I?" Dusty recapped a lipstick.

"Mothers know everything." Vivian sipped her drink. "With you stuck at that awful prison in the middle of nowhere, God knows we don't see each other often enough to suit me. But you didn't drag me down to this convention so we could share the pleasure of eating rubber chicken and listening to bureaucratic windbags. Oh, don't make a face. Your speech was the only one worth hearing. So what gives?''

"My career is very important to me, you know that,'' Dusty began, pulling at a loose thread in the sash of her terrycloth robe. "Lately, though . . . I'm thirty-five years old, and frankly, my biological clock is hammering like Big Ben.'' She took a deep breath and blurted, "I want to have a baby, maybe two.''

Vivian finished her bourbon in one gulp. "Please don't tell me you've taken back your ex, the stud of Southland Wholesale Frozen Seafood.''

"No. He's history. I learn from my mistakes. I don't do reruns.''

"Well, then, tell me about the new Mr. Marvelous.''

"Be serious, Mom.''

"I couldn't be more. Since ninth grade your taste in males has been disastrous. Everything else, superb. You're brilliant, assertive, attractive, levelheaded and better than anyone I know at beating men in their own ballpark. But your love life reads like a bad soap opera.''

Dusty tied a knot in the robe's sash, then another. "The fact is, I'm not seeing anyone.''

"Uh-oh. I think I'd better get another drink.''

As Vivian added two fresh ice cubes and a generous measure of Wild Turkey to her glass, Dusty said, "Sperm bank.''

"Well, I guess we can drop the heartbreak factor from the equation.''

Vivian listened intently as her daughter told of having made preliminary inquiries at a sperm bank in Houston. They had donor profiles, Dusty explained—race, IQ, profession, family history—to guide her selection. A single woman in her position turning up pregnant would cause some awkwardness on the job and in the press, she admitted, but nothing she couldn't handle. "This is *very* important to me," she said, her eyes pleading.

"I've never been a grandma," said Vivian, breaking into a grin. "Come, give your mother a big hug."

They embraced and Dusty sobbed quietly. "I didn't know what you'd say."

"Shh. You forget that I was your age, well, six years younger, actually, when my clock started ticking. We didn't call it that then. Getting married and having babies was what all normal women did." Vivian smiled ruefully and patted Dusty's back. "I thought time was running out. More than anything else, I suppose, that's why I married your father, God rest his grouchy soul. Here, now, let me get a tissue so you can blow your nose. Your mascara's running, too."

Dusty dutifully blew her nose, then went into the bathroom to scrub off her ruined makeup and start over. "Mom," she said, "I'm so happy."

"I know, dear. Now tell me how you plan to raise this as-yet-unconceived child properly at that damn prison. Or are you going to resign?"

"No way. It would kill my career. Governor Felsen is certain to be reelected, and that gives me four more years, five altogether. Then I'll be ready to move up. We've talked about this before."

"Yes, but without the baby variable."

"Right. Well, here it is. Please move into the warden's mansion with me for a few years. We could both take care of little Vivian. I'm naming her after you, of course."

"Oh, no!" Vivian cried. She finished her drink and walked to the bathroom doorway, glancing out the window. Dusk had arrived, accompanied by a convoy of cars streaming into the French Quarter. "Raise another baby? Not me. Been there, done that. Think about hiring a live-in nanny. You can afford it."

"Mother! Too many things can go wrong in those situations. I won't take that chance. Please just think about it. You'll—Where are you going?"

Vivian had opened the hallway door and now gave a farewell flip of her hand. "You don't need me at that terminally boring Correctional Association dinner. I'm going to my room to freshen up, then check on Henry. If he's up to it, we'll prowl the Quarter. If not, I'll go alone. The eagle flies tonight! Bye." She sailed out the door.

An hour later Vivian adjusted her wrap and knocked on Henry's door. It opened immediately. He looked splendid, she thought. The steel-gray shantung suit and red tie only accentuated his ready grin. He was a bit portly but still dashing. And looking healthy as a prize bull. Taking her hand, he brushed it with his lips and whispered that she looked gorgeous.

"I haven't looked gorgeous in forty years, but don't stop," she told him. "I love it."

Apologizing profusely, Henry said he had to postpone their date and attend the Correctional Association dinner and dance. "Have to assess the damage Tripp did and fix it," he sighed. "As well as demonstrate that I'm not hovering near death from a bad heart. This contract is not a done deal, Viv. Tonight my job is damage control."

Vivian said she couldn't abide any more third-rate food or stuffy speeches, and they agreed to meet later in the hotel ballroom. "An oldies band?" she sighed happily. "I haven't danced for years. You are a romantic old soul."

In the French Quarter Vivian headed for her favorite restaurant, a storefront on Chartres Street that boasted a live Dixieland ensemble and the best muffaletta sandwich in New Orleans. Old standbys, including the perennial favorite, "When the Saints Go Marching In," rocked the room as she nibbled through half the huge muffaletta, decided she'd had enough, and washed it down with the last of an O'Doul's beer.

Outside, the foggy street glistened under vintage street lights. A few doors away the bright entrance of the My-Oh-My Club beckoned. Its doorway barker hyped "the greatest drag show in town" before a propped sandwich board featuring glossy photos of young men with good cheekbones impersonating Liza Minnelli, Tina Turner, Dolly Parton, and Patti LaBelle. It worked for Vivian. She went inside, found a vacant, tiny table and just as the first show began, paid an outrageous price for a bourbon on the rocks.

The pressures of the day—the attack on Henry by Arnie Tripp, Dusty's desire to transform her into Granny's Day-Care Service, her own sense of having lived beyond her time—faded as the master of ceremonies began his warm-up patter of off-color jokes. The pressures vanished entirely by the time a sequined and rather muscular Carol Channing brought the house down with a dead-on impersonation of the star singing, "Hello, Dolly." Vivian applauded wildly.

It was after eleven when she got back to the Sheraton and entered the darkened ballroom. Over the dance floor a spinning mirror-ball speckled dancers and spectators alike with darts of gold reflected from hidden spotlights. A tuxedoed twelve-piece orchestra worked its way through a repertoire of forties numbers. Vivian had no idea where to find Henry among the jostling bodies around her. She hesitated, then started off to the left, threading her way among tables at the circumference of the room, eyes straining in the dim light.

Ahead a door opened, forming a rectangle of fluorescent brilliance. Two dark figures stepped through it into the hall outside, and as the door closed, she caught a glimpse of silver hair and gray shantung. Henry. The man with him was large, very large, and had a bristly, military-style haircut. A sudden sense of dread made her ears ring. It was Arnie Tripp, she was almost sure. And he was up to no good. Her instincts had never failed her, and now they signaled bright red—danger.

Quickly she reached the door and pushed it open, looked left and right. Nothing. Left, the long corridor opened into the lobby. Right, after thirty feet or so, the corridor elbowed to the left. *They must have gone this way*, she thought, and hurried beyond the angle in the wall. A bank of elevators. She stopped and checked the indicators. None was in use. Ahead the corridor took a right and, she knew, continued past the hotel's shops and ended at the exhibition hall. Which would be locked up for the night, she assumed. Perplexed, she looked around. Nobody. Where could they be?

She continued walking, her heels making muffled thuds on the carpeted floor. No other sound reached her ears. No voices. Nothing. Lights from display windows brightened the hallway considerably. Vivian sighed as her stomach unclenched. Silly to feel that light meant safety, but everyone did. An ironic quirk of genetic coding. Creatures who saw predators from afar could flee, survive, and pass on their predilection to move about in daylight. Today, she realized, light made you a better target. Shuddering, she looked around quickly. Nothing.

Dead ahead the yawning emptiness of blank pastel walls and twenty yards of corridor ended abruptly at wide double doors. Was it a hunch or purposeless momentum guiding her feet to the exhibition hall's entrance? She wondered about that and, quite naturally, came down in favor of intuition. The doors had to be locked, but Vivian gave the handles a good shake anyway to satisfy herself that she'd really taken the wrong direction. She nearly toppled forward as the right-hand door flew open.

Regaining her balance, she noticed that someone had applied a strip of clear packing tape to keep the bolt from engaging. Swallowing hard, she leaned forward and looked around. The only illumination came from a line of track lights far away on the back wall. In the murky light innocuous sales booths became dark and ominous, casting impenetrable shadows.

"If Hannibal Lecter appears," she muttered, "I'll drop dead in my tracks."

Venturing inside, she called, "Henry." Then louder. "Henry! Are you in here?" On the periphery of her vision, something moved. "Henry?" Silence. Suddenly she was very afraid but knew the shadows before her would provide more safety than the well-lit empty hall behind. She ran, glancing over her shoulder, eyes wide. A huge, menacing figure loomed before her.

"Oh, my God!" she gasped, then with an overwhelming sense of relief recognized the riot-gear mannequin. She stopped, felt her heart pounding. Crouching, she hid in its shadow, eyes darting everywhere. The only sound was her own labored breathing. She tried to stifle it, crouched lower, hoping to become invisible.

A foot. Over there beside that booth. A human foot wearing a gleaming, black-tasseled loafer. She saw its lightly scuffed sole, too, for the toe pointed straight up. And there was a black sock and the cuff of a pants leg. Gathering herself, she crawled swiftly over the scratchy carpet to what she did not at all want to see. Stopping by the forlorn foot, she looked into the face of its owner.

"Oh, Henry," she said, choking back a sob.

Eyes bulging, mouth wide open, he looked as though the Grim Reaper had clapped its hands and startled him to death.

Abruptly Vivian realized she might be next. Looked around. Nothing. Those damn booths and dense shadows could hide an elephant. On all fours she hastened back to the mannequin, remembering it was armed. Considered taking the stun shield drooping from the dummy's hand. No. Tripp would brush that aside like tissue paper. The stun gun, then. What was it the rep had said? Drop a rhino. Just the thing. Please let it be charged up. She snatched the clumsy-looking weapon from the model, held it awkwardly with both hands, pointing it in front of her.

"Don't come near me!" she shouted, voice quavering at first and then firm. "I've got a gun and I'll use it!"

Seconds dragged by. She held her breath, listening intently. A quick rush of footsteps and a whooshing sound. Vivian spun and saw the entranceway door close with a soft thud. Relief so dizzying it made her want to curl up and cry. But she had things to do.

"My friend of thirty years is murdered, and you say it's none of my business!" Vivian shouted a half-hour later, foot tapping angrily. She and a burly detective named Louis Voltaggio stood to one side while Emergency Medical Services people, uniformed cops, and the police photographer performed their tasks. In the now brilliantly lit exhibition hall, hotel officials and employees, a contingent of convention-goers, and, for the early hour, a surprisingly large number of morbidly curious hotel guests whispered to one another around the yellow crime-scene tape.

Voltaggio had appeared shortly after the uniforms and EMS crew responded to Vivian's urgent 911 call. He'd ordered the cops to string the tape and preserve the scene, then listened to her statement while scribbling in a wallet-sized notebook. As Vivian paced nervously, he spent the following hour questioning Tripp and several other potential witnesses, and talking with the medical people. Afterward he told her there was no reason to hold anyone, and as soon as the photographer finished and the body was removed, he was going to call it a night.

"Ma'am, I'm sorry for your loss," said Voltaggio, his lined, weary face lending weight to the condolence. "EMS says Mr. Armistad died of a heart attack, pure and simple. There's not a mark on him and no sign of a struggle. The coroner's investigator just told me they'll conduct a routine autopsy, and he expects that to confirm the cause of death as heart failure. I understand your feelings, but there is no evidence at this point to show that Mr. Armistad is a homicide victim."

All at once she felt foolish. Could everything that had occurred after she followed Henry out of the ballroom been no more than the vaporings of an old woman frightened of shadows? She suspected that's what Voltaggio thought. Maybe he was right. Henry probably had a booth here promoting Armistad Associates and had merely come to check on something or other when his heart gave out. She stared at the floor, turning the scene over and over in her mind. Suddenly doubt disappeared as everything clicked into place. She knew what had happened; now she had to prove it. Henry's friendship required no less.

"Detective Voltaggio, is Sparky Halligan still captain of Homicide?" she asked.

That drew a sharp look from him. "No, ma'am. He's been deputy commissioner for several years now."

"Even better," she said under her breath, then continued in a no-nonsense tone, "I'm sure he'd appreciate you taking a few minutes to indulge his old newspaper-woman friend. I'd like to ask Mr. Tripp a few questions in your presence. And if it's not too much trouble, would you please ask my daughter to come over, too? She's the tall woman over there in the green gown with spectacular red hair."

"Ma'am, I'd be proud to ask them, but I can't make Tripp come over here and talk to you."

"My daughter can. She's his boss."

They gathered in a small circle beside the mannequin, inside the tape but out of traffic. Dusty, her face showing concern, said, "Mother, let's go."

"In a minute, dear."

Tripp, arms folded, oozed arrogance. Addressing Vivian, he said, "Armistad was no friend of mine or the officers I represent, but I had nothing to do with his death and I resent you saying I did. I understand that an old, um, elderly lady would get upset, finding a body, so I'll let it slide for now. But if you keep it up, you'll be sorry."

"I'll keep that in mind," Vivian said evenly. "Let's say, hypothetically, that someone wanted Henry Armistad dead, someone who knew he had a bad heart. Someone, moreover, who had direct experience with stun guns. Someone like you, Mr. Tripp. Tell me, what would a stun gun do to a person with a bad heart?"

Tripp licked his lips, said nothing.

"You know exactly what it would do, don't you, Mr. Tripp? It would stop his heart, send it into fibrillation. Without immediate medical attention he would die."

"Those darts leave puncture holes," Tripp said dryly. "There isn't a mark on him."

"How would you know that, Mr. Tripp?"

"Heard the emergency people talking."

"Really."

Tripp sneered. "Detective, do I have to listen to this batty old broad?"

"No, you don't," said Voltaggio, his expression one of indifference. "But a person with nothing to hide would be cooperative. Up to you."

"You're right, Mr. Tripp," Vivian continued, "there

are no visible puncture wounds. Of course, they haven't yet examined his entire body.''

Tripp started to say something, then set his lips in a grim line.

''Were you going to say they won't find any wounds?'' she said. ''I agree, because this hypothetical person did not use a stun gun. He used a stun shield. This one right here. It delivers 58,000 volts without leaving a mark, that's what the salesman told us. Right, Dusty?''

When Tripp's eyes couldn't hold her gaze, she knew she had him on the ropes. ''Detective Voltaggio, you see how the shield's hanging all crooked on the mannequin? That's not the way it was this afternoon. I'll bet if you dusted it for fingerprints, especially those smooth rubber handles, you'd come up with a certain person's prints. What do you think?''

''Hey, wait a minute,'' said Tripp. ''I touched a lot of stuff in here and I probably handled that shield, too. Yes, I'm sure I did.''

''I'm sure you did, too, Mr. Tripp,'' Vivian said. ''In fact, you were the last person to handle it. So your prints will be nice and clear, not overlaid by anyone else's. Right?''

''That doesn't prove diddly,'' he said hoarsely.

''Well, let's see. I saw you leave the ballroom with Henry shortly before he was mur . . . uh, died, and I'm sure others did as well.''

''I left him there, right in the hallway, and went up to my room and went to bed.''

''So you say. Someone taped that door lock and probably wiped it clean. Someone came in here with Henry, and, much as I'd like to, I can't swear it was you. Someone was interrupted by me before he could wipe the shield clean, too. And someone admitted his prints are on the shield I think was used to murder my friend.''

Her eyes flashed and Tripp looked away. "Your fatal mistake, my oh-so-calculating Mr. Tripp, was Henry's pacemaker. Did you really believe you could shoot thousands of volts through an electronic gizmo and not damage it? Or were you so dumb it didn't occur to you? Detective Voltaggio, you will mention to that nice coroner's investigator that his office should take a careful look at the pacemaker, won't you?"

"Yes, ma'am." Voltaggio unbuttoned his jacket, revealing the butt of his service revolver. "Mr. Tripp, if the forensic evidence turns out to be what this lady says, we're going to have a talk, you and I, down at the precinct. Meanwhile, I'll have to ask you not to leave town."

He stepped forward and in a calm, friendly voice said, "I can't help you if you wait until it gets official. Talk to me now. It's your best chance to explain what really happened."

All the starch went out of Tripp. Head down, he mumbled, "It was an accident . . ."

The following day Vivian and Dusty dawdled over lunch in the hotel restaurant. "I'm so proud of you, Mom," Dusty said, pushing aside the remains of her crab salad. "The evidence of damage to Henry's pacemaker from the stun shield would almost certainly have been missed in the coroner's investigation."

Vivian sighed contentedly. "Not almost certainly, dear, just plain certainly. The coroner will find nothing wrong with Henry's pacemaker."

"What?"

"Oh, the old ones, like the one your father had, were vulnerable to strong electromagnetic pulses. But that was years ago. I did a good deal of research on the subject after his death, and I've kept up. Any pacemaker currently in use can withstand a *lot* more than 58,000 volts. The coroner's investigation will reveal that the pacemaker was not damaged."

"But . . . then how did Henry die?"

"His heart, dear. Tripp zapped him with the stun shield, just as he admitted. Henry's heart couldn't withstand the repeated shocks, went into fibrillation, and stopped. The pacemaker's tiny electrical impulses would have continued but would have been insufficient to start his heart again after a complete collapse. That's not what pacemakers are designed to do. Arnie Tripp almost committed the perfect murder."

"Except for a stubborn old newshound . . ."

"Who's going to write the story up and send it in," Vivian said thoughtfully, sipping her coffee. 'Special to the *Daily Post*, by Vivian McCall.' I'm going to follow the case, too. Who knows what else I'll find to write about at the courthouse? Watching Tripp being led away in handcuffs let me know I still have what it takes, contributions to make. Your mother" —she paused dramatically—"is back in the game!"

Dusty sighed. "But Mom, I was counting on you to help with the baby. That's important, too. That's contributing, doing something meaningful."

"Indeed it is," Vivian said brightly. "And I'll help you find a suitable nanny to do it."

"Mother!"

Vivian smiled and signaled the waiter for their check.

Abigail Padgett was nominated for an Agatha for Child of Silence, *her first novel featuring investigator Bo Bradley, who copes with bipolar disorder. Her most re-*

cent novel in the series is The Dollmaker's Daughters.
*Douglas Dennis is incarcerated in Louisiana State
Prison and works on the award-winning prison news-
magazine,* The Angolite.

ANN GRANGER

The Meredith and Markby Mysteries

"The author has a good feel for understated humor, a nice ear for dialogue, and a quietly introspective heroine."

London Times Saturday Review

COLD IN THE EARTH	72213-5/$5.50 US
A FINE PLACE FOR DEATH	72573-8/$5.50 US
MURDER AMONG US	72476-6/$5.99 US
SAY IT WITH POISON	71823-5/$5.99 US
A SEASON FOR MURDER	71997-5/$5.99 US
WHERE OLD BONES LIE	72477-4/$5.99 US
FLOWERS FOR HIS FUNERAL	72887-7/$5.50 US
CANDLE FOR A CORPSE	73012-X/$5.50 US
A TOUCH OF MORTALITY	73087-1/$5.99 US

DEN OF ANTIQUITY MYSTERIES

by
TAMAR MYERS

LARCENY AND OLD LACE
78239-1/$5.99 US/$7.99 Can

As owner of the Den of Antiquity, Abigail Timberlake
is accustomed to navigating the cutthroat world of rival
dealers at flea markets and auctions. But she never thought
she'd be putting her expertise in mayhem and detection to
other use—until her aunt was found murdered . . .

GILT BY ASSOCIATION
78237-5/$5.99 US/$7.99 Can

A superb gilt-edged, 18th-century French armoire Abigail
purchased for a song at estate auction has just arrived
along with something she didn't pay for: a dead body.

THE MING AND I
79255-9/$5.99 US/$7.99 Can

Digging up old family dirt can uncover long buried
secrets . . . and a new reason for murder.

SO FAUX, SO GOOD
79254-0/$5.99 US/$7.99 Can

Murder Is on the Menu
at the Hillside Manor Inn
Bed-and-Breakfast Mysteries by
MARY DAHEIM
featuring Judith McMonigle

BANTAM OF THE OPERA
76934-4/ $6.50 US/ $8.99 Can

JUST DESSERTS
76295-1/ $5.99 US/ $7.99 Can

FOWL PREY
76296-X/ $5.99 US/ $7.99 Can

HOLY TERRORS
76297-8/ $5.99 US/ $7.99 Can

DUNE TO DEATH
76933-6/ $5.99 US/ $7.99 Can

A FIT OF TEMPERA
77490-9/ $5.99 US/ $7.99 Can

MAJOR VICES
77491-7/ $5.99 US/ $7.99 Can

MURDER, MY SUITE
77877-7/ $5.99 US/ $7.99 Can

AUNTIE MAYHEM
77878-5/ $6.50 US/ $8.50 Can

NUTTY AS A FRUITCAKE
77879-3/ $5.99 US/ $7.99 Can

SEPTEMBER MOURN
78518-8/ $5.99 US/ $7.99 Can

WED AND BURIED
78520-X/ $5.99 US/ $7.99 Can

SNOW PLACE TO DIE
78521-8/ $5.99 US/ $7.99 Can